Insane Possibilities

Carol Plum-Ucci

Co-Pilot Publishing LLC 2024

Insane Possibilites

First-time or interested authors, contact Co-Pilot Publishing at:
Authorsassistance@copilotbooks.org
Or visit us at Copilotbooks.org

Edited by Lynn Lumpkin

Cover Design by Matthew Clark

Printed on acid-free paper
ISBN
PB 979-8-9908542-2-2
HB 979-8-9908542-3-9

First Printing: November 2024

Dedication

To Jonny, Josh, & Josie

Acknowledgments

As the saying goes, "When you start telling people you're writing another book, you end up knowing who your friends are!" I have so many that "blessed" is an understatement.

Many thanks to my initial readers, Joan Vicari, Bill Vicari, Juliet Fletcher, and Mona Parks for all your encouragement as well as interesting thoughts. Thanks to Matt Clark for a cover that I LOVE, and to Lynn Lumpkin for her most excellent proofreading skills. Thanks to Maren Hodsdon, Steve Schneiderman, and my husband Rick for the new round of publicity photos. Sorry the subject was so challenging. As I always say: "It's not the years; it's the mileage!" Many thanks to Abbey Ucci and Forest James of DISRUPT Marketing LLC for their professional consultations and new web design.

And thanks to Breandan Lumpkin, publisher. Dude, I know you don't have a magic wand, but your courage and valor intrigued me and made me want to be a part of an exciting new ballgame.

Insane Possibilities

One

The day before my eighteenth birthday, I fell ninety feet down a well.

Yes, a well--the kind with the brick sides, the roof, and the little bucket. The well was ancient, and the bucket, long gone. My younger sisters and I were fooling around, trying to look down it. We were on family vacation. We wanted to see how far down the water was.

I had been a lifeguard and a diver on two swim teams. My sisters, fifteen and eleven, were both advanced students in my mom's ballet school. None of us were klutzy. I've called it an "accident" to refer to the seriousness of my injuries, not the way it happened.

I remembered that fall like every second was split into three parts. Everyone commented on my memory when I got to the hospital—my parents, the cops, paramedics, nurses, doctors. I let all the praise keep my spirits up for the massive surgery ahead. My memory seemed perfect.

Grace had grabbed my legs to try to stop the fall, and I'd accidentally kicked her in the face *hard*. I had a split second to picture that I'd probably knocked Grace out, and Trinity had already been in the throes of one of her famed asthma attacks just from the stress of looking down. But that silence felt all wrong—somebody ought to be screaming.

I remembered to flip. It was an instinct with a flash image of hitting the water feet first--better chance of surviving. Fortunately, this old well was six feet across instead of three, or I'd have lost my scalp on the jagged wall. I only grazed one knee.

So, my first thought had been for Grace and Trinity. My second thought was for me.

My third was a terrifying fact. *Somebody just pushed me.* Running footsteps had closed in on us. My neck almost snapped at the impact of hands on my back. We didn't know anyone on vacation. There were no prime suspects.

I'd never seen so much black, like I was flying through black tar. Then the water struck like a bomb.

I'd been right to grab my knees and tuck. The water was deep enough to absorb the crash, but debris hulked beneath that surely would have decapitated me. My neck broke anyway because my sailing jacket inflated, and a rusty metal pipe caught diagonally beneath the surface ripped my right leg to shreds. The only thing I didn't know later was how I had dislocated my left hip.

The well was a sound tunnel, spiraling a man's grunts and snarls down into my ears. I could hear Trinity wheezing as he attacked her. Bodies tussled, flesh on fabric, grunts on gasps. He hollered, "Stop fighting me, or you'll be down there next!"

That was the worst part—I was helpless to save my special-needs sister, but some other person—a woman—screamed. It was a blood-curdling, upper-register screech, deafening, yet a relief. Some adult up there understood, could run for help…

And yet, the scream was creepy. Like maybe it was echoing *up* instead of *down*. Like it was coming from the water—

I could somehow hear other vacationers at the top, a man's voice, "Jesus, there's a kid down there!"

The screaming stopped when I spoke. There was no explaining that, or the calmness in my voice as the echo chamber carried my words: "Go find my parents. They're in the lounge. Dad's a diver. He's a sea captain, so he's a paramedic—"

And then the screaming started up again, and I became sure it was something supernatural, and I was dying, and this was some ghoul trying to rip off my soul. To distract myself, I went through breathing methods to ward off shock. But I have only vague memories of Dad being in the water, my coming up on a neck board, or the lights of the ambulance. It was over in an hour.

I didn't start losing my mind until I got to the hospital, hearing about my sisters. Grace's nose broke when I kicked her, and Trinity had facial injuries, a scratched cornea, and a near-fatal asthma attack.

I was awake, though barely sane. I was in pain finally but didn't dare move, didn't dare punch anything like I wanted to, like it was the guy's face, like it would help me get over the question that already tormented me: *Why?*

Why would some stranger push a guy down a well? Why skip over his fifteen-year-old sister and attack the eleven-year-old baby? Had we been attacked by that type of mad-rapist pedophile you only see on the news?

Was he possessed? Your gut instincts tell you things, and in the throes of traumatic events, the info may not make sense. But you still know. As crazy as that last question was, I knew I would return to the possession thing while trying to heal.

Here were the facts I thought were imprinted forever into my brain before being wheeled into the OR:

Grace, Trinity, and I had been fooling around at the well at the edge of our hotel.

Someone ran up behind us. His footsteps pounded.

He pushed me so hard I got whiplash.

I fell-flipped-fell and hit the water.

My neck broke. My leg broke.

I heard a man above threatening Trinity with, "Stop fighting me! Or you'll be down there next!"

A woman screamed. I told vacationers how to help. Then I started going into shock.

Ba-bang. I'm the coolest, the most miraculous fact-provider ever.

But here's the thing about the facts. They're like the characters in the funhouse that used to be on our island's amusement pier. You traded in your entry tickets for a radar gun, one that shot a neon-green electro-beam, like the light sabers in *Star Wars*. You shot at these 3-D zombies who would drop down, crawl up, or peer stealthily around corners. You could think one was dead-on in front of you, but it turned out to be a lot of smoke and mirrors. He's actually behind.

In my humble, yet now experienced opinion, we take our facts based on what we are capable of believing. And under stress, we're less reliable. They closed our pier's funhouse after the owner's kid, a classmate of mine, bought a real gun to stash under his pillow in case one of the zombies busted into his bedroom. The zombies became his facts. He shot one that "came down" from his bedroom ceiling, and the bullet shattered his sister's left heel as she stepped out of the bathtub overhead.

My trauma therapist noted early on that the way we formulate our facts overrides what's true or even what's logical. Logic and truth don't serve us as well as belief—or at least we don't subconsciously think they will.

It was after midnight when it came time to sign the police report. That's how I got to celebrate my first half-hour of adulthood. I got to sign it myself instead of one of my parents because I was suddenly of age. The half hour after midnight was filled with strange questions from the police in spite of all that I knew to be true. *Was I sure I didn't fall? Could one of my sisters have pushed me?*

And, like the cops, I had no use for spooks or supernatural notions, which I'd always been taught go against facts. Hence, there was zero discussion about the paranormal playing a role. The police let me sign the complaint with an X so I wouldn't have to move my hand too much before the team of four surgeons tried to put me back together. I just wanted the guy's ass thrown in jail forever. Happy first-adult birthday to me.

Afterwards I found myself in a physical lockdown to recover, where I would have lots of time—nothing *but* time—to play light-saber games with the facts and try to keep hold of my sanity.

Two

"Toby? Are you awake?"

I was staring at the floor when the unfamiliar voice spoke. I felt myself tighten up. Six weeks in this hospital bed, and I never got used to the fact that I couldn't spin and look at a face leaning over me.

I wiggled my arms out from between the mattresses, lowered the mirror attached to the bedframe, and saw the reflection of a man, maybe thirty-five, with a neatly trimmed beard and blue eyes.

I had the same crazy thought I'd had all week when an unfamiliar employee showed up in my room: *Could this be the guy who pushed me? Did he sneak in here disguised as a worker to kill me before I can get him thrown in jail?"* The cops had let the guy go, and a couple weeks ago they started saying they couldn't find him.

Combine that with the fact that nobody introduces themselves around here. Doctors, nurses, orderlies, technicians, social workers, volunteers, for starters—they rarely say their names and just barge in.

I had conflicting needs. I was crazy lonely. Still six hours from home, I liked to chat it up with people. If you start off with something that smacks of, I DON'T TRUST YOU AND THINK YOU ARE A SERIAL KILLER, people will give any talk time to a friendlier patient.

The mad-rapist pedophile's voice had been low and full, sort of like Darth Vader's. This guy sounded mild. *"Not him?"*

"S'up?" I croaked.

"Toby Kellerman?"

"Yeah."

"Did I wake you?"

Thunder rumbled in the distance, and I could hear rain splashing in torrents against the window.

"S'okay. We've had all these thunderstorms. They've been putting me to sleep lately."

"If you find thunderstorms cathartic, you got injured in the right summer." He smiled overtop a clipboard. *Techie?* One of the technicians on staff came in twice daily to make sure my weird bed was functioning properly. I'd gotten pretty friendly with a couple, but sometimes a new face showed up.

You're supposed to be able to see their ID's. That's great, except half the time I'm looking at them in a mirror and seeing stuff on badges like. N.R ,SRETSAMCM NNYWG. (That's Gwynn McMasters, R.N., the name of my favorite day nurse, in a mirror.)

I asked, "What's going on with all these hurricanes? What are we up to now, eleven? You believe in, like, the Apocalypse?"

"I believe we are having an active hurricane season." He grinned with a mild shrug. *Not a techie.* Those guys would launch into the zombie apocalypse, the UFO apocalypse, the Bible apocalypse. Most were sci-fi heads. Their imaginations were entertaining.

Besides, this guy was studying my bed with intrigue, moving out of view and probably checking out the generator and receiver behind me. The techies were used to all this.

He said, "They've got you in a real contraption here, don't they? I've heard of these beds but have never seen one. Are you comfortable?"

"Yeah. I guess it looks weird, huh?" I asked. My bed looks like a giant ice cream sandwich that revolves slowly. I'm between two mattresses. My arms hang out the sides but can slide in. The front mattress only comes up to my shoulders. I have a halo for broken necks, but it doesn't attach to a vest like mobile patients' halos. It's screwed into a metal bar over my head for stability. One techie told me the crown and screw made it look like the headpiece in the electric chair. Selfies verify.

"It looks like yet another salute to modern science," he said.

A motor drive turned me slowly, doing a one-eighty every half hour, turning me from lying on my back to my stomach. I was actually in a standing position for a few minutes twice an hour, only I wasn't standing, but held in place by weights.

"Thank God the thing rotates. I'd go nuts with only one view," I said.

He bent down to get a look at the front of the bed shell, which was under me now, to see the clips for the nurses' button, the tray where my meal trays or notepad could snap on, mumbling, "Wow..."

I felt for my cell phone as he touched the tray holder like many people did when it was empty, to watch it click back into the perfect upright position no matter where I was on a rotation.

"I understand you're very lucky to be alive," he said. "What's your prognosis?"

As he moved behind me again, I texted Mom quickly, "Need u." I realized the guy wasn't even wearing any hospital ID.

I grinned, trying to stay casual. "I can feel it anywhere the nurse or doctor pinches me. They tell me all the time that I'm actually going to walk, run, swim and row, though my football days are over. Every day that passes where paralysis doesn't set in means I'm one day safer."

"You liked playing football? That part sounds like a bummer..."

"I wasn't going to play in college. I got accepted at the University of Missouri Journalism School and the Coast Guard Academy. Either way, you gotta be *beyond* good."

"That's impressive," he said. "Which did you choose?"

"I'm taking a gap year to decide. At least that's why I *was taking* a gap year. Now I'm taking one to recover as well...get back in shape--Excuse me, but can you go find my mom?"

"I can. Are you in some sort of pain?"

I was always in some sort of pain, but I welcomed it. If I suddenly woke up and felt nothing, that would be the worst.

"No, it's just... I'm sure you're not Jack the Ripper. But try lying here for a few weeks and keeping your sanity intact."

"Oh. Forgive my relaxed weekend behavior." He reached in his shirt pocket and pulled a photo I.D. out. It had *Salem Medical Center* sprawled across the top of it. Fully licensed, though the long series of degrees following his name was a blur. The picture was him.

As I sent Mom a "never mind," he clipped the ID onto his shirt pocket.

"Here's something else that's making me nuts," I said, "looking at everything in a mirror half the time. I had this pretty intense English class last year where we were studying suspense in films, stories, plays—I wrote this paper on how every time a character looks at someone in a mirror, it is a symbol of, um..."

Hard words still got lost from me sometimes.

"Duplicity?" He smiled in the mirror, intrigued.

"Yeah. Like, being deceived. Whoever the protagonist sees in the mirror is about to knife him in the back. Well, maybe not literally, but, um..."

"Figuratively."

"Yeah. Either that or the protagonist is about to see a spook. Haunting scenes involving mirrors are classic in American film."

We'd been locking eyes in my mirror. And now that it was clear I didn't have an ax murderer in my room, I went to my second weird habit this week of trying to deal with the feeling of being watched from my doorway. I spun the mirror to take in the doorframe. Nobody was standing there. And yet all week, I felt so watched that I found myself doing this every ten minutes or so. *Very* annoying. I spun the mirror back to find him awaiting the end of my story.

"Anyway. I got an A in that class."

"Your mirror problems don't sound like fun. But quickly, let's run through your injuries. Your mom gave me a rundown, but I wasn't writing."

I was used to reciting my injuries, so it came out easily—stress fracture of the axis vertebra in my neck, compound fracture of my right shin bone, which now had a titanium rod holding the four pieces in place, and a dislocated left hip.

"There's no cast for this mess, at least not one that won't give you bedsores and an outrageous case of vertigo the first month you're walking again. It's not like I'll just be able to walk out of this bed. But I might be back on my feet in a week instead of a month."

He nodded and didn't flinch about my injuries like some people. I liked him for that. "I'm a fast healer, doctors say. Most people would get an eight-week sentence in this bed. I'll have gotten by with seven, so..."

"There's a lot in your favor," he smiled in an encouraging way. "Young athlete, in the epitome of good health..."

"In a week, I can start rehab. So, are you the rehab specialist?"

While he finished his writing I did it again--felt like eyes from the doorway were burning a hole into my head. Just a couple of orderlies pushed a cart past. I pushed the mirror away, telling myself to knock it off.

He finally answered my question. "No. I'm a psychotherapist. Your parents wanted me to speak with you. Again, my name is Dr. [Valparaiso?] [Vasputin?]"

I still can't remember his real name. I've just thought of him as Dr. Vapor ever since, probably because my past experience with shrinks made them seem kind of like vaporous presences in a room.

"So, what'd Mom *really* do, like, slink off to the coffee shop?"

"She did think it would be best if I spoke to you privately."

"Yeah, well. My parents think head shrinks are one of the secrets of a swell universe," I informed him with a forced grin. "My mom saw a shrink after she was adopted by her foster family at age fifteen. My little sister Trinity saw a shrink after she got mauled by a dog in kindergarten. I saw a shrink the same year because I *saw* Trinity get mauled by the dog.

Now you're here. Which might be okay, except that I saw your jeans and thought you might be someone from home."

He kept his sympathy gaze. "Your mom says you miss your friends a lot."

"Yeah. We're from Jersey."

"You guys came up to do the white-water rafting from Lake Indor or to do one of the haunted tours?"

I chuckled at that second option. "My and my two sisters' birthdays all fall within three weeks of each other. We've been coming to Lake Indor for the third weekend in June since I can remember to go birthday rafting. My dad's a sea captain, and we live on an island. So, lakes and mountains are vacation for him. I don't know anything about the haunted tours except for all the totally true stories my sister Grace makes up about the Witch of Indor while we're up here."

He laughed but kept writing. This sounded like just a casual conversation. I didn't get what he needed to write down. "My wife is on the Historical Committee of Lake Indor, funded in large part by those tours. There's so much lore out there. But I could at least tell you whether your sister is completely making things up or sticking with the stories published in the two books by the committee."

"She's making it up," I assured him. "Last time Grace read a book she didn't have to was in a past life. She says the Witch of Indor eats people and spits their bones all over the road. Some junk like that."

He looked up and made a honking sound. "False! The witch is allegedly given to scalping people. With a meat hook. There have been five recorded victims since her death in 1807. One as recently as 2002."

"Gross," I chuckled. "Copycats, obviously—"

"Unless you believe in the Witch of Indor." He looked into the corridor as I watched him in the mirror. "The historical society uses the money raised from their tours to hire a cold case detective every twenty years or so. I think the innkeepers up there would just as soon let people believe it's her. She's good for business."

I kept grinning, thinking this was almost as entertaining as the zombie apocalypse. "Doesn't she, like, make people stand in a corner before she eats them?"

"False!" He made the honk noise again. "I believe that's the Blair Witch. She's from Maryland. And down your way, you've got, uh..." He snapped his fingers beside his ear.

"Jersey Devil," I filled in. "Though our hay-wagon tours happen only around Halloween. He doesn't have the status the Witch of Indor has. Just kills chickens and cats and some bullshit...tons of sightings. But he's never killed a human being on record."

"I'm just curious...Were you and your sisters talking about the Witch of Indor just before your accident?"

I watched his blank face curiously in the mirror. *Strange question.* For one, this was the first time I'd been asked any questions about what happened *before* the accident, I realized. *Before* the footsteps ran up behind us.

"Probably not," I said, a little in awe of this utter blank. "For one, Grace's stories don't sit well with Trinity. They sent her into an asthma attack one summer. Besides, we're just getting too old to, you know, believe stuff that isn't real."

"I wish some *college* kids around town would take that view." He chuckled but kept watching me patiently, so I went on.

"I remember Grace dropped the lantern down the well to give us a view of how deep down the water was. I remember wanting to clobber her. Somehow, when the lantern broke, a fireball shot back up the shaft. Sort of like a mushroom. What in hell would cause that?"

He sniffed with a wrinkled brow like he was thinking. "Maybe there was some sort of petrol fuel in the debris below the waterline?"

"Maybe," I said. "Grace landed on top of me, trying to get us out of the way of this fiery mushroom ball that hit the little roof. But Trinity froze. You know anything about my youngest sister?"

"She's special-needs," he said, pulling up the page he'd been writing on and glancing at something beneath it. I wondered uneasily how much Mom had told him. It could take hours to paint an accurate picture of Trinity.

I just went on with the facts that were positive. "Trinity has an IQ of one-sixty and reads in four languages. One day in kindergarten she got caught reading on the playground when the other kids were playing. Guess what book it was."

"Uh…I'd guess it was something like *The Rise and Fall of the Third Reich* if I thought a kindergartener could follow that much history, regardless of IQ."

"You're close," I chucked. "It was *To Kill a Mockingbird.*"

"Wow," he said, watching me with a grin.

"She just pulled it off my mom's shelf and started reading it…decided to sneak it into school in her backpack. That's become a classic family tale, Trinity reading *To Kill a Mockingbird* in kindergarten."

"Right-brain-cognitive genius," he read off a page that must have been from an interview with Mom. "And how old is she?"

"Eleven. But a lot of people think she's not all in there. I really hate that. She's just hard to read. Grace's instincts would cause her to retreat from fire. Trinity would be inclined to stand there and stare until her eyeballs caught fire."

"Mm," he said with interest, still reading. "And she wouldn't be able to tell you later what she'd been thinking?"

I took it he was reading off Mom's interview that Trinity also had *selective mutism.* She didn't talk. Or at least not often.

"Listen, you can ask Mom all about Trinity if you want. Her problems have nothing to do with this. But I'm curious. You were asking if we'd been talking about the Witch of Indor? Probably not. But how does our conversation matter?"

"No big deal, really." He took his eyes off his notes finally and looked into mine. "There are some stories about the witch and the few old-fashioned wells around Lake Indor—one of which lies just beyond the edge of your hotel's lawn."

The well I got pushed down...

"News to me," I said, using my eyebrows to shrug with. I was almost facing the floor now. He continued to watch me in the mirror like he was waiting for a particular response. I didn't have it.

He finally said, "Some people say she jumped off a cliff after the town accused her of witchcraft and drowned in the white water. That is likely untrue. She died in January of 1702 in a blinding snowstorm. Lake Indor and the river freeze in winter. Even the roughest veins. But wells don't freeze. Some say she jumped down a well." He continued to watch me.

"She jumped down *a well?"* I wondered why on earth a shrink would bring up something like that. And to a patient who fell down a well. Seemed kind of sick.

He finally said, "Well, I'm just quoting the historical record. It's a fact that this lore has caused some problems up here for decades. Kids are having accidents because they're engaging in risky behavior—hanging out on cliffs late at night looking for 'sightings' without flashlights, while pushing and shoving each other...things like that."

I felt bad about the kids. His point wasn't clear.

He looked down at his notes and changed the subject. "Your mom tells me you had a girlfriend for a while back home."

First, the Witch of Indor. Now Sara Alton. *What's all this stuff got to do with the accident?*

"Have you talked to her? Texted with her since you've been up here?"

"No. We'd only been going out for three weeks. Let's say the relationship was all wrong. We broke up about a week before we came up here."

"She didn't break your heart, did she?"

"No. *I* broke up with *her.* Why are you asking me about Sara?"

He started writing again and said in what sounded like too casual a voice, "Some people become suicidal after a breakup. Not many, but I'm obligated to put it out there."

It took me a moment, but I understood both things at once. He brought up the Witch of Indor to make sure one of my sisters hadn't pushed me by accident while we were fooling around. Now he was bringing up Alton to make sure I didn't—.

"You think I *jumped? And did this to myself?* That's insane."

I knew from my previous shrink that they hate the word "insane." He blinked with annoyance, but I felt justified. "Not only that, but the guy's still lurking behind trees out there, I hear. Cops didn't hold him, and now they can't find him? At least, they couldn't the last time I asked, probably an hour ago."

"Actually, that's one of the things I'm here to talk to you about," he said, grabbing Mom's chair and pulling it closer. The bed flipped. Before I found myself gazing at the ceiling, I got to catch a glimpse of his face as he plopped into the chair. He looked serious. Anxious, maybe, if shrinks can be anxious.

"I'll be blunt with you," he said.

"Sure." I adjusted the mirror so I could see him again. I don't think he knew whether to look at me in the mirror and appear, uh, *duplicitous,* or avoid my eyes and look shifty. He actually got right back up and stood over me, looking directly down into my eyes.

"Toby, your family and the staff haven't been telling you the whole truth. You came out of surgery with the idea fully formed that this man had pushed you. It is *not* true that he had disappeared. It *is* true that he has not been arrested."

"You mean... they know where he is?" I asked.

"He hasn't been arrested because the police aren't convinced he pushed you."

I played the same tape in my brain I'd been playing daily for weeks. I felt like a broken record saying, "He ran up behind me. I heard his footsteps. He pushed me hard. There's no doubt."

He said nothing, which galled me. I felt my voice rise, my chest get heated. "The woman who screamed. She must have heard him threaten Trinity. She must be in that police report—"

"The police don't have any record of a female witness, screaming or not."

"Then...who screamed?" The silence resounded over the tap-tapping of rain on the window.

I can't stand people who use silence to manipulate. I was definitely not liking this Dr. Vapor. I quickly filled the air with something. "And there was a guy at the top who said, 'Jesus, there's a kid down there.' He could hear me. I told him to get my dad, that it would be faster than a 911 response— Surely, he saw the guy messing with Trinity."

"Yeah, he's on the record," Dr. Vapor agreed, to my relief. "Victor Mayes. Optician, there for a small medical seminar. He placed a 911 call while running to get your father. He said a man was hunched over your sister, but he appeared to be trying to help her."

"Trying to *help* her?" I echoed, wondering how a medical doctor could be so dumb. "He leaves my sister alone with the guy to go get help for me?"

"That's right," the doctor said. He shuffled some papers on his clipboard, which I took to be part of a police report. "Dr. Mayes said later he had no reason to believe Mr. Rune wasn't just another guest who saw a skirmish, ran over, and got there before him."

I realized I'd just heard the guy's name for the first time. "*Ruin*? That's his name?"

He spelled it. "First name, Elijah. Elijah Rune."

"Even *sounds* like a serial killer. Who has a name like that?"

He looked to the side and back, like he didn't find that name creepy. "Think of it rhyming with 'tune.'"

I thought of it sounding like "tomb" and "ruin."

Vapor said, "Rune lives on the mountain and said he often takes an evening stroll on the grounds of the Chapel Rock Inn to sort out his thoughts before bed. It's picturesque."

The Chapel Rock is where we'd been staying. That one made me laugh in awe. "He's taking a stroll to sort out his thoughts? He's a crazed lunatic who wanted to sort out the vertebrae in my spine!" I was getting loud again. "Oh, so *Elijah Rune* was just *out for a stroll.* That sounds creepy as hell. I don't see how you guys don't find that extremely suspicious."

"I understand your feelings, Toby."

"But this isn't about *my feelings*, doc," I snapped in frustration. "It's about *facts.* Creepy names and strolls at night aside. It seems the police are having trouble staying with the facts as I know them. *I was there.* Tell me. What do *they* think happened? Just so I can know what I'm dealing with..."

He shuffled some papers, which gave me time to feel my gut drop, like my spirits were dropping and pulling my gut along with them. For the past six weeks, everyone had been positive, encouraging, and making me feel great about my excellent memory and my way of staying calm and being a trooper. I'd been feeling like a hero instead of a victim, thanks to everyone's great words. I sensed some of that was about to change.

Three

"I can't tell you what the police suspect," Dr. Vapor said.

"Why in hell not?"

"Because of your condition. You're finally alert, like a healthy guy stuck in a bed, rather than an invalid who is entirely reliant on it. That's all good. But you're at probably the most impressionable phase of your brain's healing."

My body had been through hell, but I'd never thought of my mind as having accompanied it. I said nothing, and he continued.

"Nobody claims to have seen what happened—not even your sisters. It was dark. But there are a dozen or so guests and staff who heard this or that, and of course the hotel is still contacting guests from that weekend to check their phones, make sure they didn't inadvertently tape something off the balconies. Your sisters' recoveries were not as lengthy as yours, so they've been questioned a few times each to see if anything changed or grew in detail."

"The cops are doing all *that?*" I asked in awe. It had been simple from my standpoint. The guy did it: Go find him and arrest him. I was impressed to hear about all of the police attention, I supposed, but it was frustrating. *Quit dotting all your i's and go arrest him.*

Dr. Vapor went on. "So, any conjecture that police bring forth to you could become etched in stone. It could create a *false* memory. Do you understand?"

I said I did, though I knew the truth about what happened and felt annoyed.

"We need you to recall all the details yourself, without impressions from any of us. All I can tell you is facts."

"I... I told the whole truth from the beginning and nothing has changed," I said again but with less force than I would have liked. *What did he expect would change?*

"I *know* there was a woman up there, screaming at the top of her lungs," I repeated. "I don't see how the police don't have that."

"Sometimes what we think are the facts are not really the facts," he said, watching me.

"How am I supposed to *make up* the woman who was breaking my eardrums?"

"Maybe you really heard it. But that's a great example. There are some things you've consistently stated as fact that your sisters disagree with."

"Well, Grace had a broken nose and a concussion." I shrugged that off with my eyebrows and didn't mention Trinity, though a weird sense of dread settled in my insides.

"At any rate, I can present you with the truth. But I can't lead you in finding it," he said. "And I came on the weekend because your mother's become aware that, in the past few days, you've been watching the door almost constantly. She said you have an idea that someone is standing there. She said you used the word 'haunted.' You said you felt 'haunted.'"

"Hang on." I put up my hand. I was no longer flat on my back, so I could have this conversation eye to eye. "I didn't mean it *that way*. I don't believe in spooks. It's just a nag… a sensation. *It'll stop when whositsface—Rune—gets put in jail*."

"Toby, you ought to feel safe while recovering. As you suddenly don't, this seemed like a good time to try to introduce to you the notion that the man at the scene has none of the ear markings of a serial killer, in fact, the opposite. He will not break in here and get you, okay? And if your memories start to expand or change, it's best to have it all documented by a professional."

I felt my spirits drooping again.

His next words didn't help much. "You understand, Toby, that this is not your fault. Anyone who believes their life was truly in jeopardy is considered 'traumatized.' You are not exempt. I'm here to help you along with your trauma, of which these memories are a part."

I watched him write, and the scratchy sound on the paper was annoying as hell. I said, "I felt like I was in a stupor the first three or four weeks I was here. It's hard to remember much before last week except waking up a whole bunch of times, eating, texting, and hearing a lot of cheerful voices. I don't get it. Why not just tell me if they thought the guy was innocent? I mean, is it better to let me think he's roaming around? I would have argued, but what's wrong with simple honesty?"

He stopped writing to look at me again. We were eye to eye at this point. "Somehow, you got to the bottom of a well. It has to do with the implications."

"What implications?" I asked.

He wrote a few more lines. And instead of answering he said, "I need to talk to your mother in private, Toby. Give me a few minutes."

I watched his back as he passed through the doorframe and turned down the corridor. *"What* implications?" I asked myself and the doorframe, which seemed to stare back as usual, like it framed someone I ought to see standing there, though no one was there. I was more alert than I'd been in weeks, truth enough. But I wasn't alert enough to get "the implications."

Four

I started to think this shrink wasn't coming back, he was gone so long. I was almost halfway to my standing position again, which meant half an hour had passed. I thought of texting Rob Casen, my best buddy. But it was hard to come up with something I hadn't already asked him over the past couple of weeks. We would have been third-year lifeguards this summer, finally experienced enough to work together.

The phone had dinged a message from the Weather Channel while Dr. Vapor was in here. I suddenly noticed it. Hurricane over Bermuda, picking up speed. Could hit the US anywhere from Maryland to New York.

"Hear there's another hurricane, and this one might take its big dump on Port Dingo?" I hit SEND to Casen. Port Dingo was home, the island we'd been raised on.

A cool breeze crossed my right leg just above my ankle. I tried to ignore it. My doctor had been in here Friday, telling me how the last week in this bed would be the hardest because I was mostly healed. He said I'd be restless and might feel strange things. But because I felt the draft only on my bad leg, it creeped me out—like someone was blowing on it.

I focused in when Casen replied back. "Water's a total vortex. Rip tides. Five rescues in four hours. Be glad you're not here."

That made me wish I *was* there. What had brought my surgeon in on Friday was getting these sudden, crazed adrenaline rushes. They'd come out of nowhere and make me want to jump out of the bed and heave it against the wall. The doctor said that was just my adrenal glands healing, but running around the beaches and saving people seemed like a fantastic pace to be on.

"What's this storm's name?" I asked, wanting to keep my head at home rather than here.

"They named it Rhonda, if you can believe that. Gotta go, man. Can't take my eyes off these people."

Casen's "if you can believe that" meant it was only mid-August, and the western hemisphere was already up to the letter R in this season's tropical storms and hurricanes. The stormy weather this summer reminded me of my recent life. You never knew what awful thing was coming next or when you'd simply experience peace.

Dad knows I'm crazy lonely, so I'll listen to his blather. He was in Jersey with my sisters. I hit his speed dial.

"So, how many Facebook friends did you bust today for sharing fake news?" I asked when he picked up. He was home from sea all summer, thanks to Mom being up here. He stayed busy beyond what the girls needed by having elected himself the Do-Not-Fucking-Lie-To-Us Police Patrol on Facebook. Or at least that's what Grace called him.

"Today, I posted 'unreliable source' notices on eighteen shares," he said. I didn't see that as a catastrophic number. He had over a thousand friends.

"And only six were in the group of thirty-two I busted yesterday."

"Jeezus," I cringed, changing my mind.

"Toby, what is so hard about finding a media fact-checking site and finding out if your news is fake before hitting SHARE?"

Most of his fake-news examples were political, and I tended to ignore politics. It all seemed depressing when I had enough to get over my personal stuff. Hence, Dad could put me to sleep. I came up with, "How do they know the media fact-checkers aren't lying?"

I could tell by how fast his answer came that he'd been reciting it to others. "How long would an electrician stay in business if he were hotwiring houses to blow up? A business goes under fast if they're lying about what they're selling. The fact checkers are still reliable—in spite of the paranoids."

He'd decided politics was a good distraction for my recovering brain. I listened through his rant on people using their beliefs to determine the facts rather than facts to determine their beliefs. Dad could be intense.

But a likeness in our problems started to rise out of the fog in my head. "Dad, I get you," I busted in, "and your frustration because, well, the cops are telling me that my facts are false. How can a *fact* be *false?* We should be talking about *why* the truth happened or *how*. But can we at least agree on what the truth *is?*"

There was a silence, and then, "If you know the police's problem, you must have spoken with the psychologist—can't remember his name—"

"Me neither. Starts with V. Dad, I don't need the guy. I know what happened at the well."

"Well, it's not just about one memory, Toby. You've been traumatized. You need..." His words faded into *blah blah blah* about ways that shrinks help you. "If your mom hadn't had psychotherapy before being adopted by the Downeys, she likely would have been unadoptable. Look at her now! You wouldn't have fantastic grandparents and twenty-three cousins if it weren't for psychotherapy."

My mom had been in foster care from ages twelve to fourteen. She doesn't talk about her own parents much. We only know her dad had been a drug lord and her mom died of an overdose when she was ten. You'd think she was born into the Downey family. They adopted her and several others, even though they had eight kids of their own. The kids and grandkids rent out practically a whole floor at the Port Dingo Hotel each Fourth of July. We've spent Christmas with Grandma and Grandpa Downey since I was four.

My mom runs a dance school on the island while raising me, a special-needs child, and a sister who's high maintenance but thinks she's low maintenance. I'd say Mom's doing okay.

"Fine, fine. If a shrink wants to find some, like, better version of me, I'll sit and talk to him. But he won't change what I know to be true. So long as we're clear on that."

"Perfectly clear. And 'traumatized' doesn't mean lost sanity, Toby."

"Whatever."

My eyes flipped to the doorframe. The teenage girl across the hall was out of bed, studying something on her computer screen while sitting in her strange-looking wheelchair. A couple of orderlies passed by. Nobody was staring at me, though one thing I loved about Dad's tirades was that the "watched" feeling dimmed down.

Dad's words started registering in my head again, though it was hard to be interested. "Toby, people believe certain things, not because the facts line up to support them, but because those beliefs feel most convenient to them."

I thought he was still stuck on Facebook and grumbled, "Just unfollow those suckers, Dad."

"*Your* view of the facts, about what happened at the well, is very convenient. That's what I'm saying."

"Convenient to *who?*" I snapped and quickly followed up with, "*whom?*" My dad has something like good-grammar OCD. As I'd corrected myself, he said nothing.

"None of this is very convenient to *me*, in case you haven't noticed," I griped. "You, Mom, the cops, the girls—you've *all* flipped your lids."

"That may *feel* like a fact to you. But it is, in fact, an *opinion*."

"In my opinion, it's a *fact*." I ignored his steamy silence and wondered what had inspired me to call him. Of course, he would have known about this police-versus-Toby latest intrigue. "That shrink is about to waltz back in here any second. I'll call you later."

I shut my eyes as he hung up and must have dozed off, exhausted by his notions that my mind had played tricks on me. People recovering from injuries know this phenomenon well. We call it "the nods." It's not from any medication like an opioid addict's nods. You just never know when you're going to drop off at a moment's notice, and allegedly this can go on for months.

When I blinked again, I was almost facing the floor. What woke me, unfortunately, was not my mother or Dr. Vapor coming in the doorframe. It was a sensation on the top of my head, like a pair of eyes out in the corridor was burning a hole through my cranium. I tapped the mirror impatiently to see the same orderlies coming back the other way, a nurse and a technician passing them. That was it. *At first.*

The mirror was about a foot square, not small. So when I caught eyes looking at me, I couldn't always tell where they were coming from at first. Eyes watching you in mirrors are creepy.

These eyes were small and far off. *Girl across the hall.* She'd been here a few weeks and rarely shut her door, so I'd seen her a bunch. She'd never given me a glance that I'd seen. Today we were locking eyes in my mirror. I flipped it quickly away, wondering what she must be thinking of this giant-ass bed. The doctors had moved it out of its usual position that gives privacy. I was almost facing the door and corridor, since the bed came with a lot of equipment that needed to go behind it.

The girl spent most of her day out of bed, but in a contraption almost as weird as my bed. It looked like a wheelchair for people in a torso cast, only it's wrong to call it a chair because people in a torso cast can't sit up straight. It was like a wheel bed, maybe, that raised her torso up at a forty-five-degree angle so she could see where she was going. Her legs, from the knees down, could either sit on the leg rests, or she could pull her knees up under a sheet.

Since she usually had her back to me, I had noticed the website she was chronically logged into. Looked like a blog. Girl definitely was not a gamer. The wallpaper on the site was kind of disturbing, black with just a giant set of eyes. Depending on what page she was on, there would be little windows for writing or a column of type. The eyes took up most of the screen. They were serious. Piercing. Try catching that in a mirror when you're already feeling watched.

Today, she was facing me, so I decided that giving it a whirl was better than lying here listening to the air move. "That website you're always playing on with the big eyes...what is it?" I hit SEND.

A moment later she lifted her phone and looked confused. She ought to be. My overly friendly mom had taken the girl's phone a few days earlier and plugged in a text to me. The girl must have said it was okay. But I hadn't done anything with it until now. She probably was wracking her brain over to whom she'd sent "Hi I'm Rachel" three days ago.

Finally she pulled her head forward so she could see clearly and found my eyes in the mirror again. It gave me a moment to note that her injury was in her lower back, away from her neck, since she was given that much movement.

"Are you creeping on me?" appeared on my phone along with a shocked smile-face emoji.

What do I say? "Gets boring around here. Sorry."

"What's up with your bed?" she replied.

"C'mon over and I'll explain it. I can't even move, so I won't bite." I knew that last line was a bit of a sympathy tug, but I figured I'd need some help getting her motivated. She went in different directions down the hall in her wheelie thing but never even said hi to me. Not that I could blame her. It was like saying hi to Mount Vesuvius.

She just kept staring. Her hand with the phone had slowly lowered to her lap like she had to give it more thought. My instincts were telling me I'd made a mistake reaching out. But there's this thing about my instincts. While they can be amazingly right, I don't get reasons for what creeps them out. My instinct was that she was about to make my life difficult—whether it would be in a small way or big way, I had no clue.

Or maybe it was just something creepy about her stare. I changed the subject quickly to break its intensity.

"S'up with that website? Sorry, but I'm always catching those eyes in my mirror. Creeps me out."

"Thanks. They're MY eyes," she responded. She turned the laptop on the tray table until that set of eyes was in front of her own. True enough, two sets of her eyes stared back. She was a pretty girl. Hair the color of dark chocolate. Milky skin. Eyes that were bluish-purple, unique, and so you could see the distinction from her pupils twenty feet away.

A link appeared on my phone, and when I tapped it, the eyes were right in my face. Above them was another link marked, COME IN AND TALK WITH RACHEL. I tapped it, but Safari can take totally long in this hospital. I hardly ever had more than one bar of power. She sent me another text before it finished downloading.

"I'm not sure that I can come in there. So sorry," was her reply.

I stared at the comment, wondering what in hell that meant. She went down the corridor both ways easily enough. What was wrong with straight ahead?

Safari finally delivered, and I could see what this website was all about. *Ugh,* I said to my instincts. *Welcome to the problem.* The few small words on her homepage read, "I'm using my extrasensory ability to help others."

I tried not to roll my eyes, but I think I did, and I think she saw it.

It's not like I had a complete hatred for the supernatural. But a couple times, my ex-girlfriend Sara Alton dragged me along to get her "hair read" on the boardwalk. This was my only personal experience. Rejoice Illuminata, with the fake Russian accent, would braid a small portion of Sara's hair, stick the braid in this deep blue dish filled with God knows what, then watch the water and tell her what all would happen next week. I try to be diplomatic to most everyone, but watching Sara hand over a pile of twenties for a wet braid that smelled like dollar store cologne…*whatever,* must be a girl thing.

Rachel Lang-Doran was the girl across the hall's name. I was already thinking *she's a money scammer…kinda young for that, but it's not like she's loaded with stuff to do…*

I went politely to her About page because I bet she was watching for it. I read that she came into most of her talent after a car accident that flipped her family's SUV numerous times and killed both of her parents. She couldn't explain why her extrasensory ability grew due to such a terrible shock, but it brings her peace to use it to help others with their lives. Now sixteen, she said the accident had created the need for three spine surgeries and had put her in a torso cast twice now. She said her gift was new and sometimes scary to her. It also said plainly that she didn't charge any fees.

Okay, not a scammer. But she could still be crazy.

She only had a handful of reviews, but all were 5-star. The first read, "This girl is the real deal. Very young but very articulate. She will tell you honestly if she doesn't know what something means or what to do."

The cursor blinked in a box where you could write her a message, get something started. I looked at her in the mirror. She was still staring at me. Or staring past me. Her pupils had moved slightly off me.

I wanted to break her stare again.

I went against my instincts, likely my waves of loneliness nixing them. "So, maybe you could help me out with a problem?" I wrote.

She seemed to know I wasn't going to ask her to come in here and scratch the itch on my ankle. She sent back, "Sure, but no promises."

I didn't quite know how to word it. While I was thinking, she sent, "Your mom already told me how you broke your neck. Falling down a well...terrifying. I'm sorry."

"I didn't fall. I was pushed," I responded without hesitation. "The cops and this shrink are starting to imply that I fell, like I'm a klutz and an idiot. I'm afraid the guy that pushed me will get away with it. Could you, like, get any insight as to what happened? Anything that could confirm the facts?"

I watched in the mirror as she typed and deleted a few times. What finally appeared was, "What if I see something different than what you're looking for?" She quickly followed up with, "I've had a couple people mad at me already. That's hard for me. Kind of new at this."

Her honest and humble answers were winning me over as much as they were making me more leery. Since I knew what had happened at the well, I figured she either wouldn't see anything that contradicted my facts, or if she did, that meant her reviews were fakes. In that case I wouldn't feel mad, just disgusted.

"I promise I won't be mad," was all I wrote.

"Send me some recent photos of you. At least three."

"Friend me on Instagram?" I suggested.

"I need them sent. What you choose gives me some of your energy."

At least she doesn't want to dip my hair in anything, I told my smoldering instincts. And I tried not to think and just follow my thumbs. I flipped her a picture of me and Casen on the beach patrol a week before the accident, one from graduation with our class president Alicia Sims, and, eerie as it was to look at, a selfie I took of me and Trinity on the front porch of the Chapel Rock Inn, twenty or so minutes before the accident. The lights from the porch had gone weird in it, making this reddish-gray splotch over Trinity's head. But our faces were clear, so I sent it without saying anything.

I saw her tap and use her fingers to enlarge three times. She really stopped to look at that last picture of me and Trin, raising her phone slowly to get different light views, I guess, until it was parallel to the ceiling. Her eyes seemed to widen, and finally she let the phone slump and looked out at me. But it seemed like she was staring past me, past the right side of my head. That feeling of being watched struck from behind for the first time. Slowly I adjusted the mirror to what was over my right shoulder. Just the gray wall.

The arm on this mirror could make the view reach just about anywhere in the room, but I knew I had this blind spot over my left shoulder, which, sometimes, the nurses got in. It seemed her eyes froze there.

"Why are you staring like that?" I finally sent.

The intensity of her eyes moved slowly from three feet to my right, across me, and stopped either three feet to my left, or to the edge of what she could see.

I resisted the urge to shudder and texted Mom. "What are you guys discussing? How the West got won??"

I got two replies. Mom's: "We're just waiting for a pdf. Hold tight."

Rachel's: "Can you tell me about the girl in the picture?"

I'd sent her two pictures with girls in them. Before I could ask which, she sent, "The pic with the red orb in it."

I couldn't remember what *orb* meant but knew she was still focused on the picture of me and Trin. I looked at the red-cloud blob over Trinity's head. I'd just assumed it was an imperfection caused by the light on the Chapel Rock from the porch.

A different sort of anxiety rolled over me. I didn't want to talk about Trinity. Too complicated.

"She's my sister," was all I said.

"You really love her, don't you?"

I stared at the photo again, wondering how that was showing. I hate smiling in pictures. That picture featured my usual half-smirk. "Well...she's my sister," I sent with a laugh emoji.

"She's your favorite," she sent back.

So, that was true. Trin and I had a special bond that got stronger after she got mauled.

She smiled in agreement but the smile faded as she continued to stare at the picture intensely. To keep myself from getting creeped out, I went for the gold as my memory cleared about one item.

"What's an orb? Doesn't that word have something to do with a haunting? I'm sure you're a nice person and all, but you will be hard-pressed to get me to believe that a spook pushed me down a gdamn well, sorry."

Hitting the subject straight on had me feeling so watched and unnerved that I pushed the nurse's button. Their station had sixty seconds to respond to me—law. I would make up something that I needed, then ask the nurse to please shut the door. The girl was freaking me out.

Rachel's reply arrived as a response to how a spook couldn't have pushed me: "IDK."

Great. She's cray cray. My instincts were all, *sukkah.* I started the timer on my phone to go off in one minute to help me watch for the nurse. My phone buzzed again, and I looked, trying to ignore that my hand was shaking slightly.

"There was another accident. Years earlier," appeared on my screen. "A wolf or wild animal was involved?"

Okay, not bad. Numbly I shot back to Rachel, "Yeah, when Trinity was five and I was eleven, she got mauled by a dog. I saw it." I blew air out slowly, wondering whether I should be relieved by her accuracy or threatened by it. If she could accurately know Trinity got mauled by a dog six years earlier, could she be seeing something float around my room a minute ago? I tried telling myself I imagined it.

The bed flipped. I was staring at the ceiling and felt myself relaxing, like I always did after a cycle of less-natural positions. The sun was out, the rain was gone. The light made little dancing squares up there. I could see clear blue sky in the mirror. *Storm, sun, storm, sun...*it was the summer of schizophrenic weather.

I sensed Rachel staring, or at least I felt it was her eyes staring at the bottoms of my socks. I turned the mirror to try to catch her face. If she were still following invisible things with her eyes I would send an all-caps message to knock it the hell off.

I almost jumped out of my skin. Dr. Vapor's eyes stared back.

"Your mom's here with me," he said. "We'd like to talk to you together for a minute."

"Shut the door," I stammered. "Girl across the hall is some kind of psychic, or so she thinks. She's giving me the creeps. Mom, did you tell that girl about Trinity getting mauled when she was five?"

Mom crinkled her nose, then said, "We've talked a bit, but I don't think so."

As she shut my door, I caught a glimpse of Rachel thrusting her chair forward, as if to push her own door shut. As if something in this room was creeping her out.

I felt relief to hear Mom's normal feet scuffling in her flip-flops and smell her lemon cologne. The feeling of being watched also dimmed down when people were with me, and Mom was the best sort to have around. She believed in angels and Jesus and nice concepts that the Downeys had taught her, like dead people being happy in heaven. She cured the only spook-fear I had as a kid—fear of the dark in the middle of the night. She got me a fish aquarium with pretty green and blue lights, sea plants and fish that moseyed through the leaves. I never thought of night monsters again.

I put Rachel Lang-Doran's bizarre behavior away for the time being. I had to. What my mom and Dr. Vapor had to say was even more bizarre.

Five

"So, what were you guys doing?" I snapped. "Running for President? Took forever--"

"We were waiting for a pdf," Mom said. "Everything takes longer on weekends, and Sundays are tougher than Saturdays."

She touched my arm. "Look, Toby. Your dad and I really want you to work with this doctor. He's here to help you along with remembering. I don't want to stay in here—I want your conversation to be private."

I watched Dr. Vapor's eyes approach my right side. They were blue but suddenly reminded me of a doll's eyes. Blue and lifeless—

"Can you just trust us, Toby?" Mom asked. "He's not Jack the Ripper. And there are security cameras everywhere on this ward, and no one can get in here without identifying themselves." She pointed toward the window. I flipped the mirror to see what was at the other end of her point, and I saw a security camera in the corner of the ceiling. I said nothing while returning to her gaze.

"I know you're restless, hon. But the doctor and I wanted to tell you together about Mr. Rune and why it is we think he could not have pushed you. We read through his police report before coming back here. There are a few things in there we *can* share with you because they're facts. One is that--"

I didn't wait for some stupid reason. "Look, the cops found him there holding Trinity to the ground. I heard him threaten her myself."

"Mr. Rune says here..." I'd lost Dr. Vapor in the mirror and tapped it to find him following the police report with one finger under a line that was highlighted.

"...he says that your sister Trinity appeared to be trying to jump down the well after you. He was holding her down and yelling at her to keep her from doing something hysterical."

"Wha?" I'd never thought of the guy's words before without the threat to Trinity wrapped around them.

Dr. Vapor paused to read silently, then summarized. "He said when your sister wasn't strong enough to fight him and get up, that's when she started scratching her face. He said she scratched her own face so hard that it bled in several places, and that's also how she injured her eye before she passed out."

I let the silence hang this time, dense with mysteries that had long surrounded my youngest sister. I'd heard in hushed whispers from other moms since Trinity was in kindergarten, and I'd seen their faces when she looked at the ground instead of answering their questions or refused to join in and play with their kids. They only saw a sullen-looking little girl. They didn't see her fears, which were obvious to me, even though I couldn't begin to explain them.

"The face scratching..." I stumbled, "it's part of Trinity's OCD. She's been scratching herself since she was five years old."

That didn't help Trinity sound sane or this Elijah Rune sound guilty. "She only did it when she was really upset. I actually hadn't seen her do it in about two years. Have you, Mom?"

Mom was just staring past me at the blank wall. I thought of Rachel staring at that spot. It took whatever calm I had left. "Mom! Come in, Earth!"

Her gaze dropped to the floor. "Yes...two years...that's accurate, I'd say." Her voice sounded as trembly as her brain seemed to be.

"Does Trinity remember anything?" I stayed on point. Grace had been passed out for at least a minute. Trinity seemed my only hope for some corroboration, though my sinking feeling was starting to make me seasick.

"As you know, Trinity doesn't communicate very well, and it brings her reliability into question," Dr. Vapor said. At least he hadn't said, "She's emotionally disturbed." I hadn't heard that label in years. But it still echoed through my head sometimes, having been blurted by a couple of ruthless moms at football fundraisers.

I wished they had given me confirmation that they agreed that Trinity didn't do it. Screw the shrink's edict not to tell me what they were thinking.

He just said, "Here's another fact about Mr. Rune that we can tell you. Toby, the man is an Anglican priest."

"...a *what*?"

"Elijah Rune is an Anglican Priest," Dr. Vapors repeated.

I asked what Anglican meant.

"It means English. Anglicans are like...Episcopalians, sort of," Mom said.

I was hoping Anglican meant they worshipped sides of beef. Or was that *Angus?* My head fought to shake back and forth.

"And Dad and I even hired a private detective to look into his past. We can't even find something like a juvenile shoplifting charge."

I heard myself laugh instead, being that my neck was so bolted down with tongs that I could feel my head in my ass. The bed was approaching bolt upright. Dr. Vapor was almost looking up to me, rather than down from dead above me.

A tear suddenly rolled down Mom's cheek, which she brushed away with pinched lips. She said, "I'm going to talk to some other patients and try to cheer them up. All I want, at the end of the day, is the truth. We need to know the *truth. As a family."*

I watched her open my door and cross the hall to enter Hi-I'm-Rachel's room, whose door had remained open—probably because I had shut mine.

I looked at Dr. Vapor. And the pitiful look he gave back is what drove the words he'd used on his way out of here: *We can't tell you the facts because of the implications.* The implications were there suddenly: *Dad and Mom thought Trinity pushed me, that Trinity was just unpredictable enough and messed up enough that she might try to kill somebody.*

I said, "Ohhhhhhhhh, Jeezus."

But somehow, I'd long known in the back of my mind that the situation would come down to this. This shrink wanted to talk to me about Trinity.

He said, "Let's start from the beginning."

"Nothing's going to change," I said icily.

"Toby, I'm a multi-purpose visitor. This isn't just about what happened at the well. I want to talk about anything you want to talk about. Why don't you just tell me...what you've been thinking about lately."

His voice sounded kind. And I was crazy lonely.

Six

I took a cautious step, not seeing a reason to lie to him.

"Apart from this weird feeling of being watched, I've been thinking about the first accident. The one six years ago."

"Where Trinity got mauled by the dog?"

"You know much about that?" I asked.

"Your mother gave me some background." He carefully raised a bunch of pages off the clipboard to look again at what he'd been writing while questioning me earlier. "And you told me that both Trinity and you saw a therapist. You, because you were a witness; she because of the mauling itself."

"Actually, I caused it," I said.

He wrote that down. Facts were good, even if they felt bad. Not that I wanted to go into a whole lot of detail.

"But look, that was six years ago," I went on quickly. "We went to therapy, both of us, and we've moved on. It was an accident—stupid bad judgment on my part—that caused the whole thing. I'd rather not dig up a corpse."

"Okay," he said to my surprise, jotting something down—probably some asterisk to remind him to manipulate me onto the subject later. "What else has been on your mind, Toby?"

That there's a spook in my room. I didn't say it, though texting with Rachel had made the sensations of being watched more real. I had jumped from *I feel watched,* just a notion about my feelings, to *my feelings mean something real.* Not that a spook could be real. *Could it?*

This doctor would never see a spook as real. So, between him and the girl across the hall, I felt stretched out on a rack. How do you start off a conversation that you know will cut your credibility down to nothing? And why should I? The silence was growing thick.

"Why don't you tell me about Grace first," the doctor suggested.

He must have known it was easier to talk about Grace, my perfectly normal sister, but I said something completely meaningless anyway, just to stall. "Mom let Grace try out for cheer this year as a sophomore. She made it. Last week, I think."

"Yes, your mother said Grace was happy about that."

"Grace loves school," I blathered. "It seemed weird last year, seeing my sister in the corridors, the cafeteria, when we had not shared a school in three whole years, ya know?"

"Sure."

He was obviously waiting for me to switch to Trinity, my *abnormal* sister. I wasn't biting.

"Actually, Grace is a shoo-in for cheer. Mom balked at her trying out last year. She wants Grace to stay focused on dance, get in a ballet company... Let's say Grace is just trying to escape my mother's evil, late-afternoon dance clutches." My laugh sounded plastic.

"Are you close to your sisters?" Dr. Vapors asked.

The question stopped my brain for a moment.

"Yes. I mean, no. I mean…how close can a guy be to his sisters when they're three and six years younger? I'm not home a lot. Grace, I guess, is your typical teenage girl—raging hormones, big mouth—mouths off to Mom too much. When she showed up in my school last year, she tried to constantly flirt with my friends. It felt weird, like an invasion. Especially since my friends were all, '*Dang* Toby, your sister got hot.' I guess I'm wishing now I had been nicer to her."

"Do you feel guilt over any injuries she sustained at the well?"

"*Hello.* I only kicked her in the face when she was trying to hold onto my legs, to save my life. Broke her nose...knocked her out cold."

"But your kicking her was an accident," he said kind of quietly.

"Look, my sisters wouldn't have been hanging out at that well if it weren't for me and my bright ideas. These 'family birthday weekends'...everything stops for some cutesy concept of my parents. You end up hanging out with your sisters, which never happens otherwise. You forget how young and vulnerable they are because, truth be told? You *don't* really know them. You *love* them. But how well can you know them when they come in the door with Mom at eight o'clock at night, and you're on two sports, and do all this other stuff at school?"

I flicked at the mirror impulsively but only saw Mom facing Rachel, who still had her back to us, which reminded me of how quickly she'd turned away from a view of my room. I didn't feel like looking at that and texted Mom, "Shut my door!!!"

Then I spoke. "Tell me. How do you take a shit in a torso cast?"

"Mm. Not easily, I'd say," Dr. Vapor's laugh was polite but disinterested. "About on a par with how you make waste."

I peed in a jug and dumped through a hole in the back of this thing where a takeaway container could be attached. You learn to do what you gotta do, I supposed, but I wasn't really interested in Rachel's toilet-making. I was stalling.

Mom scooted out upon seeing my text and pulled my door shut. My body relaxed.

"You don't feel any closer to Trinity than to Grace?" he finally asked, and I sighed with impatience. Trinity was even three years younger than Grace. I would think the answer was obvious.

Out of my mouth came, "Trinity is an angel. She's, like, not even human"

"An *angel?*"

I guessed he knew enough about Trinity to doubt my opinion, though I was being sincere. "What else did my parents tell you about her? Besides her high IQ and that she has selective mutism?"

He paused. I was sure it was to get any sense of being stunned out of his tone before going on. "I know she's been homeschooled due to severe asthma attacks. Your mom feels it's too serious for a school to—"

"It's very serious. It's EpiPen serious," I went to bat for my mom, even though I knew better. Trinity was homeschooled for this lengthy list of reasons, and asthma merely sat in the middle of it.

"Your mom says shortly before she got mauled, they noticed that she was developing speech issues —"

"Emphasis on *before her accident,*" I said quickly, not wanting him to think I was responsible for the fact that Trinity hardly talked. "For about six months, they treated it as a speech impediment, but Mom took the speech therapist tapes. Trinity talks a mile a minute to Mom, when they're alone. And there's a couple weird Bible-thumping girls—er, homeschooled girls—in my mom's best classes. If Trinity is alone with them hanging out at the dance school, she'll talk a mile a minute to them. Speech disorders aren't selective like that."

"So, they went with *selective mutism*," he said correctly. "The problem is...she doesn't talk to *you?*" He raised the question softly and in a compassionate-type tone, but it still felt like he was twisting a knife.

"Or Grace, or Dad... or anybody else in the universe," I sighed.

"Look, you won't understand Trinity from anything I tell you. Nobody does. Except for me. And that's only because I can read her mind—" I stopped, realizing I'd just told him I didn't really know my sisters anymore.

"—when I'm paying attention, that is."

"So... your sister is a categorized, right-brained genius with selective mutism, asthma, and some OCD behaviors including cutting—the face-scratching would be considered a subcategory of cutting or self-harm." His tone was informative, not insulting, but it made me defensive anyway.

"It's very complicated," I confessed. "But only if you don't know her. It's all just…Trinity. I'd tell you she worships the ground I walk on, but anything that isn't a fact is going to make you think I'm exaggerating to protect her."

"Not necessarily," he said gently, but I wasn't backing down.

"Add this to your bank of facts. Trinity might be homeschooled, but technically, she's a high school graduate, with more languages, physics, computer coding, literature and…whatever than I'll ever have. But they said her type of genius is like a spotlight on a stage. The sharper the light, the darker the surrounding areas."

"In other words, they can't predict types of behavior her intelligence would cause." He put that 'delicately,' I would say.

"It means her IQ could cause the OCD and the problems with talking that other kids don't have. They were not caused by the mauling, and they certainly have not made her violent."

He smiled in a jolly way, but I felt like a crab trying not to wander into a crab trap. "Anyway, I'm not responsible for her shyness or any of those other problems…only a few scars in and around her…" I stopped. I was used to seeing Trinity's scars, and so it only hit me occasionally what a completely disgusting place on your body it was to be chomped on by a vicious dog. "…in her left armpit."

He watched me in the mirror. I watched him back.

"Have you seen her," he finally asked, "since you've been here?"

"No. She was in this hospital for a week herself." I thought about the conversation I'd had with my parents about this, and Mom's words: *Toby, I don't think we should bring her in here, hon. You know how her asthma can be tricky…*

"Do you *want* to see her?" he asked, and I watched his eyes some more.

I didn't realize how badly I did until he said it, but I went with another fact.

"No, no. She…has this weird habit of losing her shit when she sees dead birds or squished cats in the road, stuff like that. We had a problem with dead birds in the yard a few summers back. We'd no idea why birds kept dying in our yard that summer, but I got in the habit of heading out there every morning before Trinity woke up to make sure there wasn't another one. Or she would cry and end up on her asthma nebulizer half the morning."

"So, their feeling is that her seeing you in a special-facilities bed for a spinal cord injury would be detrimental to her own health… given her personality."

"Right." I watched his concern in the mirror but argued, "No, I really don't want her in here, all looking at me like…" I shut my eyes, trying not to remember.

He was merciless. "Like what?"

Like the night in June when I woke up in a sweat over this upcoming family weekend. I always got skeeved right before them, had nightmares, woke up sweating. Something terrible had happened once. Something could happen again…"

Mom and Dad had always felt that Trinity getting mauled had nothing to do with us being on vacation. Accidents can happen anywhere, they'd always said. *Ta ha-ha.*

I get up out of bed and tiptoe down the hall in the dark. I'd been doing this three times a year, maybe—with a nagging feeling that I have to look in on her and make sure she's still breathing normally. I look in her room, and my brain goes a little on the fritz. All the furniture's piled up in the middle…the mattress stands straight up like a monolith, like it has eyes, like it's laughing at me, whispering, "Not here, Mr. Weird."

I'm jumpy, backing out again, remembering. She's sharing a room with Grace while Mom re-wallpapers, between everything else she has to do. I never go in Grace's room unless I have to. She could wake up…ask what the hell do I want with busting her out of her beauty rest, in that whiny voice of hers…

But I'm sucked to the door like a magnet, and something's making my heart slam… Grace is mean to Trin. Impatient. Spouts too many hormonally charged rant fests lately. For Trinity, sleeping with Grace would be like sleeping under a wet, electric blanket. I don't know how I know this. Trinity certainly never told me. She never tells me anything.

Grace is facing the wall, thank God. Trinity's on her back. I move up silently beside her and stare down. As blond as Grace and I have stayed, Trinity has gotten darker and darker.

"She's a throw-back from Grandma Rose," my blond mom loves to say. My blond dad loves to agree. "My mother also had a very high IQ. She was a brilliant poet."

What they don't say is that Grandma Rose was in and out of a mental institution most of her adult life for schizophrenia. But I don't think Trin is schizophrenic.

Maybe Trinity's reincarnated. I don't know. I just know she's like something divine. A little angel. I usually only see her with her hair pinned tight to her head because that's how she comes home from ballet. Unless it's the middle of the night. It falls all around the pillow.

Her arm is over her head in these summer PJs with no sleeves. The moonlight pours in.

I can make out one of her scars in the moonlight because I know exactly where they are. Most people's armpit is shaped like a hollowed-out egg, but Trin's is shaped like a hollowed-out cone. It comes to a point. Three lines reach out, though I can only see the one that runs down her arm. A second is about six inches long, running toward her waist and a third one stopped a merciful few inches from—I haven't seen that last scar in years, and I'm glad I can only see one now. One is enough.

It's the totality of surreal, to be awake when you should be asleep, to be silent when you want to speak, to never know what to say.

She's blinking. Her head moves slowly to the side. She's looking to make sure Grace is asleep. Then it moves back again. Her mouth spreads out in this little grin.

Homeschooled kids... Grace goes on and on AND on about them.

Grace has threatened to stick stuff under Trin's pillow, if she doesn't start showing any interest in knowing what sex is. Dirty pictures off friends' computers or something like that. A couple times I've checked under her pillow, though Grace swore it was all frustration talk, a reaction to her ever-present question with no answer: "Why do I have to have a weird sister that no one can get close to, instead of one I could hang out with and tell secrets to?"

Trin's smiling but doesn't move. I think I should just turn and leave. She's breathing. Grace hasn't tied her to the bed or anything. I never know what makes me think Grace has it in for her. Grace is fourteen, has a life of her own, doesn't hit her, kick her, or any of that stuff Casen's sisters do to torment each other—though his sisters are thick as thieves.

*Whenever Trin wakes up to find me checking in on her, she'll smile, like she's doing now, which completely annihilates me. Usually I wave, then turn around and leave, and she seems to get it, that I'm just making sure she's breathing normally and isn't...I don't know what...*isn't dead of something else that nobody saw coming?

I feel annihilated because I'm also trying to say something:

I'm sorry, I'm sorry, I'm sorry. Why won't you talk? What's with this exclusive little club you've got going on that includes Mom and a few homeschooled, ballet Bible thumpers? What about me and Grace? And Dad? Why won't you forgive me? Me first, but Dad and Grace, and all the normal kids in the world, too?

She sits up, but the bed doesn't creak. Only the sheet rustles. Wings of angels. She gets upon her knees, lays her head on my chest, wraps her arms around my back, and hugs me totally tight.

Trinity has rarely been able to get out more than five words at a time to me. This is how we talk; this is how she tells me, "I love you. I never held it against you. I don't have it in my heart; my heart wouldn't know how to stay mad at a person."

This is why I keep coming back in the quiet, in the dark, because of what she can't seem to goddam say once the sun comes up—

"I don't want her in here…finding ways to tell me that it's all okay." I heard my voice rising in volume slightly. I didn't want to look at images of reality. "Come over here, where I can see your eyes with my eyes."

He stood up, disappeared from the mirror, and then looked down over me. The bed had flipped again at some point, and I hadn't even noticed. The mirror moved with a swipe of my hand I couldn't seem to control. Somehow, I'd caught the deep hazel eyes of Rachel. Mom had moved on.

"I told Mom to shut my door," I snapped.

"She did. Apparently not all the way. It just opened a minute ago by itself…"

There was nothing creepy in his voice. It was a news-brief type of fact that defaulted immediately to some breeze having done it. He shut it, but not before I caught Rachel's eyes for a brief moment looking from my eyes to something immediately beside me, on the other side of Dr. Vapor.

I couldn't hold back anymore. I decided to blame my stress on Rachel. "That girl across the hall? She thinks I've got a spook in here."

I watched his eyes find mine, then quickly move to the door. The silence made me wonder... "Is she your patient too?"

"I can't tell you that," he said with an easy shrug. "Doctor-Patient confidentiality."

I supposed that meant she *was,* or he would have said, "no."

"Tell me, Doc. What do you do with a patient who thinks they're sensing spooks? Don't you automatically think that's some sort of, you know, weird psychological symptom?"

He barely blinked before giving a complicated answer. I supposed this wasn't the first time he'd been asked.

"We don't believe that every supernatural encounter is psychosis, no. Plenty of psychotherapists belong to houses of worship. We worship *God."* He shrugged. "The leap to other things is seen as rational so long as the patient isn't exhibiting signs of disordered behavior—"

"But there's a big difference in believing in a God, and, say, believing in the Witch of Indor."

He was back again, eye-to-eye. After a moment he asked, "Have you always believed in ghosts, Toby?"

I thought back and said slowly, "Not since I was a little kid. I was afraid of my Grandma Rose. She died in a mental institution when I was about five. I kept feeling like her spirit was in my room for a month or so following the funeral. My mom solved it with a fish tank."

"Your fear of that death dissolved with your mother adding some life to your room."

"Yeah, I stopped feeling that way, what with the fish."

"And there's been nothing since."

"No."

"You haven't had any paranormal beliefs until recently."

I almost laughed. "Since maybe, like, half an hour ago. Honestly, that Rachel girl freaked me out. She was acting like...like her eyes were following something in here."

"Her eyes were following something."

He was "parroting" me. My other shrink had done it constantly—repeating you to keep you going. "We were texting. But her eyes kept shifting all around my room."

"That's a very subtle thing for you to see from all the way across the hall."

True enough. But I *had* seen it. "Her eyes, they're kind of an unusual bluish. You can see them move more easily than brown eyes against black pupils."

"Okay," he seemed to buy that. "So, Rachel is having some effect on your belief in the supernatural."

"Well...maybe." The conversation had started making me nervous. It was bringing invisible eyes out of the walls, like, making me feel watched from everywhere.

"Possibly because meeting her isn't the only thing that happened half an hour ago," he finally said. "You also met *me* half an hour ago. *I* was the one who brought up the Witch of Indor."

"So... you're saying any belief I might develop in a spook may have something to do with meeting you..."

"I'm not trying to tell you what happened at the well, Toby," he said. "I just want you to be aware of not only your thoughts and memories but also your thought *processes.* To develop a sudden belief in the supernatural...I'd see that as related to your dilemma."

I thought of my dad saying, "Your memories of what happened at the well are very convenient." I supposed he and Dr. Vapor would think I was bringing in a spook to keep anyone from blaming Trinity.

"I think I'm done now," I said tersely. "Would you mind shutting the door on your way out? Tightly?"

I thought he'd insist on staying his full hour, but maybe all that waiting and reading with Mom made him think it was okay to give me my way. He stood up.

"Would you like to do some writing this week, Toby? If you were accepted at a prestigious journalism school like the University of Missouri, you must be gifted. People usually enjoy using their gifts."

I think my having been accepted to Missouri had less to do with my good grades and more to do with a screenplay I wrote junior year. It had won a national screenwriting contest for high school upperclassmen. Mine had been about a lifeguard who saved a little girl next door from a vicious female child molester. I think they liked the female part. It was original, and that's why I won. It had been totally fun to write. Or maybe I should say totally gratifying somehow. I made myself laugh and cry while writing.

"I'm not trying to be difficult. It's just the nods. You know…I'm still falling asleep every twenty minutes."

"Maybe if you found some way to keep yourself awake during the day, you'd sleep a little better at night," he said. "Try to write down every memory you have of the night you went down the well, starting from the time you arrived at the Chapel Rock Inn. Writing slows the mind. You'll be amazed at the details that will come clear. Does that sound good?"

It didn't. But he shook my hand and said he'd be back in a few days. He walked out and shut the door, but it kind of bounced back open without him seeing it.

"*Jesus God,*" I muttered, so exhausted by this lockdown where I couldn't even shut a door that I didn't want open. Rachel was staring.

Since I was still close to lying flat, I needed the mirror. I stared back at her eyes, wishing she had the good sense to wipe that disturbed look off her face while swapping stares. It was like I was growing horns before her very eyes.

"Do you mind??" I yelled, not even bothering to text.

She tore her eyes down, her face turned bright red, and she moved forward to shut her door. I'd made her feel bad. I didn't care. I might have just wasted a friend but didn't care about that either. I figured I would write down memories that would get Elijah Rune (what a sick name) locked up. Plenty of priests had done evil things to kids. I still felt convinced, and couldn't wait to put a sane, organized, detailed and factual version of what happened in Dr. Vapor's email box.

Seven

WRITTEN ON: Sunday, August 7, 3:32 pm

SUBJECT: My Accident My Most Embarrassing Moment

It's actually no longer 3:32 p.m. I've fallen asleep three times while trying to write this shit, and it's now 5:17 at night. Dinner's here. Meatloaf that looks like Purina Cat Chow and green beans the color of baby poop. I don't want to write and don't want to eat. I only want to sleep.

I had told Dr. Vapor I would be too tired to write much of anything. But I'm actually thinking about something that won't put me to sleep. If I'm writing it, at least I won't be cutting logs while Trinity rots in Suspicion Limbo.

The guys I hang with had been swapping stories all spring about their most embarrassing moments. Who knows how you get on certain subjects. Mine is pretty good. When these shoot-the-shit fests actually started giving each tale a score around Memorial Day, my story was voted second best: A nine.

It had to do with forgetting my money on my very first date in seventh grade. Other guys had started to ask girls out, but their idea of a date was to invite them to play video games and then lurch on them at some critical point. Either that or they would "hang out" by going walking, and they would end up in the dunes, where everyone from Grace to my parents and their friends got their first kiss.

Instead of luring Jana Klein out into the meadow grass, I would be very sophisticated and take her to the Port Dingo Hoagie Shop for dinner. We could walk there, and walking home, we could walk *through* the meadow grass, and just maybe I would find some nerve, blah, blah. I'd had the whole thing figured out.

We were eating Italian hoagies in Dingo's Subs when two terrifying thoughts struck me at once. First, I'd left both my money and my cell phone on the kitchen counter and couldn't pay for this, and secondly, Trinity was at home in the throes of a bad asthma attack. I wasn't sure how I knew this second thing. I had a little of Mom's ESP, at least as far as Trinity was concerned, and once that year I'd found myself leaning over her in her bed, banging on her rattling chest to loosen it, and *then* waking up. She was six.

But this no-money thing was a curveball to the gut. I shot up in the booth and sent our coke glasses into Jana Klein's chest, that sort of grabbed hold of her breasts like she'd just sprouted binoculars. Then I choked and shot an enormous glurt of chewed onions and salami into her hair. It was at that point that I realized I could hear Trinity wheezing because she was standing right behind me. She was holding out my wallet and phone.

She wasn't supposed to leave the yard with her bike—Dad had just taken the training wheels off two weeks earlier. And she was never supposed to leave the house without her inhaler, ever. So, I had to call Mom to come pick up her and her bike, then deliver Jana home to her door, drenched and drowning in what clearly resembled puke. I'd been chewing that hoagie bite a long time, too

nervous to swallow.

And I'm too sensitive, yeah, yeah, but it was

sophomore year before I actually kissed a girl,

and probably only then because it was inevitable.

Casen had practically been beating girls off him

with a stick for a year and a half, and we were

always together. (The overall Most Embarrassing

Moment Award went to Matt Sykes, who got thrown

out of the locker room naked in eighth grade, and

there's this whole gaggle of Little League Varsity

Cheerleaders practicing out in the corridor—and it

was really cold.)

Trinity—that's why I thought of this story.

That's the type of little girl she was. I mean,

wouldn't most sisters have fallen down on the

ground and laughed their sides off, all, *my

brother's about to get arrested in front of his

first date ever?* I mean, wouldn't some sisters

have gone down there *without* the money, just to

watch their big brother get arrested? She risked

her life, essentially, to protect my dignity, even

though I'd ruined myself socially for at least a year before I even saw her.

My phone vibrated with an incoming call. "Anonymous" appeared, and the time: 7:11 PM. I had a couple of telemarketers trying to sell me wheelchairs, and they always called right after seven. I know this because I had nothing better to do than remember shit like this. As they always showed a different phone number so I couldn't block them, I figured this was them disguising themselves.

"Hello?" I said. No response.

"*Hello?*" You know you're slightly off your gourd when you're hoping the telemarketer didn't pick up another call first.

I heard a crackle of some sort and said, "Hi there. I'm stuck in a bed for seven weeks. How's life with you?"

The same sort of crackling came through… Could be a bad connection. "Are you a beer salesman? I'm not a huge drinker. But a cold beer would sure taste—"

I stopped, realizing I was actually hearing *something* rhythmic. *Inhale, exhale, inhale*…I had a deep breather. I listened through three more raspy inhales with guttural exhales. *What the hell?*

"If this is someone from home, you're not funny. You could be actually giving me someone to talk to."

More deep breathing. I started to fume. Just after the accident, Alicia Simms contacted everyone who knew me from football, crew, diving, NHS, and student government. For the first two weeks I was hospitalized, she arranged it so that I got a text every twenty minutes except from midnight to six a.m. One of the highlights of my day was seeing who all texted each time I woke up. But the texts and calls had dropped off after a couple weeks. I was lucky to get a text a day, and since everyone had summer jobs, it was hard to get someone's actual voice on the other end of my phone.

The deep breathing had these raspy inhales and exhales, like someone was being strangled. It almost sounded like... *an asthma attack?* I'd certainly heard enough of them over my life that, even though the "anonymous" made no sense, I automatically said, "Trinity?"

It sounded like a girl's voice that whispered, "She's trying to kill you."

That gave me a not-fun adrenaline rush. I looked across the hall as my chest lit fire. Two nurses were in Rachel's room, and she was listening to them politely lecture her that she shouldn't want to go to bed this early or something like that.

Not that Rachel would make a call like this, but *who would?* When friends called, they were generally a little too serious, intimidated by my situation, and I was the one who had to cut all the jokes at first. Who was drunk and disorderly? *Whose party?*

"Very funny," I said, though my hand was starting to shake. The breathing did sound just like Trinity's in the throes of it. But she wouldn't do this.

"She wanted to kill you. She *will* kill you… "

"Who is this!" I demanded. "I'm going to count backwards from three. If you don't tell me who you are, you sick little fuck, I'm hanging up." *Breathing, gasping…*

"Three…two…one…" I ended the call and immediately hit my dad's number.

"What's up?" he asked. "I'm trying to get tickets to come up, but the airlines want twenty thousand a ticket for last-minute flights tomorrow."

I said, "You're kidding," to get the pins and needles out of my skin before I told him about the call.

"I'm exaggerating. But it may not be possible to come to you." He blew out a couple curses. I chimed in with a couple myself. Dad's got good-grammar OCD but believes in freedom of speech, big-time. So you can use a swear word so long as you use it properly in a sentence.

"I just got a prank fucking call," I finally blurted.

"That's interesting, using an i-n-g word as an adjective. I'm wondering why you didn't splice your profanity in before 'prank,' thereby using it as a traditional adverb."

He could be so annoying sometimes.

"I just got prank called," I huffed.

"Really? By whom?"

Smart as he was, my dad could also be an idiot now and again. He laughed at himself. "Well…maybe it was a telemarketer."

"It wasn't a telemarketer. Caller ID said 'anonymous.' Where's Trinity?"

"Upstairs in her room," he said. "Why on earth would Trinity prank call you? That's not in her pay scale." It's not her personality type, he meant, and he was right. But she could figure out in a second how to do anything with a cell phone, including mask a number, if she wanted to—not that she would want to.

"I don't know, Dad. I'm grabbing at straws here. The person sounded like she was having an asthma attack. I just wanted to—"

I heard his chair creak and steps as he moved across the floor. "Strange, very strange…I just don't understand why she would call you if she were having an asthma attack when I'm right here in the house."

I didn't mention the "she's trying to kill you" part directly. I just said, "She's afraid of the Witch of Indor. And since she never says anything on the phone to me except an occasional 'yes' or 'no,' I can't begin to tell you what her mind is dredging up, but it could be that the Witch of Indor is trying to… to get in here, to get at me…"

"The crank caller mentioned the Witch of Indor?" Dad asked. I didn't answer, just listened through what sounded like his footsteps going upstairs. I heard a door creak and, "She's in the shower… Hey, Trin?" He knocked on the bathroom door, and I heard shower water get louder, like he'd pushed the door open an inch to be heard. "Are you having an asthma attack?"

My sister's little voice said, "No."

"Did you just call your brother?"

There was a long pause, though I took that to be surprise and confusion. Trinity hadn't called me all summer. She just listened to me talk for a minute when Dad called me, and she texted me pictures of the beach and ballet class, and stuff like that.

Finally, "No."

I knew sometimes she jumped in the shower when an asthma attack wasn't already off the hook. The hot steam helped clear her chest.

After all I'd just written I was even less likely to suspect her of anything but decided to end any doubts I might have later.

"Dad, get her phone," I said.

I heard the bathroom door close. "I already have it… "

"Did she make a call three minutes ago to me?"

"No," he said, and then, "Grace?"

I could hear his footsteps moving back down the hall as he said, "Trinity has no sense of humor. If it's a prank call from anyone in this house, it would have been Grace."

Grace could be a practical joker, but she wasn't *that* evil. I listened to Dad ask if she'd just called her brother and listened to her whine back.

"No! You said *not* to call him. You said we're not *allowed to* call him until he remembers what happened at the well!"

That got me pissed. "I know what happened at the well!" I shouted, but it got mixed up with her loud mouth. "Somebody said *what* to him?? That's sick! Look at my phone. The only person I called was Wiley, *why?* Because we're going to a party! I'll find out who pranked him. What a shithead. Gimme that… "

Suddenly her voice was in my ear. "Who prank called you??"

She could be an idiot, too. She added, "…about the Witch of *Indor?"*

"What have you been saying to people down there?" I demanded suddenly as a thought struck me. "I just got an earful today of something you probably already knew. It was about the Witch of Indor dying by falling down a well. I don't want to become island gossip, Grace. *She* falls down a well, and now *I* wind up down the same damn well…" It dawned on me that whoever it was, this all could have started with Grace's big

mouth—

"I swear on my life, Toby. I would not do that to you! I do know

that story. The coincidence is creepy, but I would not stir the shit like that

for you…even though it's driving me crazy to be answering 'How is your

brother?' every ten minutes all summer. God, give me some credit."

Her tone was adamant and sounded genuine. It could have been that

she told the story at some bonfire two summers back about the witch

falling down the well, and some knucklehead put it together when I fell.

"I'll find out who it is, though," she said. "Everyone will be at this

party tonight. Wiley and me, we'll make everyone hand over their phone.

If someone won't do it, they're the suspect."

"How are you going to do that without bringing up the Witch of

Indor?" I asked. "Be *careful,* Grace! When I come home, I want to forget

this, not answer everyone's bullshit questions for the next ten years."

"I'll be very careful," she said. "You will come home to zero island

gossip. Even if I have to break my own back making that happen."

"Thanks," I said. That was nice. I wondered if she was turning over

a new leaf. In my thinking, Grace hadn't had an unselfish thought since she

was like twelve. Mom, with her way of finding the silver lining, had

mentioned once last week that a trauma like this makes everyone grow a bit. I felt my chest relaxing, my smile even spreading slightly as I said, "Anyway, uh…whose party?"

"Not telling," she said. "It'll just make you wish you could go. Hey! When you come home? Me and Wiley will throw the biggest party for you that you've ever seen. Right, Wiley?"

I heard Wiley's grunt through the phone. Mom doesn't let him in Grace's bedroom, even though he's been friend-zoned since they started hanging out in third grade. I wondered what else Grace was getting away with since Dad was in charge. Had he even bothered to ask whose party?

But Wiley grabbed the phone and furthered my suspicions about trauma making people grow—even Grace's half-wit bestie. Part of my parents' problem with Wiley had been his chronic three-word vocabulary, even when he was eating at our dinner table. Here they are:

"Ayeeee." Wiley's version of "yeah."

"Nayeeeee." Wiley's version of "no."

"Mmmyahnayeeee." That was "I don't know."

Because we had Trinity's speaking problems, we probably put up with him better than another family could have, even though his problem was just not caring what he sounded like. I could see him in the school corridors chatting it up with other people, but I'd rarely been in ear shot to know what he was saying. Grace's defense always was, "Wiley's really sweet, you just have to get to know him."

Here it was, like six years later, and he was talking. "Yeah, bro, like… a *total* party. We're gonna get you a band. Like…who do you want?"

"Thanks, guys. Is Dad okay with this?" When Wiley said, "ayeeee," I asked for Ridgewood, the band that played at my prom.

I could hear my dad saying, "If these plane tickets don't break me," which meant yes, and made me smile bigger. Even Wiley was growing up, and I was having a major bash once I could get out of here.

"Take it easy," he said. "We'll get working on this one. You know everyone on the island will come."

"Take it easy, yourself," I said, smiling hugely.

By the time Dad took the phone back, I was telling myself it didn't matter exactly who called me if it was just an island prankster. Drunks get sober; that was probably the last I'd hear. Dad's tread squeaked on the stairs as he said, "I finally blocked some guy on Facebook tonight. Ya proud of me?"

It was his turn, now that he'd promised me a band. It was hard to fake interest with my mood suddenly in the outer stratosphere. "Yeah. Totally. So what sort of lie was he telling?"

"*Sharing,*" he corrected me. "Even though sharing a lie is the same as telling a lie. Isn't it?"

I supposed.

"Here's the problem with social media. Most people are not conniving enough to think up a really good lie and know how to spread it. But suddenly…there's *all* these lies. It's like a smorgasbord! All you have to do is pick some tale that tickles your fancy, tell yourself it's true, and hit SEND. You don't even have to burn a single calorie."

I chuckled. Dad could cut the tension with his poor excuse for problems. "Which lie was this guy sharing?"

"I'd have to call this guy 'legion,'" he said. "He's got a hundred. There's a space station on the bottom of the ocean where Atlantis sunk. The school shootings near Boston were a hoax. The Trade Center was blown up by the President. This time, he shared a video of a protest in Oregon where the alleged liberals were shooting up the conservatives with guns. Who ever heard of liberals having guns? The premise is ridiculous even before you Google it."

"It's pretty hard to fake a video," I pointed out.

"The video was twelve years old and shot in Indonesia," he said. "It's not so hard to write a lying ident."

"How'd you find that out?" I asked. "I'm impressed."

"Oh my God, I can't believe you're my child," he snapped back. "I just googled a description of the picture. Took five seconds! *Five seconds,* and people would rather poison their neighbors with lies than take the time."

"Dad, this is not really a problem," I said, feeling myself come back down to reality. "Here's a problem: I can't just Google 'what happened at the well' and copy and paste it and say, 'see?'"

"Mm..." he said. There was a long silence. Rachel's door was now shut, and I watched the line of light under the door turn black, like she was going to sleep. I felt the threat of aloneness wafting over me, what with everyone at home going to a party. I probably wouldn't get any texts I could turn into calls.

"Toby, everything that's bad starts with a lie. Think about it."

I didn't want to. I just responded likewise, "Mm."

"Somebody up there is lying. You figure out who that is, and you'll have your truth, your peace."

"Yeah, it's that Elijah Rune," I spat out. "Mr. I-Went-For-A-Walk-to-Sort-Out-My-Thoughts."

"The most dangerous lies of all are the ones we believe because it's *convenient.*"

I sighed. "I don't suppose it would be very convenient for the police to arrest a priest and have to defend their actions."

"Just don't *you* believe anything because it's convenient."

"I won't," I said.

He stayed quiet a long time, like he didn't quite believe me. It was kind of galling. I was getting ready to just hang up when he finally went on. "I need to pack Trinity's nebulizer and medication. You know what flights do to her. And I need to find airline tickets. I'm believing in faith that I will find three tickets for which I don't have to mortgage the house. Hey. What's the difference between me believing in faith that three airline tickets are coming my way, and someone believing that aliens have a space base on sunken Atlantis?"

He often knew the answers to the questions he asked. He just wanted to see if I did also. A thought that was mushrooming, one that started with an image but was blowing up into a full-blown memory. It started when he mentioned Trinity's name.

I said, "I'll call you later…"

As he hung up, I took a deep breath and stared at the nothingness in my doorframe that always felt all wrong. Then I pulled the laptop close and just started writing again.

Eight

WRITTEN ON: Sunday, August 8, 8:01 pm

SUBJECT: The Night of the Accident

The huge lawn in front of the Chapel Rock Inn had been extended this summer, the forest cut back across the road to circle the well. It was all in cut grass now and slightly lit with torch lamps, like maybe the owners decided the well had been dangerous, so covered in bramble on the other side of their circular drive. A "secret discovery" has more allure than what's out in the open, maybe, and they were looking to avoid an accident. *Oops.*

Darkness was falling fast as Trinity and I hung on the porch, which ran the length of the inn and was lined with a dozen rocking chairs. Beyond the woods rose two mountain peaks, and the moon sat between them like a big light bulb, a perfect circle, throwing its glow onto the lawn. The moon glow reflected off the silhouette of the well, almost to the black woods, and the rope that cordoned it off. A little sign hung from the rope, and a little spotlight barely made it visible. I couldn't read from where I was, but I knew from passing it as we arrived that it said, "Do not go past this sign."

"Calling all stupid kids," I muttered to Trin, a laugh squirting out my nose. "They ought to just…*not* put the sign up. It's like a drawing magnet. Wonder why they didn't just fill the well in with concrete or something. Brain seizures, maybe."

I toed Trinity in the ankle with my sneaker, not that I expected a response. She'd trailed me out here like a lost puppy while Grace went to check out the spa, the rafting launch, and any kids she might be able to turn up, though most people wouldn't be arriving until the next night, which was a Friday. Dad had wanted Mom to have a day to visit the masseuse and "lie about." He said she needed it, though Mom was not the lying-about sort.

Mom and Dad were nowhere in sight—probably still up in their room getting dressed to go to some adult party in the lounge. I was supposed to be going with them. I'll generally only spark something at a party, but Casen had given me one joint as a going-away present, and I thought of going to smoke it down by the waterfall. Let's call it lounge-lizard-music protection. But Trinity had followed me outside.

I sat down in a rocker, patiently, figuring I'd get my chance later. I was watching her lean on the rail in front of me, staring at this well. I could only see her back, the bottom of her ponytail swiping her butt, and her super straight posture, all of which were familiar from Mom's post-grade-school ballet girls. What in hell went on in her mind? I could get Trinity to talk sometimes.

"What're you thinking about?" I tried.

A quick shrug. The usual.

"Why aren't you with Grace?"

Not even a shrug this time. If I didn't adore this kid so much, I would think she was downright rude at times.

"Don't you want to go in the pool?"

A headshake.

"Why not? It's fun. It's not the ocean. There's no sand, no seaweed. It smells good. It's fun, you know, F-U-N."

She grabbed her throat. Good sign. Words were on the way. I just had to wait. That's what the education specialists advised us of when she started all of this back in kindergarten. Mom called it, "losing her words." It meant she had to re-find them, I guessed. *Now, where in my brain did I leave all those words?*

Trin's trouble getting words out had only grown slightly worse after the dog mauling, but another development made the situation a lot tenser. It had started in the house one day—

"Trinity! Stop, hon!" Mom's stunned voice makes me look around the corner from the TV room into the kitchen. I watch, confused, as she goes on. "It's just folding wash, honey! Who cares if you can't fold the shirts as perfect as Mommy—"

I'm seeing what will become a household ritual. Trinity's scratching at her face. She puts her palms up to her cheeks, fingers covering her eyes, and she scratches up by her hairline. She's stomping her feet in frustration and hissing between clenched teeth. Sounds like a snake. It'll happen so often over the next few years that Grace and I will simply call it her snake-thing because the sound is worse than the sight. Mom's afraid she's going to poke her own eye out or draw blood.

So she tries to pull Trin's hands away, and it becomes a battle. Her fingers are still working, scratching at the air in front of her forehead. And Mom has no choice but to stand there, holding her up off the floor by her wrists until the spell is broken. She'll get tired and eventually collapse on the floor in what looks, to Grace or me, like a trance. That's the snake going back into the cave. Until tomorrow or the next day, when Trin can't color a picture the way she wants or make her bed without wrinkles--

I was a little past my straight-up position. So I stared straight into the corridor, realizing I'd gotten an irrelevant flashback in the middle of writing a relevant flashback—of the Chapel Rock porch on the night of the accident. My head was swimming. You can't think of two things at once and not feel crazed.

I breathed out slowly while glancing at Rachel's door to see the black line under it. My hope was that she would have peaceful, zero-drama sleep. As for me, I realized if my surroundings couldn't present any drama, I could do it on my own. What with the burst of adrenaline the irrelevant flashback caused, my fingers shook too bad to get the memory onto my screen. *If it's irrelevant, how come it screwed with you so much?* I wished

my thoughts would come out in chronological order.

Cracking my knuckles, I willed my thoughts to five years later, back

to the porch of the Chapel Rock. It wasn't too hard, being that Trinity was

in a much better mood in this flashback. At least she was when—

I pried her fingers off the porch rail, the

ones she wasn't using to grip her throat, thinking

about what Dad's brother, Uncle Todd, had figured

out one Christmas dinner. He had spent a lot of

years traveling before settling down as the head

of youth ministry at our Port Dingo Presbyterian

Church. He knew lots of languages. He discovered

that when Trinity "lost her words," she could get

them back faster if she said them in French,

German, or Latin first, the languages she'd picked

up easily just from software. Then, she could

leapfrog over to English pretty quickly most of

the time. Go figure, but it often worked.

I shook Trin's fingers once I'd pried them

loose from the porch rail and said, "Come on. Say

it in German."

She shook her head. I followed her eyes to the well.

Being that she could get this tense over squished, dead seagulls in the road, I wondered if she wasn't imagining some animal falling in.

"There are no dead animals down there," I said. "Animals are smart. They stay out of wells, out of harm's way—"

"*Ich wäre lieber bei dir, wenn du nichts tust als bei irgendjemand anderem.*"

I'd taken four years of German. She didn't have to translate, though she could have knocked me over with a feather. "*I'd rather be with you doing nothing than with anybody else.*"

She was still staring at the well, but I could see the shy smile rising in her profile. I stood up and put my arms around her shoulders from behind.

That's when I took a series of selfies of the two of us. I held my thumb on the button and got around ten shots. Unfortunately, all of them had this red splotch over Trin's head, which, at the time, I took as some weird reflection of the porch's lantern lights. But I didn't take more pictures.

A lot of little girls kind of worship their big brothers, I suppose. And yet she looked right through me in the house when Mom or anyone else was around. It was like our little secret—the fact that she loved me—and it was so mysterious and unexplainable.

The bottom of Rachel's door caught my eye as the line turned from black to yellow again. I'd been writing for about an hour and a half, but I'd seen this happen before. Around an hour after falling asleep, she'd have a nightmare. It would wake her back up. I'd overheard the nurses talking to her about her REM sleep cycles being messed up. They'd said the nightmares would subside once she was getting more exercise.

I hoped my rudeness earlier hadn't given her anxiety, or worse, that my room was giving her terror dreams. Two nurses entered her room, which means she had hit her button. The nurses would often get her back in her chair, leave all the lights on, and place her laptop on the tray, all of which seemed to snap her out of it.

I prayed they'd just leave her in bed this time. I mouthed a silent curse as they pulled her wheelie thing over to the bed to get her into it. She'd asked to face the window, *thank God.*

I started fixing typos as a way to slow my memory. It's like I knew something bad was coming next. It seemed easier to fix all my half-sentences into full ones. Rachel stayed on the same page for at least ten minutes without typing, and the webpage eyes were staring at me out of the otherwise black screen.

And with her not typing and being so still, I was able to see that she was using the black screen like a reflector mirror. *The girl was staring straight at me.* Watching me type in my journal.

I can't find the words to describe a black screen with the enormous eyes and, while knowing they're photoshopped and can't really see you, you're *still* being watched. And by some shadowy, black replicants beneath them that blink and stare and then blink some more. It felt like a cold breeze blew through the mattresses. The ice cream sandwich bed was turning to ice cream.

I fumbled for my phone and sent her a blunt, IT'S NOT POLITE TO STARE. I pushed the mirror away when she reached for her phone. I didn't want to see any reaction. *Screw all eyes, visible and invisible.*

Pick a winner, Toby: your weird new acquaintance from across the hall who sees spooks, or your weird sister who—

I put my phone back in my pocket after taking the selfies with Trinity and stared across the lawn with her. It had all been very boring until Trinity spoke. In plain English she said, "I don't want you to go over there..."

"Over where?"

"Don't go near the well."

I felt surprised. It had probably been a couple years since she spoke directly to me without stammering. "I wasn't planning on it. But what are you afraid of, Trin?"

"She will push you..."

"Who?" I asked.

Instead of answering, she pointed. Just slightly above and beyond the well. Like she was seeing something in the black mass the well had become as a cloud covered the moon. Her finger was shaking.

"Are you talking about the Witch of Indor?" I asked in disbelief.

"She wants to push you." She didn't stop pointing emphatically.

"Trinity." I tried to spin her to face me, but she turned to stone. I only got her shoulders halfway around. Her chin stayed straight and away from me. "Listen to me. That story is a crock, okay? There is no Witch of Indor." All the bits of data I'd picked up from Grace came out in a blast. "It was some poor orphan girl from olden times who got falsely accused of witchcraft by a bunch of hysterical people. Okay? Let her rest in peace, wherever she is."

"She's at the well."

Ba-am. I got a text back from Hi-I'm-Rachel. "I'm sorry. I didn't mean to stare. I'm really sorry."

If my brain weren't in six pieces, I would have felt bad for her. She'd been having nightmares, and God knows what else. The situation brought relief in a strange way. I wondered how many times she had done that sneaky staring, and even though it was weird, maybe it was the cause of my feeling watched all the time. Maybe my subconscious had seen her doing it many times, though my eyes couldn't pick it up. Maybe the sensation would go away now.

I didn't reply though. I couldn't get distracted now, when it was all coming back like some sort of a sand trap:

```
"She's at the well."

"Look at me, Trin."

"She's going to push you in."

"No, she's not. Figments of people's
imaginations don't push people."

I had managed to turn Trinity, who hugged me
around the chest so tight I could barely breathe.
She whispered into my shoulder, right by my ear,
"She's telling me to push you in—"
```

I choked on my spit as the place where the wall meets the ceiling came into view again. I then let out a yell because my throat seized up.

How could I have forgotten all of this? I hadn't remembered talking at all about the Witch of Indor the day we arrived at the Chapel Rock. Plenty of past years, Grace had forced us to listen to her jacked-up version of local Indor rot she found on the Internet or got from guests doing the spook tour. Trinity got skeeved out and wouldn't even laugh. But on the porch that night, Trin had brought up the witch on her own. Grace wasn't even there. I couldn't remember what came next, at least not while I was choking half to death.

I'd had a couple gasping-choking spells before, always when I was coming to my straight-up position. The doctors had eventually shrugged and said, "Expect anything." The choking always stopped once I was tipped forward slightly, but in the meantime, I kept making a sound, while trying not to panic, like barking.

From the corner of my eye, I saw a shadow dart into the part of the room I couldn't see. To my left.

"Who's here?" I managed to get out between two chokes.

I was in the straight-up position and felt my throat starting to relax. But nobody answered, so I scanned the area behind me with the mirror. It was a jolty and dizzying look-about due to my hand shaking. I saw no one. And yet, the presence of someone was a fact. I waited to see if someone would move out of the blind spot on my right, but the complete silence made me jumpy. It's not normal to see a splash of something and hear nothing.

"Carly?" I croaked, thinking my favorite night nurse might be behind me in my blind spot. No answer. I'd stopped choking and finally got my fingers around the nurse's button.

But I dropped it in a new panic as eyes stared at me. They were the blue, disturbing eyes off Rachel's laptop. Only they were four feet below me. Rachel was in here, watching me, looking nervous as hell.

Nine

"You were choking," she said. "Do you want me to get the nurse?" She gripped the sheet that covered her torso nervously.

"No!" I said quickly, clawing for the button again. "Just tell me. Who's here with us?"

I watched her eyes go to either side of the bed and slowly back to my face. "I don't see anyone."

"Can you look behind this contraption? It's bulky— "

I knew this sounded crazy, and she just looked down to the floor and back again.

"There's no person. I'd see their feet."

My feet hung out the bottom of this bed probably looking like two socked, dead fish, but I felt one of them twitch. I could wiggle my toes lately if I wanted to, but I had other things on my mind. Now it was the sensation of someone breathing on the back of my neck—which was impossible. There was a mattress back there. I tried breathing out and reminding myself of the doctors' edict to "expect anything."

"Sorry, I just had these flipped-out couple of memories. Got me all confused—"

She watched me, her compassion registering. But it was mixed with something else—something that dragged her gaze to the left side of the room. Something was making her tense.

"Are you all right now?" she asked, then grabbed her wheels like she might speed on out. I didn't want her to. My heart sort of focused in on her, probably so I wouldn't have to focus on me. She was kind of frail anyway—not a big-boned, muscular, soccer-playing girl. Before grabbing her wheels, she'd been clutching a big bunch of her sheet, and it now lay on her stomach, a mound of wrinkles.

I remembered Dr. Vapor's word, *traumatized.*

"I'm sorry," I finally said. "I didn't mean to be rude earlier. I know you've been through a lot. I know you're kind of scared of this room. And whatever it is you're afraid of, you can imagine what it's like being alone in here, what with nothing to do but imagine. I hope you're not...so scared right now that you're thinking of leaving."

She glanced around for a moment, and let go of the wheels, and folded one hand into a ball while the other clutched it. Her knuckles stayed white. "I'll stay."

I heaved a sigh of relief and wanted to say something. But everything seemed wrong or awkward. I just grinned, and she asked the first question.

"How much longer do you have to be in that bed?"

"Just until Friday. Like, four-and-a-half more days."

She glanced into the corner again, and I moved into big brother mode to distract her from whatever she was fixating on with normal questions: "How much longer will you be in your cast?"

"Three weeks."

"And on your About page, you said this is your third surgery?"

"Yeah. I ruptured a disk in the accident. It was my only bad injury. But when they fused my spine, they discovered I had scoliosis."

"What's that?" I asked.

"Curvature of the spine." Her brows went from crunched to relaxed. She didn't look at the corner this time but watched my face curiously, swallowing sort of nervously. She went on after a moment. "It was a semi-bad case. If they didn't straighten my spine, the fusion might not hold, or I could wind up crippled. So, that meant two more surgeries."

"Bummer," I mumbled, though she shook her head like it wasn't so bad. She opened her mouth to speak, but there was a few-second delay before anything came out. It reminded me of Trinity a little.

"I could have worn a back brace for a couple years instead of the two surgeries. But the surgeries kept me from going to school. I can't stand being in school..."

Most people I knew also hated school, but they wouldn't have chosen to stay home for too many days.

I encouraged her on with, "I have a home-schooled sister," which made her gaze into my eyes with interest. "Trinity—the one who got mauled by the dog—not that the mauling is in any way related. School wasn't working for her either. She's got a one-sixty IQ. Schools are supposed to be able to work with anything these days. But there's always exceptions."

"One-sixty," she repeated in a whisper. "That's incredible. Definitely, I don't have that problem." She laughed nervously, playing with the top piece of the gripped sheet that stuck out from the top of her fist. Her smile faded.

"So…tell me *your* problem," I said.

Her mouth twitched, and finally she said, "It's too complicated."

"I bet it's not," I said, thinking of Trinity's problems. "It's not like we got places to be and people to see. Take as long as you want."

I tried a smile, and she actually smiled back briefly again before opening the gate a bit.

"When I was a little girl, I used to see auras maybe once a week. That's a light around somebody's body. I thought everyone could see them. I didn't know it was, you know, weird. Also, I'd suddenly 'know' something about someone maybe twice a month. The 'knowing' thing…it was like some fact just registered with me, like I'd heard it on the news, only…I hadn't heard it anywhere. I just *knew.*"

She watched me, wide-eyed, like she was waiting for me to approve before going on.

I could only think of, "Okay..."

"So when I was twelve, it got to be that I was seeing auras once a day and 'knowing' something about people maybe three times a week. But then, after the accident?" She relaxed her hands and used the wrinkled part of the bed sheet to wipe her sweaty palms. "...it was just about everybody I came within three feet of. I would 'know' something about them. One time a girl bumped me in the arm. I 'knew' she had a serious bone disease. She didn't even know yet."

"Wow," I breathed in sincere awe. "Did you try to tell her?"

"Not at first. But I finally made the decision to tell her, thinking, you know, maybe it would help her get to a doctor faster."

"What happened?"

She seemed to have forgotten about the corner. The conversation was nerve-racking enough, I figured, and I watched her cheeks light up. "She was not thrilled. She was an athlete. It was the last thing she wanted to hear, and... she told a whole bunch of people. Posted it on Instagram that I was a morbid, um, *freak*."

"Sorry. Wow. That *does* sound like too much to be around."

"She didn't find out about the cancer for over a year. By then I was long gone, and nobody put it together...what I had said and what happened to her." She inhaled deeply. I could hear her breath shake. "School was exhausting. The surgeries gave me an excuse to do home study."

I thought of Trinity again. But I didn't want to explain Trinity.

"Sounds like the right choice for you," I said. "So, does it help to be around a few people at a time instead of a couple thousand?"

"It does," she said. But her face clouded over again, and with some tension in her voice, like she was trying to say something casually that was bothering her. "But there's some added, um, *features.*" She bit her lip, and I watched her cheeks blush. "Sorry. I'm probably talking too much. I, um, don't get to talk to somebody my own age very often."

"No, it's interesting," I said, but with an edgy feeling, and simply rolled with the question in spite of it making me edgier. "So what do you mean by 'added features?'"

Her lips were kind of meaty and when she quit biting the bottom one again, it sprang up. She'd be cute if she weren't so...dreary. I almost wished she wouldn't answer. But after a minute she went on quietly.

"I hear things and see things. I'm not always sure what they are, or what I'm supposed to do." Her lips spread in a flash of a smile that died away just as quickly. "It's a bit like driving a new, fancy car—one that has all those dashboard features after you've been driving an old bomb car for years. I just...I never know what will happen next."

"Doesn't sound fun," I said.

She looked into my eyes for a second   "Could you, um, do me a favor?"

"Sure. As long as it doesn't require lifting and hauling."

The smile flashed again though her eyes stayed serious. "Could you just...read me that funny thing that you were writing at first?".

" Uh...was I laughing? Smiling?" I flicked at my screen until I was looking at the words that represented my Jana Klein debacle.

"No."

I watched her eyes for a moment, which I could see without the mirror, coming toward the floor. "So, how'd you know it was something funny?"

She didn't answer that—just cleared her throat and scratched one foot with the other. "I would like to laugh too...if you don't mind, that is," she said.

I read her the thing. When I got to the part about the spilled cokes on Jana Klein's boobs, she did laugh and kept smiling really big as I finished. A night nurse came down the hall and stopped long enough to do a double take at her in my room, laughing and smiling over something funny. She smiled herself and kept on going.

Rachel's smile lit up her whole face, a really pretty smile. It was a shame she didn't smile more often. I felt like I'd known her for years— maybe from staring at her from across the corridor for weeks and getting to know her habits. The connection of us both being immobilized—that was huge too.

I tried to keep the conversation light and fun. "So...do you see a shrink too, and does he make you write dumb stuff?"

"I see your psychotherapist. I saw him come in here today. He doesn't ask me to write, just talk. He said I'm traumatized. From the accident. I guess that's obvious. But I'm not a sociopath, a schizophrenic, and I'm not bipolar. I'm just...." she shook her head a little. "They don't have a word for 'second sight' in psychiatry."

Her eyes swept over to the wall again and back to her lap. "You wrote something else," she said, "About your favorite sister."

Wow.

"I'm not sure I'm ready to share that," I said as nicely as possible. "It's about what happened that night...at the well."

What if, as I'm reading, you suddenly 'see' what happened differently than I know it? I didn't at all believe Trinity could have pushed me. But the writing of the flashback had been weird enough.

"Oh...I won't see anything," she said easily. "You're, um, not readable right now. I just thought I could listen as a friend. Even if, you know, it wouldn't make me laugh."

"What do you mean, I'm not readable?"

She glanced over the top of my head this time and at my feet. "It could be all this equipment. Maybe it's cutting off your energy. It happens sometimes—a person is behind a locked door. Most people are behind, um, open doors. I don't know why."

Her eyes moved slowly sideways to the dreaded corner. She quickly glanced down, but the smile was gone. She swallowed hard. I'd no idea what was upsetting her, but I rarely knew what was bothering Trinity either. Rachel brought out the big brother in me, who always tried to humor my sister when something upset her.

I said, "You know, sometimes, if you say what you're afraid of, it makes it go away. Did your mom ever tell you that?"

I clenched my teeth too late, remembering her mom died in the accident. But Rachel erupted in a nervous laugh. "Yes, she did used to tell me that. I miss her telling me that."

At least I'd brought her smile back for a flash, I thought.

She finally broke the silence. "She realized I had some sort of a gift, back when I was twelve. She made me, you know, very comfortable with it. Unfortunately, she's gone now, so..."

"So, do you live with somebody?"

"Sure. Orphaned doesn't mean homeless. I live with my Aunt Jess. She's a surgeon in this hospital. You've probably seen her in my room a few times."

I did remember seeing a woman in a white jacket with dress clothes underneath, often sitting with the chair pulled up to the bed and talking to her.

"That's your aunt?"

"She pulled strings and got me on the rehab ward as an inpatient. I could be recovering at home with a couple of nurses. But she's always here more than she's not, and she can see me more this way."

"She looks nice."

"She is. But she's not my mom. She doesn't, um," she cleared her throat and her look darkened again. "She doesn't exactly believe in extrasensory ability."

"That kind of sucks."

"I wouldn't say she's completely *against* any belief in it. She just doesn't get it, doesn't want to talk about it. You know?"

She was splitting my heart open, gripping that sheet with her skinny, white fingers again, an anxious orphan girl with all these surgeries and maybe no one to understand her gift. Watching her, I thought of the elf girl Arwen in *Lord of the Rings,* only Rachel was frail, and the actress, Liv Tyler, looked pretty strong in that role. Rachel had that same intensity, same knowing, only hers was wrapped up in so much anxiety.

I went for the distraction, even though I didn't want to. "Maybe you could get your mind off it by helping me. I'm really not readable?"

"Right now, you're not." She glanced around at all the equipment, then slowly put out her hand. "Touch me. Sometimes that will help. Though it might not be that this room is some sort of energy block. The block could be coming from you personally. No promises. Right?"

Reluctantly, I stuck my hand out, grabbed hold of her wrist, and she grabbed hold of mine. I felt an actual chill rush up my arm and work its way slowly across my body. I had to remind myself I'd written a whole screenplay, and so my imagination was in prime condition.

She stared off with an intense focus. "Let the fog open where it will..."

The next thing was even weirder than the cold chill. What flashed through my head was a memory, but one I hadn't thought about in years. And I couldn't imagine a reason to pull it out to reflect on it. But it played through my head like something beyond me was forcing it, like I was watching it on a screen or something...

Grace and I had been five-pound babies, but Trinity was a ten-pound baby, and at two-and-a-half she's still roly-poly. I loved to catch her that summer in nothing but a diaper and sink my face into her fat cheek, her fat stomach, her enormous thigh. It's always cold fat, and I've got her turned upside down on the couch, blowing bloops on her fat thigh, and she's screeching, a real ear-bleeder.

"Honey, let her go. You know how she hates to be held down." Mom's ironing t-shirts in her bathing suit.

But Todd Casen grabs her from me. He's come over early. We're supposed to go to our third-grade sailing camp, but it's high tide, and he wants to schlep around the bay for an hour or so first. He's not in love with Trinity's fat like I am, but there's this other thing all my friends find irresistible.

He's got her box of a hundred and one crayons, which doesn't make her happy. She lets out another blood-curdling screech until he lets her down, standing between his legs, and he sets her box on the floor. "Hey, Trinity. What color's this? Is this purple?"

He's pulled out an aqua crayon and waves it in front of her eyes. She takes it from him, looks at the side, and puts it in his hand.

"Aqua, aqua, aqua. What is…the matter? You must have noticed…what purple looks like."

Mom's told us not to laugh at her, but the way she puts words together cracks me up sometimes. A laugh squirts through my nose, but she's moved on to another color and isn't paying me any attention. She looks at it sideways, puts it beside the first. "Indigo, indigo, indigo. Stop it! You mustn't do that! You are supposed to do it this way."

He's curling his fingers, and she wants his hand to stay flat for some reason. She rubs her fat palm over his hand until she gets it how she wants,

and drops the two crayons back on it, reaching for a third. She turns it
sideways.

"Cadet blue. Cadet blue. Cadet blue." And another. "Sky blue, sky
blue, sky blue."

"Mrs. K, swear to me she's not reading those crayon colors off the
side of the crayon," Todd says, losing his grin.

Mom looks up from her iron and smiles absently. "I think she's
reading the first two letters or so and remembering the rest. That's what
she was doing last week. Ask me next week."

"Trin. Say it in Spanish." This is the part he couldn't get over last
week. She ignores him, studying the side of another bluish crayon. "Come
on, big girl. Say it."

She won't look. I know Mom's been letting her click around in some
of Grace's software games, and there's kiddie games in Spanish and in a
couple other languages. You click on the color or the shape or the item and
the computer says it and spells it in that language.

She takes the sky-blue crayon out of his hand and like she's lost in
thought says, "bleu de ciel, bleu de ciel, bleu de ciel… "

We've been taking Spanish since kindergarten. He looks confused.
"That's not Spanish."

I sit there gazing at my sister, kind of stunned—not so much because
of any words Trinity could learn off a computer game or even how to put

them together. It's more this little smirk she's got going on while she puts the crayon back in his hand, like she knows she just played him. It's like she's well aware he asked for Spanish and she gave him French, just so she could be this little bit of a rebel.

I whispered, "Having a memory. It feels forced—"

"It's a happy memory," she murmured.

"You can see it?"

"Only the shadows. But I can feel it. It's your favorite sister, right?"

Not bad. "Yes. Can you see how old she is?" I asked, still somewhat dubious.

Rachel shook her head once. "Only that...you're seeing her purely. You're seeing her before any of her issues took hold."

"But what I thought of, I hadn't thought about in years. I wouldn't just think of that. Did you *cause* that?"

"No..." She let go of my hand and rubbed her palm. "My subconscious asked, and yours responded. Probably means you'd like to see her return to that state."

"Uh, she was a baby."

"Not her age...her *state*. I can feel your love for her. Like...you would sacrifice anything to bring her back to that state again. You feel responsible. Ugh..." she groaned. "She's got scars. Surgical scars?"

Mom said she couldn't remember telling Rachel anything about Trinity's accident. But she could have put it together from the dog mauling. It gave me more chills anyway.

"So..." I paused, but then the words seemed almost forced up my throat, like they'd been yanked up on a string. They contained a question I can't remember having before. And it's like I was hearing myself say it rather than saying it.

"So, is this about justice? Could she have pushed me down the well to even the score because I accidentally got her mauled? Or something horrible like that?"

"How did *you* get her mauled?" Rachel asked.

I didn't want to chase that memory right now. Enough was already pouring through my head. "Long story," was all I said.

She jerked her head in half a shake, staring into the wall above her knees, straining her neck forward, like staring harder would help something come clear in her mind. She put her hand up again, waggling her fingers to let me know she wanted mine back. I dropped it in hers, and this time I didn't feel anything chill. However, I was thinking about the well again suddenly.

But after a long silence I asked, "See anything?"

"Not much," she grimaced in frustration. "It's the night of your accident... There are just so many shadows..."

"It was really dark, especially after Grace dropped the torch lamp." I just went ahead and gave her the image in my head to work with. "I was leaning into the well. That's the last thing I remember before hearing running footsteps and being pushed. Grace was leaning over with me. We were trying to read something on the inner wall."

"Something yellow. Yellow, like, spray paint."

Wow. The bed had inched forward, and I tapped the mirror until I found her eyes again, staring into the space in front of her knees.

"There were the three of us. And then there was this guy named Elijah Rune. Can you see him? Like, when he came up?"

"Shadows are lifting a bit," she whispered and blinked a couple times, still concentrating into the white sheet covering her knees. She started shaking her head slowly. "There were five people there."

"What?"

"Five people. You, your sisters, a man...and a woman."

For a moment I felt relief. The woman screaming, whom the police didn't write down and Trinity and Grace forgot about. "Who's the woman?"

Rachel craned her neck forward again, just staring at the wall. She finally said, "I sense one of them is very good, very saint-like."

Elijah Rune was a priest, though I wasn't sure that meant saintly.

"The other is..." She pulled her neck back as her eyes grew wider, like she could actually see something physical.

"The other is what?"

"A...an..." she whispered the word, "*abomination.*" She jerked her wrist out of my hand and sat there massaging it, as an image formed in my mind of my sisters and me being sided up to by an--

Abomination. It was a weird word, one you'd know but never would use, not unless your normal words were in no way cutting it, and you were grasping for one to hold up a thousand-pound image. The concept seeped through my head...*meaning what?* Millennial witches can be considered just another type of American citizens, and kids go to horror flicks and scream and laugh at every species of demon, zombie and spook. What's an *abomination* today?

And it was like being through the Looking Glass, where you're wondering about people you never considered real, and you're relieved by your terror.

"At least, um, if it was an *abomination,* it wasn't Trinity," I heard myself say.

Her response seemed just as surreal. She had her head back and her eyes had shut. Her lips moved like she was either praying or calmly swearing. A tear ran down her face.

"What's up?" I asked. "I didn't mean for this to upset you."

She opened her eyes, glanced sideways quickly and said, "It's not you."

"What is it? Is something scaring you?"

She nodded.

"Something here? In this room?"

She swallowed and opened her eyes, staring into the blob of sheet she gripped, and she whispered her previous words: "Sometimes, I see things, and I don't know what they mean."

It was the last place I wanted to go while trapped in this bed. But I thought of Trinity again and kept staying in big brother mode.

"Are you seeing something now? Can you tell me what it is?"

She breathed, "I see it in here several times a day. It's why I've been afraid to come in here."

She couldn't keep her eyes from darting off to that left corner of the room every ten seconds, and as they bounced back for the third time, I turned the mirror to look over there. Since the hospital had relocated my bed to the middle of the room, there was just an empty space and a nightstand beside where the bed should have gone, and a mirror on the side of the little clothes closet. There was a magazine, brought in by Mom after dinner last night and some lotion they often put on my feet, which were shedding skin for some reason. I couldn't see anything else.

But when I tapped the mirror back to see Rachel, she was staring at me, all wide-eyed—more at the bed, back almost into the same emotional condition as when she wheeled herself in here.

"Do you see a person?" I whispered.

After a moment, she whispered back, "Not yet. I haven't seen any, um, dead people materialize or anything like that. *But I know it's coming...*" She blurted that, and wiping a tear away with shaky fingers. I tried again to keep her in the present.

"What are you seeing?"

"Just...an aura."

I took it by how she kept glancing in the corner, this was not *my* aura.

"Auras usually surround people," she whispered, like maybe this aura wouldn't hear her or something if she whispered. "This one is in the perfect outline of a person. But the person's not there."

She stared at the ceiling wide-eyed. I prayed to God in heaven. I didn't know what else to do. *God. Please. This is nuts. Protect us. Please.*

"Strange color," she whispered.

Please protect us.

"It's smoky. Like a gray, and there's red in it. Most auras I see are like crayon colors."

Happier colors? I got out a few more silent lines of begging God, and then stopped, watching her.

I whispered back, "It's still there?"

"Yes." She glanced swiftly to the left again and swallowed.

I held out my hand to her, just to give myself something to hold onto, and just to give her the same. She cupped my hand in both of hers, after wheeling herself closer, and held it tight to the top of her cast. I didn't think of whether I was giving her any more fodder by touching her.

I just whispered, shutting my eyes, more to God than to her. "Just tell me Trinity is not involved in this."

To my surprise, she said something fairly loudly, in an even voice. "Oh...she's *involved.* She's *very* involved..."

I cleared my throat, trying not to feel annoyed. "Look. We can't have both the Witch of Indor and one of my own sisters trying to hurt me in the same dramafest. That doesn't even make sense."

With that Rachel looked directly at me. I could see her in the mirror, but she stared at my profile, so it was weird, feeling some heat from her gaze on the side of my face but with the illusion of her looking off somewhere else.

"*What* in life *does* make sense?" she whispered. "This is how I help. This is what I do for most people. I'm just starting to realize, it seems to...to come down to the same pattern, same thing with everyone I help."

I whispered back. "Which is what?"

"It's a recurring theme. *Life is never as it appears. Don't hang onto the first narrative that runs through your head... It's usually something close. But it's never that complicated...* I... I help people find that thing— that thing that's close but *not as it appears*."

I didn't have a clue how to use that advice.

She let out a long exhale. "It's gone," she breathed.

But she didn't seem less nervous, and she'd said it with her eyes shut. How would she know without even taking a look around?

"I'm sorry." she pulled her hand away, glancing at the corner before becoming wide-eyed and panicked. "I just can't be in here. I can't come back here. I just can't."

She grabbed her wheels, backed away from me and turned toward the door.

"Rachel," I spoke to her in my normal voice, "don't just completely lose your shit—"

She said in a glurty, overly fast way, "You're safe for now, I never see it in here except for every few hours...don't worry.... I just can't—"

I felt myself start to panic. She might be lying to get out of the room, leaving me alone and trapped with God knows what. "You're going to pull some crap where you scare the hell out of me and then up and leave? That is so not right."

But she was out the door, yelling, "I'm sorry. I'm so sorry."

I rolled my eyes, pretending impatience was the worst thing I was feeling.

Ten

Thunder groaned in the distance as Rachel managed to shut her door. I swiped up my phone to see the time, 11:37 pm. Who could I call that would be awake and home and wouldn't mind?

My gut instincts were to reach for a live voice, so I called Grace. I had only texted with her this summer, and like only once a day. I'd had nothing interesting to tell her. She'd send me pix I'd already seen on her Instagram page with a cheery couple of lines. I was trying to think of when the last time was that I had actually sat down and tried to talk it up with my sister.

Last year's family weekend, Grace and I got in the habit of sitting on the long front porch of the Chapel Rock Inn, waiting for the parents to come down for dinner. We took side-by-side rocking chairs for about twenty minutes every night. I looked back now with regret. We'd stared at our phones the whole time. If I ever even asked a simple question, I don't remember it.

And once on a rainy Sunday between spring crew and my summer diving team, we watched a movie together in the family room, but we fought the whole time because Grace has a real stomach for horror flicks. Trinity's laptop stays in the kitchen because Mom thinks she's too young to be roaming about the Internet in private. Hence, Trin was often in earshot of the family room TV. If I wasn't snapping at Grace that we should put on something happier in case she was listening, I was snapping in awe of her thick skin. We were watching *The Ring*.

She sat there glazed and blinking when that girl-creature crawled through the TV screen; she blew off my disbelief impatiently with, "Duh. It's not like it's *real...*" About Trin, Grace snapped back in a whisper, "She's *always* in the kitchen! Does that mean we can *never* watch something scary on the big screen? Find her some earbuds."

I might have limits to my imagination, but Grace had none to begin with. And because we talked so rarely, viewing *The Ring* was one of the first times I got the notion that Grace had grown to see Trinity as a dominating, chronically trumping force in our house. I saw Trinity as weak and needing protection. I wished we had talked more.

I touched her name and watched the phone light up. It went to voice mail. I felt irked. The only place Grace didn't take her phone was in the shower. She'd probably seen my call and passed on it. I tried again. Straight to voicemail. I knew from my last call with Dad that she'd been told not to talk to me about the accident.

She texted. "I'm sleeping! What?"

She forgot she already told me she was going out partying with Wiley. Grace could tell a lie and forget she told it. That's how she often got caught, especially by me.

"You're at a party, liar, and I'll just have to lie here awake by myself," I sent, feeling my guilt over using the pity play. I didn't want to manipulate anyone. I just wanted to not be alone.

"Sorry, but you know I'm not supposed to talk to you," appeared on the screen.

"I won't talk about the accident. I know the police think that guy didn't do it."

I watched my phone remain lifeless for about a minute before I glanced into the corridor. I didn't need the mirror. I was almost straight up. A couple of orderlies were coming out of Rachel's room. One of them hit the light off and closed the door. They must have just gotten her back into bed.

I glanced to my left where she had kept looking. Everything appeared normal and unmoving, though it was dim with night shadows.

My phone lit with an incoming call. I hit the button. "Grace."

"What? You know I'm not supposed to be talking to you," she said. Music and a bunch of voices came through in the background, a bunch of loud, happy voices.

"You are so allowed to talk to me," I countered. "Just not about the accident. There's like a thousand and one things we *can* talk about, because I am your brother, you know." She just breathed in response to my stumbling. "For one... whose party?"

"Uh…Tesla's." I heard her swallow. "Me and Wiley decided to make an appearance." Mark Tesla was *my* friend. But Grace had been showing up at more and more stuff generally reserved for upperclassman. It helps to have a big brother.

"What's up? *Are you okay?"* she asked with a sudden urgency.

"Yeah, yeah. I know it's weird I'm calling you. You'd have to think there was something wrong, right?"

"No...it's okay," she said. "Lemme move outside. *Hey Wiley! I'm going out!"* she screamed in my ear, probably alerting him across a roomful of bodies. The background noise dimmed way down, though she took her sweet time to get where she was going. I heard pounding surf in the background and figured she was in the dunes.

"Yeah, no..." she finally said into her speaker. "It's really nice that you called me."

My turn... I cleared my throat. "So. You're getting a hurricane?" *When you don't know what to say, start with the weather.*

"Not for three more days. Dad says it will hit north of here. I'm not worried." She laughed. "When do I worry?"

Never. "Dad said you guys might fly up here."

"When did he say that?" She sounded truly alarmed. "Not that he would tell me until it was time to walk out the door. I'd disappear. You know...hide under Wiley's bed or something. Sorry, Tobes. I hope you understand. I'm not exactly anxious to go back near that place."

Salem Medical Center was actually forty-five minutes away from Lake Indor. I'd been choppered here from the local hospital, but I understood.

"I get it. I can't wait to get home. I'm just lying here racking my brain for people to call or text and bother."

"You've only got a few more days," she reminded me. "And Mom said there's a girl across the hall. Have you been talking to her?"

"Some," I said, not wanting to take Grace's brain apart with the conversation we'd had. "I'm not sure about her..."

"Is she a total dork? I wouldn't be too picky."

"Right now, she's probably sleeping," I said, studying the black line under Rachel's door, wondering if she'd passed out from exhaustion after what she'd allegedly seen in my room. But Grace has this way of honing in on what you don't want to talk about, almost like she's part psychic herself. "So, she can't keep you from feeling lonely right now. And you're awake, all by yourself, and it's creeping you out."

I laughed nervously.

"I'll keep talking to you," she said, which was a nice gesture, being she was having fun at a party. Definitely time to stop ignoring my sister and reconnect. My high school years were over. "So, tell me about the girl."

I rolled my eyes. "Her parents' SUV spun out and rolled. Both parents were killed. She was fourteen. This is her third spinal surgery in two years. Last one, I think."

"That's horrible. But so was your accident. Sounds like you'd have that much in common."

"She has a website. Says she's got second sight."

"That's weird. Think she's lying?"

"She freaked me out today. Told me our family had been involved in a previous accident, something to do with a dog."

"Wow," Grace responded loudly, then simmered down for the rest. "Bro, that is creepy. But maybe Mom told her."

"Mom's saying she didn't. The girl also tells me I got a spook in my room."

"What? That's crazy. And it's a dumbass thing to say to somebody who can't move."

"Grace, I never was paying much attention, but you really loved those Witch-of-Indor stories when we were on family weekends. What do you know about her?"

"You sure can change your tune quickly. A few hours back you were telling me never to mention her name around here."

"This is just between us," I snapped. "I need to know, is all. I just found out today, a couple hours before I talked to you, that she probably died falling down a well."

"Nobody knows that for sure. It's just part of the…the *happy bullshit,* you know. I do love those stories. But it's not because I *believe* them. They aren't real. But who would bring her falling in a well up to *you?"*

"Actually, the shrink."

"He sounds like a real rocket scientist. What was he doing, telling you that?"

"He wanted to make sure the accident wasn't caused by the three of us having gotten carried away with some spook story that made us, you know, too daring and kind of spastic."

"So did you tell him I'm Second Soloist in Mom's conservatory, and you're a champion diver?"

"Grace, I wanted to snap his head off his shoulders. What a crock."

She changed the subject quickly. "So, why this massive turnaround? When we were on vacation, you used to hate when I told those stories."

"I hated what they did to Trinity. Remember the night a few years back, you jumped out from behind the tree and screamed, and I had to run up three flights of stairs and throw her inhaler to you guys over to the balcony?"

"Please don't stoke the flames of my guilt. I've gotta change my evil ways. No more picking on Trinity."

"I...think that would be really great," I encouraged her, but she sighed in frustration.

"Tobes. You gotta understand. Think about it. If it weren't for her, we'd have a perfectly normal life. Between doctors, and shrinks, and homeschooling, Dad being at sea half the time, and Mom's overly protective vibe toward her...I feel like I get, like, *one-quarter of one parent."*

I'd heard Grace blasting Mom with some complaint like this a few times. I'd *heard* but hadn't been *listening,* if that made sense. I was too busy worrying she might throw a b-word out at Mom or Trin. She had a point.

"It never fails, Toby! If I'm managing to get *one quarter* of Mom's attention, just for one hour, here along comes Little Miss Asthma Attack. Remember the time, before my eighth-grade dance, I *almost* got Mom to actually go to the mall with me to shop for my dress? She started saying we should take Trinity with us. I was all, 'Mo-*om!'* As soon as she agreed to leave Trinity at the Twardy's and, *miracles,* take me to lunch just the two of us, what happens? We...have an asthma attack!"

The Twardy sisters were Trinity's homeschooled friends from ballet, to whom she spoke normally. I sort of remembered that day. Trinity ended up on her nebulizer for half the afternoon, and Grace went to the mall with another girl and her mother.

"When we've been on family vacay, and I'm, like, stuck with her all day and night, I get to feeling like, 'You want an asthma attack, you little freak? I'll give you an asthma attack.' Toby. I *know* that is so wrong..."

I felt a stab of guilt about ignoring Grace's feelings for years. Grace just kept plowing along in life, bouncing around school like Tigger, but living with this feeling at home. I said, "Hey, you're entitled to your feelings. I don't see having a sister like her as a bed of roses, either. She never talks to me, Grace."

"Me neither. Or Dad. I'm not as bothered by that as you are, though. I figured if she's going to dominate our lives so completely, I don't need to *hear* her, too."

I laughed quietly. The windows lit up with lightning, though the thunder was far off. It made me feel on edge. I accidentally went where I shouldn't have again. It seemed so natural.

"The parents, the shrink, and the cops, they sort of think, uh, it could have been Trinity that pushed me."

She didn't say anything, and I finally realized she was crying. She sniffed up tears and gulped in between sniffs.

"Just so you know—*I* don't believe that," I continued on. "I'm sure it was Rune. Either that or it was that Witch of fucking Indor—"

"Oh..." She sniffed again. A link appeared on my screen. "Have a blast," she said.

It was a link to some website called Haunted Tours of Indor.

She sniffed really hard. "I know that thinking there really is a boogeyman--and the boogeyman might have pushed you--that is easier than thinking your little sister might have done it."

Ba-am! Grace wasn't known for being subtle. I didn't want to tell her that Trinity pushing me was beyond my imagination—not after I'd dragged her out of a party, got her crying and all depressed. My question sort of flew into the air, and I recognized my own voice in the echo. "Grace, do *you* think Trinity is capable?"

It hurt my insides to even say it. I figured Grace would quickly tell me she wasn't allowed to talk about this with me. She either forgot her orders or felt like I did, that the breach was necessary. She said around sniffs, to my dread, "Most days...no. Some days...*yes.*"

"Like, which days do you think yes?" I couldn't help asking.

Grace said in a much weaker tone, "Like, when I remember...about her guinea pig."

I pinched my eyes shut and found myself breathing in that way that wards off an adrenaline rush. *I'm holding Mr. Stubbs' body as Mom holds*

Trinity who sobs, and I'm telling her, "Trin, six years is old age for a guinea pig. It was his time. Everything dies, Trin." And I don't know what else—something about pets going to the Rainbow Bridge—while I'm realizing the pig's neck is dangling, much longer than it's supposed to be... I don't want her to see Mr. Stubbs' head flopping over and so far down like that—like it's on a spring. But she must have seen it already. But how in the hell would a little guinea pig get a broken neck?

She'd been home all by herself. Mom had dropped Grace at the mainland mall, then took me to the pre-season boat races. Dad was at sea. We pulled into the drive just as Grace was opening the door with five bags in her hands, so we collectively found Trinity curled up in the corner of the kitchen holding a furry black ball—

"Grace, I still think the pig died of old age," I said. She sniffed and said nothing until I couldn't stand it. "Why? Tell me your thoughts."

"Just that...that you have this really convenient way of deciding things, Tobes."

Ba-am! The sting wasn't because my dad and a shrink had just said the same thing, but because it seemed like I cared more about what was convenient than what was true. And I *did* care about the truth. *Totally.* Didn't I?

"You already know what *I* think," she reminded me.

The pig had died in early June this year. I'd heard Grace try several ways to explain her feelings, not that any of them was perfectly clear. The worst was something like, *Trinity has two personalities; one that would kill an animal, and another that would grieve like crazy over its death.*

This much was true: Thinking about the Witch of Indor *was* less scary than thinking of my sister having pushed me.

Grace let me talk to people inside Tesla's party until her phone was down to two percent. It was great taking a half hour to tell everyone I might be home in a week, and look out for the party. It was great to hear people's genuine excitement. I supposed finding the source of my anonymous call had gotten lost in the shuffle, but I wasn't too bothered by it.

I was more bothered by the night sounds of the ward as, hanging up, I realized how long this night could be. Thunder was louder. It wasn't a good time to be striking links to the Witch of Indor, but I was almost *glad* to, *glad* to feel eyes watching me from the door. I could still hear those footsteps running up behind me. Nothing had changed there. But I was pushing links and watching intently as a pair of blue eyes, far icier than Dr. Vapor's, came clearer and clearer on the page Grace had sent to me.

Eleven

A drawing of a blond girl in a red hood stared back at me, looking familiar, and I realized I'd seen it on several websites and in brochures on our many vacations at Lake Indor. It was like Little Red Riding Hood's hood, the old-fashioned kind. Her eyes looked troubled, reminding me of Rachel's, only hers were a light blue and not like Rachel's violet. The fine print underneath it read, "Original Missing Poster: Elizabeth Ainsworth, 1704."

It looked like there was actual history behind the stuff Grace would make up. This copy was attached to a blog, written by a guy around my age, maybe younger, you could tell by his pictures that faded in and out of kids our age hanging out in the woods around Indor, pointing out strange gashes in the trees and footprints on the ground. The heading above the drawing read, MY 411 ON THE WITCH.

Below the heading the type was small. The kid, Justin McDaniel, had written this:

The Witch of Indor, our token local resident she-demon, haunts Lake Indor. She had been orphaned as a teenager in the early 1700s.

Around a decade after the Salem Witch Trials, the people of Salem had calmed down and were actually sorry about the hangings and accusations that had gone on. But the people of the woods between Salem and Indor—they were still jumpy. At fifteen, the orphaned Elizabeth

Ainsworth was accused of doing weirdnesses with chicken blood and five-pointed stars and was thought to have been the culprit when all the hens within a twenty-mile radius mysteriously died.

People didn't know about bird flu back then. But their fake news still spread like a plague. The people of the woods went out to her cabin to hang her. She picked up a meat hook to defend herself and took out the midsection of one of her attackers, which would have sealed her doom had she not been a fast runner. Her accusers burned her house down and then refused to let her in anywhere, in spite of it being twelve degrees outside in a blinding snowstorm.

In the darkness before dawn, three of her accusers claim to have heard a scream that got farther and farther away, like a girl had jumped off a cliff, but there are no cliffs in the mountains over the Lake. Some say she ended her sad life by jumping or falling down one of the wells at the foot of the mountain.

She was never seen again. Her bones were never found.

That feeling of being watched was hitting me like a tidal wave, of course. My eyes moved to the floor, halfway between myself and the spot Rachel had kept staring at. I figured I'd see anything move in my periphery, and if there was some spook there, I didn't want to give it the satisfaction of looking directly into it.

I could see in the corner of my eye the magazine Mom left there and the lotion bottle on top. Nothing was moving or looked any different. I went back to reading, glad to hear only the pinging of rain and not some thunderstorm dramafest out the window. The guy turned out to be a good writer.

In every spook legend, the spook has that sort of tragedy-type story. But they also have their signature movements, such as Bloody Mary materializing when you call her through a bathroom mirror.

Here's the signature move of the Witch of Indor, part of which I've already explained in her reputation of literally never being seen again. She always comes up from behind. Victims claim to hear her, and suddenly they smell decaying flesh. Then she starts to lure them into dark death under a cloud of confusion, which can prevent them from finding their way out of some abandoned house or off some abandoned road and back onto the highway. Many have heard that far-off falling scream on a dark night. If you're among the most unlucky ones, she suddenly drives a meat hook into your spine, snaps your spinal cord, and you're left to feel her rip your scalp off with the meat hook when you're completely paralyzed and left to die.

Well, of course that got me feeling so cheery that I wanted to puke. And it made me wonder about whatever Rachel saw. If nobody ever saw the witch, I decided even a girl with sixth sense probably wouldn't get that lucky. Maybe Rachel had seen something else. *Maybe Rachel is a loon-o and I should never let her in here again.*

Just as I thought that, the light turned from black to yellow under her door. I wonder if she felt watched like I felt watched.

"Can't sleep?" I sent her, feeling too lonely, forgetting that quickly I just called her nuts.

I saw the message was delivered, but not read. I thought she was being good to her word to avoid my room—and me also. I stared for a few minutes at the spot on the floor where I could see the dark left corner. Nothing moved. Finally, a nurse's aide came along the corridor and stopped with her back to me, having seen the light under Rachel's door, and she opened it. I could see Rachel asleep in her chair facing me and the aid's hand reach for the light switch.

"No, don't," I said, trying not to be loud enough to wake Rachel up. The aid looked at me and I mouthed quietly, "She probably wants to sleep with the light on."

The aid shrugged and gave me a friendly grin. I ignored the watched feeling while returning my eyes to read about having your spine snapped by a witch and an invisible meat hook.

There are those bits of truth, those historical realities, which people love to tie into a legend. There's been a history of scalped murder victims around Lake Indor, long after the settlers and the Indians had quit scalping each other, around 1810. Two were found in the 1890s. The victims could not have been the work of one serial killer unless he lived to be a hundred because two more were found in the 1970s.

Then there was a guy in 2001. Copycats? So say some, but not if you're a believer in the Witch of Indor. And there were a few more disappearances and, of course, a thousand and one "sightings," if you want to call them that. Because no one ever sees her. They see her footprints on the snow or meat-hook gauges in the sides of trees, or they smelled decaying corpse while lost and confused on a mountainside. Even the bullshit artists know that a claim with a visual sighting would take away their credibility.

Thunder grumbled overhead, and as I was finishing one final paragraph of the blog, I saw something move in that corner of the room again. I was almost completely facing the floor and could no longer see that part of the room without the mirror, just the very periphery, where I would swear, I just saw something scoot.

A shadow...a flash... I slowly turned the mirror and took in the normal scene. Some of Grace's goofball friends had a name for seeing something from the corner of your eye that isn't there when you look full-on. It's called "caped air."

My eyes were drawn to the yellow light shining under Rachel's door. I watched, unconcerned at first, as it was broken by what looked like the shadow of two feet walking past... *Rachel, on her way to the bathroom.*

Then it struck me: *Rachel can't walk to the bathroom.* My heart sped up. Two footsteps *had* just passed by. I hadn't imagined it. A minute later, they passed by the other way.

A scream rumbled up my chest, but I stopped myself. Maybe a nurse had gotten in there in the short time between when the last nurse shut the door and walked away. The nurse would have gone in unnoticed by me, which was almost impossible when my eyes and ears are this hyper aware. No way.

Maybe a spook wouldn't hurt her or wake her up. I didn't want to alert Rachel and scare her like she'd scared me about the strange aura in my room. As for getting help, I pictured one of the night orderlies would come running, open the door, wake Rachel, and we'd see nothing. I'd have the shrink back with me again tomorrow and the whole staff would laugh, but little else would happen. I had no idea what to do.

I shut my eyes and asked the God I recently started praying to *a lot* about sending an angel to help Rachel out, and I decided no matter what, I would not open them again until morning. Maybe it was stress, along with having stayed awake for six hours straight today. I was good to my word.

Twelve

Monday, the sun poured in the windows, leaving warmth on the back of my arms. The ward bustled with doctors and every kind of worker until Mom showed up at eight o'clock. The bed had just flipped, and I was on my back. Mom's smile loomed over me. The sight of my beaming mother sucked any remaining dread out of the room.

"Did you remember the gift certificate you gave me for today?" she asked, beaming.

"Yes." I'd forgotten until now. Since I hadn't spent much of my lifeguarding money from last summer and had no chance of spending any on myself now, I'd called the hotel on Friday and gotten her a gift certificate to the spa for today. She was supposed to take a day off from me, get a massage, and lie by the pool. She'd been so touched that a tear spilled down her face. The weather was perfect for once, and she looked excited.

"Let's just hope the weather holds," I said, forcing a big grin and some enthusiasm.

"Believe it or not, it's supposed to rain in the afternoon."

"Got to be the rainiest summer since I was born," I griped, flipping at the mirror until I could take in the blue sky with maybe one cloud. I moved it to check out Rachel's door. It was open. I saw the two orderlies in there who often had gotten her washed up and out of bed. She was alive, unharmed, and probably sane, as I hadn't heard any screaming.

"I may have a surprise for you when I get back," Mom said, and I wondered what could make up for having to spend six hours alone here with my eyes darting from the left corner of the room to Rachel's door. *I just won't do that,* I told myself.

Writing in my journal could at least get my head out of this room. When Mom left again after breakfast, I figured I'd do some writing about happy memories from our house. I thought I would write another journal entry like Trinity and the crayons.

I turned on my laptop and checked my email, as somedays, someone from school would email what was going on with them, which was pretty nice. Today, there were none. As I opened a blank Word doc, my mood suddenly turned so dark that I checked out the window again to see if the sun had moved behind new clouds. It hadn't. But it's like there was a physical element to this mood swing.

I gave Rachel's door one furtive glance before typing out what rolled through my head.

WRITTEN ON: Monday, August 8, 10:35 pm

SUBJECT: Who Knows, Except it's the Middle of the Night at my House

Our house was built by one of the first sea captains to settle on Port Dingo. It was not considered safe to live on the barrier islands a hundred years ago, as there were no bridges to them, and you had to haul your food and medicine and everything in a boat. But around 1910, five sea captains all decided to build these big old Victorians on Port Dingo, and they could have each other's backs, watching each other's houses when some were at sea. Our house is one of those original five. Most people love my house. Some say it looks like a haunt.

Mom and Dad took out the long, dark corridors downstairs years ago. But upstairs, there's still four corridors, two short ones on the south and north sides and the longer ones on the east and west sides. The kids' bedrooms are along the outer wall of the west corridor, and the other wall this far north is a balcony. Mom and Dad's bedroom is on the ocean side, across the balcony. The upstairs corridor, along the north side of the house, looks down over the living room. At night, you can hear the grandfather clock chiming from beside the fireplace. It dongs on the hour but doesn't usually wake us up. We're used to it.

Mom has stopped telling us just recently not to roughhouse in this corridor in front of our rooms. She's long been afraid of one of the kids going over the rail and splattering on the living room floor. But we're getting older now. I'm more afraid of Trinity falling over it in the middle of the night. She's been known to sleepwalk. Or maybe she's awake. It's just that Dad complains sometimes of rolling over in his sleep, opening an eye, and she's just standing in the middle of their room staring at them.

This night, the clock wakes me up, donging three times. I notice it because the pounding surf dulls any other noises in our house. But tonight, there is none. It's one of those windless, waveless nights where even the air isn't moving. Feels like nothing on this whole island is moving.

I'm a light sleeper anyway, or I have been, since I've become aware there's something big wrong with Trinity—and has been since around the time she was bitten by the dog. I hear her nighttime asthma attacks. I hear her turn over in her goddam sleep sometimes, even though the turning was no longer laced with groans and cries like it was for a month after the accident. It's two years later. Trin is seven.

Which is probably why my eyes flip wide open. A splotch of white floats slowly past my door. I sit up, watching the door frame. I call for her, but she doesn't come. I call louder. No sounds.

"Trinity, what are you doing?" I'm out of bed, walking into the corridor. There's no sight of her. But I go down to the bathroom and flick on the light.

It's Grace, not Trinity, who flips on the faucet and splashes cold water on her face.

"You okay? I thought you were Trin."

As the water drips off her red cheeks, her blue eyes are popping in horror. "She's got her own bathroom. We don't. What the hell would she be doing down here? Why didn't you hear her this time? She's up. She—"

She points back into the dark corridor. She had been whispering, but I can hear my mom stirring in their room across the landing. She sleeps like I do—one eye open, maybe one ear—but Mom's and Dad's light hasn't gone on.

The bathroom light sheds a path down the corridor, and I let Grace push me along, back toward Trinity's room. She thrusts me through the doorframe. I see Trin's not in her bed. As I approach the bathroom, I can see only the outline of her white nightie. It's the same as the one Grace is wearing. Grace hates it when Mom dresses them alike, but at night it's okay. Trinity's standing back from the sink in the dark, like she's looking in the mirror, only it's too dark to see.

I hit the light and all but jump out of my tree. I can hear the yell rising out of me, annoyed, frustrated, pretending not to be terrified. Her face is covered in streams of blood. It's run down onto the front of her white nightie. Her hands are covered in it, especially the nails from her longer fingers. She's holding them in front of her, squinting.

She turns, whimpers like a scared animal, and tries to stick her face into my chest. I let her, but Mom's here now.

"Did you scratch your face again, silly willy? What were you dreaming?" Mom pulls her up to the sink, runs water over a white washcloth, and I stand there watching as the cloth and the water turn pink. So, Mom's seen her draw blood before, scratching her face. This is my first experience in seeing it, and obviously Grace's too.

Trinity says nothing, so Grace, who's behind me, pipes in. As I pull off the bloody t-shirt and dump it in Trinity's hamper, she says, "That's too weird. I can't do this anymore." She's sniffing up tears and running, and I understand it. There's a side of me that's like her, that wants to shout sometimes: TRINITY. WHY CAN'T YOU JUST BE NORMAL??? JUST. ACT. NORMAL, GODDAMIT.

It's just three scratches along Trinity's scalp line, each not a quarter of an inch long. They bubble over each time Mom dabs at them with the washcloth.

"Head wounds sure can bleed." Mom is putting on her normal voice, like this is nothing. Well, guess what? *It's not nothing. This isn't normal.*

I stumble down to Grace's room, where she's crying into her pillow. "Why didn't you hear her this time?" She sniffs up tears. "I'm always the one to hear her when it's something really gross. I get to hear her yell in her sleep when she's saying something awful. I can't stand it anymore."

"When did she yell in her sleep?" I ask in frustration. I can't change what happened to Trinity two years back. The only thing I can do to make up for it is care now. My gut knows this and generally wakes up, even if it's just for a moment.

"Last night and tonight!" Grace whispers. "It was something in French. Or German, or some shit. It goes like, 'It wahz boozes compt!' Trinity kept saying it over and over until I got up and went in there and told her to shut the hell up. I swear, Toby, I thought I was going to smack that weepy-whiny little voice box into her ass."

"All right, you don't have to turn into a sailor."

I supposed my friends and I started cussing up a storm around age ten, but it didn't sound great coming out of my sister's mouth. And it gave me something else to focus on while the hair was rising on my arms, as the translation was arriving of "*Etwas böses kommt.*" I hadn't taken any German yet. But it had come from the mouth of a demon-possessed German girl in a movie Casen and I had watched around Halloween, and a priest translated it for the girl's mom.

Something evil comes.

Had Trinity been listening to the movie from the kitchen? I suddenly didn't care. I was going to march back to bed and not say a word to her, freaked out as I was, but my heart melted as I saw Mom bringing her out of the bathroom in clean pajamas, with three mini Band-Aids on her forehead, her hands and fingers clean, her hair brushed and shiny. Her eyes were swollen, yet trancelike.

I leaned into the doorframe, grabbed her hand and shook it. "So, what now? Do we have to make you wear mittens to bed? You want to be the abominable snowman in July?"

My tone is jokey, which makes her stick her lip out, her way of stopping a smile when she wasn't ready to. She turns, grabs her throat, and finally whispers, "I'm sorry I woke you up."

Slay me. I mean, she'd just had to cope with the Stephen King version of herself staring back in the mirror, and now she's sorry for waking me up.

"Listen. Do not ever be sorry for waking me up. Do you need me to stay awake with you? I can sit in your rocker."

"I'll finish sleeping in here," Mom says. Mom sleeps in Trin's room a lot when Dad is at sea. He's back this month, and he'll gripe if she does it much. "I sleep in a bunk for six weeks straight. Now I have to come home and sleep alone also? Toby, can I pile into your bed? Can I snuggle you to sleep??"

Ew. We'd laugh.

I flop back in bed, trying not to whip myself for not hearing Trinity tonight or last night. Grace hardly ever hears her first. She doesn't care as much.

I rubbed my fingers, which felt tingly from hammering so furiously in those last paragraphs. I could now hear rain drumming on the windows. The time on my laptop read 11:57 am. I muttered some profanity, thinking Mom couldn't sunbathe, and tried not to think too deeply about *why* I'd just remembered this scene I hadn't thought of in a few years.

Who would *want* to remember? *My sister is a cutter.* It was something I'd long known, that specialists put her face-scratching in the category of cutting. Why was I reminding myself of that? What did it have to do with the well?

Quickly I thought of Rachel's mantra, *things are never as they appear.* I supposed I believed that, and it left me with a slightly calmer feeling, though varying thoughts blew through my head like storm debris.

I decided to text Casen, see if he'd even had work today, or if they'd shut down the beaches already. I shot him the question, then googled Hurricane Rhonda for an image. If this was the outer bands threatening us six hours north, it was a monster—hopefully one of those large eaters that took a little bite from everywhere but a huge chunk out of nowhere.

The image reminded me of Hurricane Sharon, which struck Port Dingo when I was twelve, a behemoth that caused a lot of flooding from New York down to West Virginia and especially on our Jersey barrier islands, which got the eye. It had caused us to get a new roof. Hence, I wasn't worried about our house getting eaten. The standard rule with hurricanes is if you have a new roof designed for hurricane intensity, whatever is underneath it will survive.

Casen texted me back. "Looks like a *spidercane.*"

"Woe," I replied. That's a more rare hurricane that's shaped like a spider, with bands that reach in every direction for hundreds of miles.

"You're getting the top of one of the legs. We're between a couple. It's sunny, calm, and the water's actually better today. If the eye is coming here, they won't evacuate 'til tomorrow."

Things are never as they appear... A hundred years ago, nobody would have seen squat coming from those skies. Massachusetts might have thought it had something to worry about, and Jersey would have been the sitting duck. It kind of amazed me how calm the sea could be just hours before a hurricane showed up.

I reread my journal. The flashback had distracted me from this room for a couple hours, but with a three-a.m. horror that I'd been able to mentally avoid for years. Seemed like a trade-off. I glanced over at the corner, and while nothing looked out of place, its energy felt swollen, pregnant with notions of some aura materializing. The rain and frothing summer wind outside weren't helping.

I saw my earbuds over in the corner by the dresser and considered pushing the nurse's button to have them brought to me. They'd been there for six days, since I started realizing that plugging my ears made me feel twice as claustrophobic and tied down.

I jerked my gaze back onto the screen. I had two things in writing now: My Embarrassing First Date, and My Sister the Nocturnal Cutter. I supposed Dr. Vapor would not see much relationship between the two, or maybe he would see a lot. Because I was suddenly seeing the truth: Neither made Father Elijah Rune look the least bit guilty.

Just maybe Rune had merely been there to help, I reasoned for the first time. I wasn't buying it completely. I was just willing to look at the notion of him at the well doing a good deed.

But if so, *who was the abomination?*

I didn't let myself look into the corner of the room again. I just closed the file and chatted endlessly with the kitchen person who had brought my lunch. I watched the corridor for one of the aides to call out to, but none came past. I decided to send Rachel a text as she had not opened the door except when the orderly delivered her lunch next.

"You okay in there?" I asked. A friendly concern couldn't hurt. At least she would know I wasn't still infuriated by her dramatic exit the night before.

"Yes, just working," she replied. "Two new clients to my website."

So whoever, or whatever, had been in her room last night hadn't caused her any harm. *I need some sort of clients,* I thought jealously and did my usual escape with a nap.

Thirteen

Mom's smile peered down at me for the second time that day. She had sun on her cheeks—and a wet umbrella in her hand.

"How was your massage?" I asked.

"I got a pedicure." She adjusted the mirror until I could see her bright pink toes. "I wanted to take away something sunny that I could keep, like summer nail polish. Thanks again, my angel child."

"Good enough. You bring me anything? A milkshake?"

"I can get you one, but I brought you something better."

"A new body?"

"Not quite. But it's a *body*. It's at the foot of your bed. Just arrived special delivery from Jersey."

I flipped the mirror. Grace was making a funny face at me. Dad hadn't called me back last night. He must have beat the evacuation order in time to catch a morning flight.

"Sweet Jeezus. I thought your game plan was to hide under Wiley's bed!" I held out my hands.

"I forgot you looked so jammed up. It's not a strait jacket, but almost," she giggled. "Can't hug you. I'll just have to kiss you. Ew. Kissing my brother. Here goes nothing."

She kissed one cheek, then the other. I hadn't seen her in a month. At the time, she'd still had traces of her broken nose, which included some remaining purple under each eye.

"You look great," I said.

"Actually, Dad got me here by bargaining with me. He said I can get a nose job this fall if I got on the plane to come see you." She grinned, turning her face sideways. "I was thinking of getting a pixie nose like Audrey Hepburn."

Grace had a thing about the Sixties actress. "Your nose looks like it did before the accident," I noted.

"I have scar tissue. I snore. I wake myself up!" Grace insisted. "It's grody. Anyway. Dad says I can get a new nose. Maybe I'll just be like Mickey Mouse and have a black ball implanted on the end."

Mom was shaking the umbrella out over by the sink.

"Just open it, Einstein, and let it dry open," Grace said.

Mom grinned at us. "Didn't you know that's bad luck? To open an umbrella while inside— "

Grace sauntered to Mom, took the umbrella from her hand, and a crack resounded as it opened. You could see drops falling everywhere.

"What about that recital dance you made us do back in sixth grade, where we all had to dance with umbrellas on stage? Stages are indoors. We're all still living."

The thing I'll never find perfect words for is what a blast from home can do if you've been tied down and locked away from it. The blasts take you back to those places you didn't appreciate, even though they defined your normalcy, your strengths, your things that make home a great place.

And they can include stupid things. I'd long noticed around here that Mom smells like lemons. If you think a smell isn't important, lie for a month away from all the smells you knew. Grace smelled like baby powder. I'd just never noticed before, but now it filled the room. It was like her dancing, which she started right in front of me, and for the first time in years I actually watched.

She was nervous, being here, as she'd predicted last night on the phone. She compulsively did dance moves whenever she was nervous. She wasn't ready to fully take in my condition yet, so she started to twirl with that umbrella in the stage-size space where two beds could be.

Grace could twist herself up like a pretzel and straighten herself out like an arrow. It had always been part of the scenery. Friends I had over would be all, "Oh my *God*, Grace," while I'd stopped seeing it. Now I was watching her pick her leg up behind her, pull it into the back of her head so her legs made one straight line while twirling the umbrella in front of her.

Watching that move brought on a flashback of a conversation I'd had with her last fall about whether she should accept this one junior's invitation to the fall formal or ask a summer kid who had allure and mystery.

"I know I'm going to remember stuff like the fall formal when I'm sixty, right? I *have* to make it good," she was saying. I was marveling at her sentimental view of this choice—not that she was splitting her legs on two chairs, one in front and one behind. And the center of her was dipping lower than either foot.

My only comment as I'd walked away: "Grace. Don't break your ass."

Home rushed at me as she did some nervous twirls, and Mom commanded from her chair, "Don't sickle your foot..."

It was part of my *normal.* I could suddenly smell the house, feel the little grits of beach sand under my feet on the wood floor, feel the salty breeze blowing in my face as I left the house for work. I made a promise not to take cool stuff for granted once I got out of Oz-Hell and back to Kansas.

I promised myself I'd spend more time with each of my sisters and notice everything they did.

As she came out of this kick-thing that took so much control that it looked like slow motion, I even said, "Grace, maybe when we get home we'll have to start calling you Grace-ful."

Her eyes widened and she smiled through another twirling pass and said, "You mean instead of Sarah Heartburn??"

I cringed. It was a nickname we'd given her for when she used to whine about stuff,

like not having a ride if Mom had already promised me a ride somewhere else. I'd always figured Grace whined a lot. I hadn't figured I was being self-centered a lot.

Changes coming, I promised.

Grace shook the open umbrella one more time, in the middle of the floor in that left corner where a bed would have normally been. Pleased with herself, she curtsied and then stared at my bed like she'd drained enough anxiety to show interest.

"Is that fun?" she asked. "Is it like being on one of those Disney rides?"

I laughed. "Anything but fun."

I explained how everything worked—the weights which were behind, the motor, timer, and clips that kept everything in my reach. I even knew about the generator and the receiver behind me, now that I was more awake and alert.

I hoped my calmness might calm her, but she studied the bed with her hands pulled into her chest.

"So…what keeps you from sliding out the bottom?" she asked. We'd explained this to her the last time she was in here a month ago, but she still had a concussion.

"There's like thirty of these elastic straps, each carrying a certain amount of weight. It's all computer generated." I watched her look hesitantly around on either side of me. "Don't worry. I can't even feel them."

Mom encouraged her with, "Honey, ask him anything. It's okay."

She swallowed. But then in usual Grace form, she just let fly. "How do you pee?"

"In a jug."

She crinkled her nose, still looking confused, and twirled some more. But she launched in with everything from, "What keeps this bed from falling forward and dumping you on your head," to, "How do you shower?"

I answered everything calmly, and she went from three twirls at once to one. I hoped that meant she would reach the end of her questions soon. I really didn't want to spend all afternoon talking about my own dilemma. I wanted to forget it.

"So, like, the nurse has to undo *thirty straps* every time you get washed? Or do you just not wash those covered parts of yourself?"

"No, I'm perfectly clean, I assure you," I said. "The computer unlocks the bed, and all the straps open in one movement. It's pretty cool to hear. Clip-clap-clop. All the nurse has to do is rehook them once I'm clean and dressed. But if she even leaves one unhooked, the bed won't close. It's pretty amazing."

"And this happens every day," she said, watching the side of me.

"Every other day."

She made a face, saying, "Uh-uh… "

Mom and I cracked up. Grace's hair was as long as Trinity's, and through these long grooming processes, she managed to keep it silky. But she went through shampoo like crazy. In spite of Mom yelling about it, she used up like three bottles a week.

I'm just worried, is all. This is my *brother*. What if he, like…suddenly falls out of that…that *sling?"*

I cracked up. Mom said, "Now, how would he do that?"

"I don't know! He just said that all those clamps or whatever can just open at once. What if he's hanging there facing the floor and starts hearing clap-clip-clomp…"

I assured her that the bed only opened with the key and the nurses were well-trained to make sure I was lying flat.

"Looks almost like a cannon from the very front. That thing can't suddenly propel his body out into the corridor like a rocket, right?"

I didn't think that was worth answering. Her face finally relaxed and she sat Indian style on the floor.

"Well. Only four more days, Tobes. Then, your life can restart. Hey, guess what? After we walked to you last night, we called Ridgewood."

The band from my prom. "I'm going to be at this party and thinking I'm dreaming it."

"You won't be dreaming it. If we can't get them, we'll find somebody else. We had to leave a message. But Dad says it's cool, so… "

I could barely fathom that party. I focused in on what had been keeping me buoyant. "And come Friday, we're all gonna walk out together. Remember when Casen had that cast on his leg two springs ago? The doc took it off. He walked out."

"That cast was to his *knee,*" Grace reminded me emphatically. *"*Are you delusional?"

"Could you humor me just a little? Doctors keep telling me I've got amazing healing powers. I am *not* using any stupid wheelchair." I rolled my eyes. "I'll surprise you all."

Grace looked out the door as a nurse's voice drifted in.

The nurse had opened Rachel's door to give her a couple of pills. She had deep lines under her eyes, though she forced a little wave at me in the mirror and I made a polite peace sign at her. After the nurse closed the door again, Grace giggled.

"So, that's the extrasensory girl," she guessed.

"Yeah, that's Rachel. She's driving me a little batty right now. She was actually in here last night."

Mom gasped with a pleasantly surprised grin. I ignored it and just blurted the harmless part, not wanting my willies to come back. "Some invisible energy or something in this room keeps scaring the crap out of her. I don't think it was cool for her to mention it since I'm locked in here."

I felt guilty for leaving out Rachel's abject terror but not enough to want to discuss it. Grace glared out the door. "Maybe you shouldn't let her in here. Do I need to go punch her out?"

"Uh, no." I smiled. I couldn't remember Grace being funny as a kid. This year in school I'd sometimes see a crowd of people laughing, with her in the middle of it. She'd come into a sense of humor somewhere along the way.

"So, I suppose Dad wouldn't leave you home alone, fearing some gargantuan hurricane party," I said. Grace stuck out her tongue.

"You guys are here; that's all that matters," Mom said. "Hurricane gave us a reason to be a family until it all blows over. Dad is at the hotel. With Trinity. They're coming to see you tomorrow."

"Trinity's here..." It struck me. I glanced over at Mom with hesitations. Having written about Trin today, I wasn't sure how I felt. I didn't want her scratching the hell out of her face over seeing my condition up close.

"It was a last-minute decision," Mom said. "She keeps nodding, *yes, she wants to see you, and yes,* she understands about your condition and the bed. We think she gets it. Even still, I would have said no. You know what flights do to her asthma. She's still on the nebulizer back at the hotel."

Grace countered. "She's been coddled too much. Sorry, Mom. I know you're doing your best with a really weird situation, but think of it. You and Dad keep saying she can go to Princeton and be a theoretical physicist. She hasn't even seen the inside of a classroom since kindergarten! How's that supposed to work?"

"Princeton has thirteen homeschooled students as we speak," Mom said. "We'll make it work."

"And she doesn't talk!"

"She talks," Mom said. "She talks to me. She talks to the Twardy sisters, and other girls at dance."

"The Twardy tarts." Grace rolled her eyes.

It was also good to hear normal school-type talk in here, even if it was scrappy. Trin's best friends, Mila and Eloise Twardy, showed up at

Mom's school for their privates a couple of hours before the schooled kids piled in, and they hung out with Trinity. And they were from a family so religious that they probably thought my family couldn't make it into heaven. They went to a church on the mainland where there was a rock band instead of hymns, and people prophesied and laid hands on those who fell down in the aisle. So the rumor went.

"What do they *talk* about?" Grace wondered, going back to the umbrella, picking it up, and spinning it like a roulette wheel. "Like, how to keep your sock drawer organized, and *Caillou?"*

Mom cleared her throat and said cheerily, "I don't think Eloise and Mila are allowed to watch much TV, but they and Trinity do seem to find plenty to talk about."

This winter and spring I could sometimes hear Trinity blathering on to them over the phone at night and giggling and stuff. From the sounds, you'd think she was just a normal schoolgirl facetiming. Usually she was in her room with the door shut. Once I stuck my ear to the door. But Trinity's voice is half whisper, even if you can catch her motor-mouthing. I couldn't hear her words.

Grace was on my wavelength. "Maybe they talk about the Bible. Who begat who. Or, like, maybe they think the Prophets of Old are hunks or something."

"Who begat *whom,*" Mom corrected her but kept sounding cheery. "I think we should be thankful that the Twardy girls like Trinity, and Trinity likes them."

"Mom. They're like eleven and twelve and still think you pray for a baby!" Grace griped.

"Well, I think *all* people should pray for a baby, along with everything that comes with conception," Mom persisted cheerily.

Grace walked away from the umbrella as it slowed to a wobble, and she picked up the bottle of lotion on the nightstand, staring at the ingredients.

"Honey, go out in the hall and get a chair!" Mom begged her. Grace had trouble sitting still sometimes. I wondered if she could make Mom more weary in an hour than I could, recovering from a broken neck. I chuckled at the thought but bit my tongue.

"Why don't you take a walk? Go buy him that milkshake," Grace said over her shoulder. "Cm on. I haven't seen my brother in a month. And I know you hate school gossip, but I've been saving all mine until I saw him again."

"Uh-oh," I said.

Mom stood up slowly, taking her time doing something I couldn't see. I flipped to the mirror and found her stepping around the open umbrella and fixing her hair in the mirror above the dresser. It was me watching her in a mirror and her watching me back through another mirror. Mirror to mirror. There was something surreal about it, even though I liked the idea of seeing my *mom* in the corner of the room as opposed to whatever had sent Rachel flying out of here. Finally Mom left, flipping her flip-flops and reminding me she'd had a relaxing morning already which included someone painting her toes.

Fourteen

"So, what's going on at home?" I asked. "I want to hear everything."

Grace started with, "In fact, this is the most drama-free, boring summer I've ever experienced, except for needing a t-shirt that says, 'MY BROTHER IS DOING FINE, QUIT ASKING ME BEFORE I PUNCH SOMEBODY.'"

She put the lotion down, went to plop in Mom's chair, and went down slowly instead. "Mom's hovering. What the hell."

I tapped the mirror and saw a second nurse entering Rachel's room and leaving the door open. Mom was sticking her head in to say hello and make nice-nice.

"I told her to take a walk to the first floor and buy you a milkshake. She's across the hall instead?" Grace asked. "I don't know how you stand her being with you all day and most of the night. She's like a helicopter. Flying up your ass, chopping all your organs to smithereens."

"You're pushing it too far," I smirked. "She picks up what I drop, gets me what I want from down the hall, and doesn't bother me too much. You and her...I don't know. Maybe once you're done being a...a *sullen teenager,* Grace, we'll all say you're too much alike. She used to say she was loud and rebellious. Remember that?"

"Yes," Grace admitted sullenly. "But I'm not rebellious, and I'll be sullen 'til I'm ninety. Part of my charm. "

The bed flipped, and Grace watched, going, *"wwwwoe..."* until I was facing the ceiling again. "You're *sure* that wasn't fun?"

"Wasn't fun. I promise." I decided it was time to get on to something important. Thought I'd take the indirect route, though. "Sorry I upset you last night...even if you were at a party at *my* friend's house."

"So sue me," she said in annoyance and then changed her tone. "It's fine that you called. We're not supposed to talk about it, that's all."

"I don't see how it hurts to talk about Trin's guinea pig," I muttered. "I don't see how it hurts to talk about *any* of it."

"It's like that doctor said…whatever he said. I can't even remember."

"I don't like him. *He* should try lying here, day after day, when there's a psychotic out there loose, who pushed me down a well. He's got me believing in the Witch of Indor... Next it'll be the Jersey Devil. Is head shrinkage supposed to be emotionally healthy? I thought shrinks were supposed to help along your...your...*emotionality.*"

"Is that a word?" she asked, digging out her phone and entering her password.

"Hell if I know. I'm just glad I'm done with the SAT because I can't remember big words...except I *do* remember what happened at the well."

Her thumb was scrolling Instagram, but her eyes were glued to the door, like she was scared Mom would come barging in.

"Look, um...since we're not supposed to talk about this at all, I'll just say it fast. I don't remember that Elijah Rune priest-guy showing up soon enough, Tobes. It was dark. I didn't hear anything that would mean a stranger came up beside us. That's all I want to say."

I remembered clearly hearing his footsteps and *then* feeling the thrust of a hand in my back.

"You didn't hear footsteps run up behind us," I watched the door intently in the mirror myself.

To my amazement, she sighed. Finally she said, "No."

I wondered how she could *not* have heard them. They'd been clear as day to me—the part that was more clear than any other. I said quickly, "What about Trinity? Does she remember running footsteps?"

She stopped her scroll to like a picture Wiley posted of himself with a seagull net. She finally said, "No."

"Jeezus..." I muttered, dazed and confused.

"*Don't* tell Mom I told you that." She blinked furiously like tears were going to fall.

"Sorry," I said.

"That's fine, it's...maybe I'll get out of therapy if I cry some. I just don't want Mom coming back in here to find me bawling. I'll find some other way out of it." She cleared her throat with some determination.

"Mom and Dad didn't make you go to therapy?"

"Too worried about Trinity!" she hissed between her teeth. "Do some things never change? I always get overlooked. But in this case, it's good. You know how I hate talking about my problems. I'd rather go...catch birds with Wiley."

Wiley Mathis would catch endangered birds that had wandered out of the bird sanctuary up at the north end of Port Dingo. He would take them back down there in his trap and let them go. It's one of those things we figured Grace meant when she said, "You have to get to know him, he's really sweet." A guy with only three words in his vocabulary *could* catch endangered birds and return them, we supposed.

"Daddy does want me to go to therapy before school starts. It's mostly because I haven't been able to cry. He thinks that's awful."

"You cried last night," I said.

"Maybe you can be my witness. I know I should have cried before. But people handle their challenges in their own way. I'm just as worried. My way's different, that's all. I feel like if I cry...somebody's going to die. And we're all alive! So, why put the stress on my tear ducts?"

"You think Trinity pushed me." I forced myself to say it, though it was like taking a punch in the gut from an invisible fist. The silence all but slayed me. She just kept rubbing her eyes, staying quiet. "*Everyone* thinks Trinity pushed me. Mom hasn't said it yet. Nobody's said it *plainly* yet. But that's what everyone thinks."

She just stared dropped the hand with the phone in it between her legs and stared down at her sneakers. I thought maybe some truth coming from me would help her along. "I was alone with Trin for a while. You hadn't come out from the pool yet."

That got her looking at me, in a concerned way. "Was she acting weird?"

"Yes. Very."

"What happened?"

"You remember," I said vaguely. "I was harping on it. She was telling me the Witch of Indor was at the well." I stopped short of telling Grace about *the witch told me to push you.*

Her eyes were starting to look swollen and glassy from all the rubbing. But she didn't look surprised.

"Look, Tobes. I can't say she did or she didn't push you. But what are the options?"

I thought of Rachel's very scary words from the night before: "You, your sisters, a man, and a *woman.*" The room darkened a bit as clouds rolled in front of the sun. I pushed my mirror around to see them. Grace could see them in the mirror too. "Sun was good while it lasted. It'll be back."

I turned the mirror to the dreaded corner, catching only a blast of purple umbrella fabric. I went on, "I don't know what causes people to get the creeps. But I have them constantly. I feel watched. If I'm alone in here, I get creeped out looking in my mirror. It's like, you know, some spook will be staring back at me. Rachel's not helping. She saw something in here—"

"Stop," she said, flopping back in the chair. "Rachel is traumatized, you just said it. And we can't go there, Toby. We just can't."

I persisted anyway. "Sometimes I feel like something...someone...is blowing on my leg."

She didn't freak out on me, but the look in her eyes told me she could at any moment.

Her voice was still calm. "Didn't your doctors say to 'expect anything?' I'd be creeped out in that almost-strait jacket, *ugh*. Who wouldn't? Look. I loved the Witch of Indor stories because it's fun to scare people. Especially Trinity. I know you think she's a direct descendant of God Almighty, but I get sick of her chronically getting all the attention for being *weak*. You and me? We have to be *strong* to make up for her being *weak*, and it's unfair. She's *fun* to scare. God, such a walking, breathing *victim*. My point is...I don't believe those stories. *She does.* You know how Wiley and me can go see a double or triple horror feature, and I'll just go home, drop into bed, and sleep the whole night?"

That was another thing that made us dislike Wiley Mathis, the guy who could do two or three really gross horror movies in a row and walk away yawning. This wasn't the time to bring up how Mom and Dad thought he'd been a terrible influence.

She finished with, "So, please don't go there…don't start blaming the Witch of Indor."

"Look. I know how crazy this all sounds. But it's like, I've got my choice between my sisters, a priest, myself, and a dead witch. I've got nothing but insane possibilities, so why not pick what's least likely to hurt any living people?"

Grace was leaning forward again, bouncing her heels off the floor pensively. She looked down at them, watching one ankle rise and fall, and then the other with her chin in her hands. Finally, she got up and wandered over to me, staring out at Rachel's closed door.

"What we want to pick is the truth," she said. "No matter how messed up it is."

"I know. But I know Trinity. I know she would not hurt me."

"Here's what you know, Toby. You've always felt guilty about the dog attack. She has a special place in your heart. That's nice and all, but special places can screw up how you see things."

"She's not violent. She wouldn't do this."

"Here's a solution for you, one that is still sane."

"Bring it," I said, adjusting the mirror. I was looking up at the back of her head. She turned and locked eyes with me. She came closer to the bed, letting one arm fall on the plastic casing around my chest. She beat on it with her palm lightly on the outer coating of the bed top. "That it was an accident."

The silence echoed until she went on.

"It was an accident. She didn't mean to do it. It just happened. It would explain a lot. Why she scratched her face so much, why her asthma almost killed her that night. Smells like guilt to me."

I opened my mouth but didn't know what thought to go for. I settled on, "Why wouldn't she just confess and say it was an accident?"

"So, I'm not saying it was *that* kind of an accident. I mean, I don't think she bumped into you with her fingers accidentally taking a claw shape and striking you in the back. I'm talking about some sort of... *urge,* something...that isn't normally there but can come over her sometimes. Just sometimes. That kind of accident."

Like an urge *to drop the guinea pig on the stairs.* Dad had found a guinea pig fur ball on the stairs, about halfway down. Maybe he was right. Maybe Grace was onto something that I was blind about. *Get some urge, do something crazy, then cry about it like you have an evil twin—*

The thought brought spit to my mouth.

She sighed, saying, "Goddam. I wish I could cry—"

Her lip was trembling. I reached out for her hand. She shouldn't be leaning on this bed anyway. It was set for my weight, and I wasn't sure how it could malfunction.

She put her hand in mine and took a step back. "I mean, bro. Do you mind if I say... we've known for years, hey, our sister is way strange? Whatever goes on in her head is a mystery to me. Don't think I don't have my guilt too! I feel horrible that I scared the crap out of her all those years with the Witch of Indor stories, given how things went down. But, like, if you have no idea how she thinks and what she thinks... I should not have scared her at the well like I did. I should have left it alone."

She was talking about one of those swiss-cheese spots in my brain. I decided I needed answers more than I needed to protect Trinity. Or maybe the best protection of Trinity would be to come up with some answers.

"Were we talking about the witch while we were fooling around at the well?"

She blinked at me, and then her eyes widened. "Yes, Toby. We were *very much* talking about the witch at the well."

I must have looked confused.

"Well, if you don't remember, then I'm not telling you."

I searched my head but with a wariness, like something might jump out of my brain and rake my face. "I remember you dropped that lantern down the well to see how deep it was."

"*That's* how you remember it?" she asked. "I dropped the lantern on purpose? Just to see how deep it was?"

"Didn't you?"

"You really *don't* remember. Do you?" She unclipped the remote and flopped back down in the corner chair. "Let's watch TV. Don't you ever watch TV?"

"I usually stream movies. Or I have to keep moving the mirror. Gets to be a pain. But I'll watch something with you. Nothing scary, please. A comedy or something."

"You just picked the genre, which means I get to pick the movie," she said and went with some comedy that was so boring and not funny that I fell asleep about fifteen minutes into it.

Fifteen

Grace's voice, softly, over my head, was saying in a soothing tone, "Remember all the detail. It's okay. I'm here. I'm with you."

Only it wasn't actually Grace. It was a voice in my dream that only sounded like Grace, until it grew distorted, like someone slowing the speed of a recording, and it changed into a groan of thunder. I knew I was dreaming, but any efforts to pull myself out of it were not with my real body. I tried touching my face but couldn't feel anything. But then I floated across that Chapel Rock Inn front porch toward Trinity, and suddenly, nothing else was real except what Trinity had just said to me. "She's telling *me* to push you…"

Grace has suddenly come up on the porch, wrapped in a towel, stinking of chlorine, and watching us. She wraps the towel around her waist tightly, having a white long-sleeved t-shirt over her bathing suit.

I take Trinity by the shoulders and force her to look at me. "Well then. We have nothing to worry about, do we? Because you would never do a thing like that."

"What are you guys talking about?" Grace asks. I ignore her.

"No," Trinity says. And in German, "Ich würde nie, hören immer zu ihr." "I would never, ever listen to her—"

"What'd she just say?" Grace demands, stamping her foot impatiently. "Tell me."

She can't remember what she learns in her English classes let alone French, and even if Grace weren't ditzy, Trinity has picked German. She hates when I understand Trinity and she can't.

I ignore it again but don't like how Trinity stares at me wide-eyed, like she isn't giving up on this the-witch-is-at-the-well idea. I hate seeing her scared and all turned around like this.

I finally say to Grace, "She's getting herself all creeped out." Then I pull Grace over to me by the arm and say to her while staring at Trin, "We are going to ignore some no trespassing signs so somebody can learn there's nothing weird down there."

We leave Trinity on the porch. Within five steps, I can hear the faintness of her wheeze. She wheezes under stress.

"Grace, what the fuck." I all but bruise her arm, giving her a good shot with my elbow. "You're filling her head with those Witch of Indor tales, you moron. You know how easily she gets spooked. Are you mean or just plain stupid?"

"I have not mentioned that story this year!" She elbows me back just as hard. "We've been here four hours. Give me a chance to wind up. I have my priorities. Pool first, hot tub second, three decent meals at least. Then I start scaring the shit out of everybody."

I almost laugh. But the idea that Trinity can get that amped up without any fodder from Grace has me really concerned. I say it in my *head, the thing I'd thought about but never say out loud:* I don't know my little sister. *I have no idea what goes on in her mind, if I'm being honest. This time I add the silent question:* Could she hallucinate a voice—a voice telling her to push her brother??

"I'm worried about her," I say.

"You need to settle into it, bro. I'm very sad that I have a mental case for a sister, but I learned to live with it. You need to, too. It's time."

"She's not mental. She's just..." I trail off, words having failed.

"Just what? Look. I think you're confused, Toby. I think you're afraid that if you admit she's got a screw lose, that means you can't love her as much. For me? It means I love her more. It means that I don't have to be blind and deaf, like Mom is—"

She halts because of running footsteps behind us. I turn, but Trinity stops about twenty feet short of us and watches us smoothly climb over the chain that held the sign. I make sure I don't even pause.

"Care to join us? You're welcome to come." I say evenly, then mumble to Grace, "I think you're lying to me, you little shit. You told her something just to watch her squirm. She thinks the Witch of Indor is in the well—s"

"Why do I chronically have a target on my back?" She's raised her voice for that much but then lowers it again to a grumble, her molars clenching. "I'll tell you why, Toby. Because it's easier. It's easier for you

and Mom to think I did something to her than to think of what she's capable of dreaming up in that...that very locked little mind of hers..." She knocks on the side of her scull so hard I can hear it. "... without any help at all. It's okay. Blame me! I'll bounce back. I always do."

"Grace, don't be a martyr—"

I woke up to white sand on the TV. But the remote wasn't in its clip. Grace wasn't trained to bring everything back to me when she was done with it, and I spotted it with a sweep of my mirror, on the arm of her chair. The chair was empty. A quick sweep of the room told me that she and Mom were not in here, though the umbrella still was. I groped for the nurse's button under its clip. Before I got my fingers around it, I grabbed my cellphone to look at the time. *Nine-thirty?*

The last few weeks I'd spent all day and all night sleeping about half an hour, then being awake about half an hour. This week, I was staying awake longer, which probably meant I was sleeping longer. *But four hours?*

There was a text from Mom. "Didn't want to wake you up. Trinity's asthma improved enough to take the girls out to dinner but not for a potentially stressful experience like the hospital. Call if you want me to come back afterward."

I couldn't blame Mom for wanting to spend a night as a normal family in a normal restaurant, even if it didn't include me. I got a stab of Grace's feeling, that Trin could run the show in the family. It was annoying. I found myself wondering if she could fake something to avoid seeing me.

I pushed the nurse's button. The rule was that the nurses had to get to me in one minute, but I was going to check Instagram to fill those extra-long seconds. The feeling was back already—the one of being watched.

But when I picked up my phone again, it registered in my brain that there was a text from Rachel as well. It had come half an hour ago, and I'd slept right through the ding.

"Sorry I was such a baby and ran out on you last night," it read. "That was really selfish. I didn't want to bother you earlier, sending this while you had company. Hope you got some laughs, and again, I'm really sorry."

I looked to see if there was any light coming from under Rachel's door, but there was just a black line. She was probably asleep, and being as I hadn't answered half an hour ago, she probably thought I was still mad at her for the sudden desertion.

I didn't want to wake her up, but just in case she was awake I made it short, "It's fine. I understand."

Half a minute after I sent it, the black line under her door turned yellow. I guessed she wasn't exactly asleep. She also couldn't stick her head out the door and just say something to me.

A text dinged. "Are you mad?"

I wasn't sure what I was feeling. I supposed the words "high maintenance" would apply to Rachel if someone wanted to be her friend. My heart went out as I remembered her gripping that sheet and being all amped over things that didn't make sense to others. But having a needy friend was kind of off my grid right now.

I typed "no" but hesitated. One-word text replies can sound pissy, and I didn't want to her to go to sleep feeling bad. I added, "Didn't even have time to think about it. My sister Grace showed up with my mom. Great to see her after a month."

I sent it, and the ellipses showed almost immediately as she was typing. "Anything happen in there?" appeared with the ding.

The question was too vague to get whether she meant socially, psychologically, physically, or something worse. *Paranormally.* I sighed and shot another glance into the corner, then rolled my eyes slowly to the TV, still creating sand.

"Are you talking about my room?" I hit SEND and felt impatient that no nurse had shown up yet. The one-minute thing that was a rule, tonight it had probably been two. The silence grew overwhelming, as it was late, and there were no visitors, no daytime personnel making a clatter in the corridor.

Rachel hadn't responded and wasn't typing. Did she fall asleep? Great, creep me out and leave me alone a second time.

"Say something," I sent, refusing to say the TV was sandy over here. Might give her a heart attack.

The ellipses popped up quickly. She finally replied with, "Never mind."

My instincts said to leave it alone. With her scramming out of here last night after creating oh-so-much drama, I didn't trust much of what she would say, but ever Mr. Nice Guy, I felt like I was already into it. "No, tell me."

"It's nothing."

"No, it isn't."

I should have left it lie, except I knew the nurse was coming in a minute. I wouldn't be alone. "Did something happen that scared you?"

"Sort of."

"Tell me."

"Okay. I saw the aura again, the one with no body."

I figured she must have seen it in her room as I remembered the footsteps that passed back and forth in the line of yellow light. So I typed, "Did it do anything? Try to hurt you?"

After the ellipses showed a few times, the text popped up. "I didn't see it in here. I saw it in the corridor when your Mom and sister showed up."

"Okay..." I honestly didn't know what to think. I remembered the nurse opening the door to give Rachel medication or something, and leaving it open a few minutes. If Rachel wasn't out of her mind and was actually seeing something factual, it could be the thing that pushed me, and Trinity was innocent.

I let her type, and this appeared: "It followed them into the room. Then it floated between you and your sister when she was talking to you."

That sounded stone-cold nuts. I was speechless. If it was real, it hadn't hurt either one of us—that was my second thought, though I felt like my brain was on a pendulum. Would the thing try to hurt Grace next? Would it try to hurt Trinity tomorrow? And of course, the biggie: Was what Rachel saw the same thing that pushed me down the well? And if so, why me? Why not some lazy-ass, couch potato, uncoordinated sucker, the kind who totally believed in spooks and would scream all the way down?

I had not screamed. Not once. I'm a lifeguard and a diver, and my sole thought had been if I could manage to land feet first instead of headfirst, I'd triple my chances of surviving. Doing a one-eighty in a six-foot-wide passage is not as hard as it sounds. *I don't need to think, I don't need a light. It's in slow motion that I straighten out... because it dawns on me that this water could be only a foot deep—*

I hear the shatter of glass from the lantern, but only for a split second. There's debris down under me, but what I find out later is a six-foot rusty pipe somebody dropped down there, probably years ago. It shatters my thigh... I hear the break, even from under water. My neck breaks from the pressure of the sailing jacket expanding on impact. It shoots me up like a rocket, and I feel like I've been hit in the base of my neck with a sledgehammer. My brains are on fire. But even then, I don't scream. I know a scream could kill me.

Elijah Rune is hollering, a woman is screaming. I hear them but still don't scream. "Stop fighting me, or you'll be down there next!" A minute later I'm answering some guy's questions in a regular voice that echoes, actually kind of pleased with myself that I'm able to say, "Get my dad, Tobias Kellerman. He's a seaman. He's in the lounge."

I know there's more I can't remember, but I've remembered enough to wonder, what kind of fun would *I* be to a spook?

Rachel sent another lengthy apologetic text, saying she couldn't get out of bed by herself, but if I needed anything, anything, she would text with me. She would sleep with her phone in her hand.

I glanced at the sand on the TV, but only through my mirror. A blast of relief shot through me as I heard footsteps coming this way finally, I just wrote back, "Okay, sleep tight."

"What the hell is up with the white sand, Toby?" Carly Sames, my favorite night nurse, breezed past me to the TV.

"Remote's on the nightstand. My sister left it out of my reach."

"She's adorable," Carly noted. "And funny, too."

"Yeah, she's getting to be that way," I grumbled.

"How'd you guys get so lucky, to get in a family with looks *and* charm?" she asked.

I just cleared my throat and mumbled, "Thanks." I didn't say, *You've only met two of us,* though in my mind, Trin looked more like an angel than me or Grace could ever on our best days.

Carly snatched up the remote and jumped down a couple of stations. Still white sand.

"I'm not a techie, but..." I lost sight of her in the mirror for a moment as she bent down behind the chair. Whatever happy movie Mom and Grace had been watching was over, and Golem, the little savage from *Lord of the Rings*, was staring out of the screen, rocking on his heels in a cave and smiling.

"Plug wasn't all the way pushed in. Huh. Did somebody kick it?" Carly stood up again.

If someone kicked it, they would have seen the TV screen turn to sand when they were in here and fixed it. *Duh.* I asked, "What took you so long? What if I'd been choking on something?"

"Were you choking?" she asked knowingly, smiling like I wasn't in the mood for.

"I could have been. Sorry. I'm not trying to go rude on you. But you try lying here for weeks."

"No thanks. The good news is...you've been upgraded. We now have three minutes to get here from the nurse's station. That's what happens to patients who are almost better. You'll get a chance to exercise more *patience* this week, oh *impatient patient.*"

I smirked. "Hey. I'm starting physical therapy tomorrow. They're bringing me some bar to push on with my feet."

"I heard that. You'll have all your leg strength soon. You a Tolkien fan? You want me to leave this on?"

I actually loved Tolkien. But I didn't need close-ups of Golem staring at me on top of all these confusing thoughts roasting in my brain.

"Just turn it off. I'm probably going to be awake for a while. Might as well do some writing or something."

The screen went black, and she put the remote in its clip on my bed casing. "So. You promised to take me out dancing once you're out of here." She reminded me of this every few days. "Coming up soon!"

"Four more days in this bed unless something goes horribly wrong. I'm gonna swing you over my head like one of those disco people."

"I'll wear a parachute, just in case you get carried away," she smiled big, cracking gum. Carly was twenty-two, chronically chewed gun, and was the closest person I had to a contemporary on this staff. She didn't have the seniority to get on day shift. Though she was kept busy, on slow nights she'd kill a half hour talking to me.

"Hey, Carly, you know anything about the Witch of Indor?"

"From up yonder around Salem?" A smile bloomed slowly, revealing the gum between her molars, and she plopped into Mom's chair. "She's like your Jersey Devil, ya know? Everyone's got either a personal story or knows a friend who knows someone who's got one."

"Right," I said. "Do you have a friend of a friend with a story or—"

"My story is actually personal," she said curtseying to pretend applause. "One of my ex-boyfriends was a wannabe film producer and bigtime camper."

"Uh-oh," I chucked with her. "That sounds like a deadly combination of hobbies."

"Exactly. So he'd spent nights, entire weekends up there, trying to lure her out. He had night vision equipment and a thermal camera and all this stuff. He kept saying as soon as he sold his evidence to one of the ghost shows on Destination America, we would get married. Guess I dodged a bullet there. He was way too into the paranormal stuff, and it was creeping me out. Just before we broke up, I went with him once."

"Yeah? You see the witch?" I asked.

"No. But that's not saying much, considering nobody sees her, right? We were asleep in the tent, and around three a.m., woke up to this smell, this...ugh. It was like a thousand sunbaked road-kills. I can still smell it sometimes, like when I'm stressed out. Like, it's been forevermore stuck in my nostrils and just seeps down sometimes."

"Gross," I said. "So you think it was her?"

"Well, of course Lyle went flying out of the tent. He said his thermal reader was going crazy—hit by a hot spot or something. But his camera caught nothing. We got in a fight. I wanted to leave right then, and he wanted to stay. He won the fight, but I didn't sleep another wink, even after the stink blew over. And three days later? We broke up. I don't mind donating a weekend to possibly getting haunted, but I didn't want to dedicate my life to it. Why are you asking about the Witch of Indor?"

"You, um, you ever heard of her pushing somebody down a well?"

She flinched after a moment, revealing her gum again. "Ooo! I thought you were just bored and looking to talk about something. Why get her all involved in your accident? That's not going to help you heal up."

I just couldn't *not* go there. "I've got some severely limited options as to how I got to the bottom of the well."

"Toby, you need to get your life back. You need to get out of this bed."

"Tell me about it. But right now, it looks like my little sister Trinity is going to get blamed for pushing me. I can't believe she did it."

"Your sister..." she went on with a surprisingly accurate description. "... the one who spent a week on the fourth floor, with the bad asthma and the scratches on her face and her cornea?"

"You work down there, too?" I asked.

"No, but you know, nurses talk to each other sometimes, just to get a load off."

I didn't like the sound of that but couldn't help but understand the reaction. "Everybody thinks she's crazy. 'Cept me. I love her."

She shifted in her chair uncomfortably while blurting, "Don't get me wrong. They weren't speaking ill of her or anything, Toby. They were just concerned, you know, that she couldn't seem to tell them when she was really uncomfortable. She utterly stonewalled the staff shrink--like she was in a trance or something. That's hard to do. He's a great shrink."

I wondered if it was Dr. Vapor, but since I couldn't think of his real name, I didn't bother asking. It would have been nice for him to tell me he'd seen my sister also.

I didn't exactly care what the nurses thought at the moment. I cared what I thought. And what I couldn't think of. "I'm suddenly starting to remember more stuff."

"Okay," she said. "That's normal. That's good."

"But it's like... not in order. Instead of remembering things in order of how they happened, I'm remembering them in order of easy-to-handle to difficult-to-handle. Or something like that. The really hard stuff? I'm getting close. But it's like...I'm afraid to remember. Like...it's going to be off-the-wall crazy and involve a witch. That sounds crazy, doesn't it?"

To my surprise, she didn't look the least bit disturbed. "Toby, we see one accident victim after another on this ward. And it is very normal for them to not remember details and suddenly remember them while they're here. It's part of the healing process. As for our patients seeing strange things, we're so immune to it that we don't form opinions. Lots of people in your condition recall seeing angels. One guy said he saw a devil--I remember that." Her eyes widened for a moment. "If you want me to sit here with you—sometimes it helps to have a nonpartisan person with you, so you don't feel alone with your thoughts, you know? If it'll help you get rid of the Witch of Indor—God. What a concept."

"Do you have time?" I wanted her to stay primarily because I didn't want to be alone with my willies.

"Let's just say I don't have time to sit here and help you scare yourself half to death over something that's, yeah, a bit off the wall. We're getting a car accident in from post-op. I gotta spend most of the night keeping him stabilized."

In other words, she couldn't sit here and baby me.

"I'll do what we do for lots of other patients who want to remember details—for insurance companies or to stop some unhelpful family blame-game. Give me your hand." She reached out, and I put my hand in hers.

I could feel myself relaxing already as she said, "Just start talking about what happened in a real monotone voice, almost like you're watching it happen instead of being in it."

I said slowly and smoothly, "Grace and I had left Trinity and gone on past the sign. The idea was to look down the well, fool around, and come back unharmed to show Trinity there was no witch down there. Trinity was kind of obsessed with her that night."

I'm not sure if I even said anything else aloud.

Trinity's wheezing has gotten closer. When I look, she's leaning against the tree trunk behind me and Grace. There was a torch lantern hanging there a minute ago. Now it's gone. I could only make out Trinity's silhouette, stiff, tense, and ready to run.

Light comes from my other side, but the moon is behind a cloud. You can barely see the sign with it. Grace has the lantern. It's the oil kind that they hang from some of the tall trees around here to make things look prettier at night. It's making the sleeves of her white t-shirt glow neon, like she's a spook.

Slowly she lowers the light into the shaft. I see—

"Grace. There's writing down there. Some creepy, glow-in-the-dark letters. Gimme the lamp. Or lower it down—"

"Use your phone!" she says.

"Use yours! I'm not dropping mine down a—"

"Oh, your phone is sacred, and mine isn't? The lantern is enough. Ooo-hoo. It's the witch," Grace says somberly. "She wrote something. It's a message for us. Oooo—"

I can't lower the lamp because Trinity decided at this point it was time to jut forward on her knees and hold my hand. She's kneeling beside me, wheezing in my right ear.

Grace lowers her arm with the lamp. "What does it say? Hurry up, or I'll set fire to my favorite new surf shirt—"

It looked like graffiti from some stoner asshole—but the words are coming clear. I say them...

"SHE'S DOWN THERE..."

Grace scream-laughs like there is something glee-worthy out of what just scared the life out of me. "How'd he get down that far? Like, with a rope?"

"Stoner," I say aloud, at a loss for other words. The writing's in bright yellow, about twelve feet down. My hair is standing on end.

"I don't think he was a stoner," Grace laughs. "Had to be a mountain climber pro or something. Hey! The witch wrote it! Shit, now she's burned my knuckles—"

The quiet voice of Carly rolled in with, "What do you remember?"

"Grace. She dropped the lamp because it burned her," I said, more to myself than to her. "I always just thought she dropped it to see how deep the well was, but it's like anything that night—anything to do with the Witch of Indor got completely wiped from my brain."

Carly groaned, squeezed my hand, and said something like, "Don't do this to yourself, Toby."

But the light of the flame becomes a pinprick as we hear the splash, when it finally hits the water. Then, BA-AM. It explodes in orange and mushrooms back up the well.

"Look out!" I push Trinity down and throw myself on top of her.

Grace jumps away, screaming curses and laughing. And the flame mushrooms out under the little roof. It's gone over Trinity's and my heads—

"Carly. How does a flame hit water and explode instead of being immediately burned out?"

"Not sure. It could have been the well water was compromised...full of gasoline or something. Did you see what you're after, like who pushed you?"

I'd leaped over it, had gone down the well.

Staring into a big flashlight beam from the top, I realize I'm alive...I'm breathing. Not oxygen deprived. I'm not floating in gasoline. It's water. But standing water, so it stinks, but I can barely notice it because my right leg is exploding with pain along with my brains.

I heard myself groan, not wanting to be in that blackness, agony, and abject terror—

"Let me just ask some perimeter questions," Carly said in monotone. "Who rescued you?"

"My dad. Came down on one of the hotel's climbing belts. He's a seaman. Great diver. Not afraid like the medics were."

"How'd he bring you back up?"

"I was in hypothermia and can't really remember. Later he said it was your basic plastic stretcher for neck injuries. They're compact—"

"Try and stick to what you can remember. How long were you down there?"

"Half an hour, but it felt like two days. I was in the chopper a half hour after that."

"Fast, wow."

"Treated it like a climbing accident. There was some plug and chug to it..."

"What did you do down there?"

I could feel again how badly my head had hurt while having to shout up to describe my injuries. I can remember the screeching, coming and going and making me wonder where it was coming from.

I didn't want to think of being down there. Not only was it the hardest thing I'd ever done, but it wasn't helping me see how I got there. I brought myself back up, to the point where Grace dropped the lantern, followed by the explosion and the ball of fire coming up.

I couldn't help replaying it over and over. Something about it, something about that flame had seemed alive, like it had a mind of its own.

"Carly, what in hell came up out of the well? What in hell came up with that flame?"

"Okay! That is enough for now." She stood up. Carly could get just as authoritative as the other nurses. But I'd only seen it occasionally. "I have to go take care of my post-op. You slept through your dinner and your bath. The bath will have to wait. Are you hungry?"

The normal questions still couldn't jar me out of the sight of that explosion, over and over. "No. Not hungry."

"If you change your mind just push the button. Now, look. I'm going to put cartoons on this TV. Kid cartoons, where nothing scary happens. If you're going to be awake, I want you to watch them with your little mirror and quit thinking about counterproductive things, okay? Because if you don't, I'm going to have to call your shrink and tell him you think the Witch of Indor pushed you down a well."

Which he would say was just a form of denial about Trinity. It made me think of Rachel, and how isolated she must feel in a world of people who will only go so far in their beliefs. Nurse Carly had been willing to rock my world with stories of the Witch of Indor—until it got too personal, too real, too medical.

Now, she was placing the remote over by the TV so I couldn't change the channel, and I had to watch *Mutts 'N Stuff*, where real dogs mix with real people and animated characters. And uh-oh, it looked like the star, Calvin Millan, didn't know how to roller skate and didn't have the nerve to tell his dogs and toddler friends. Hey, that's a real problem!

Carly patted my arm before leaving, and I stared at that remote in the mirror, wishing I had the power to float it over to my grip. But Carly had a point. The shallow nonsense and blah-blah made by these characters really did make me relax, and the tension left the room. I supposed nurses could be smart.

I wished that sense of childlike peace could have lasted for more than twenty minutes. But when I was starting to give into the nods, the screen turned to white sand again.

Sixteen

The gel in the mattresses seemed to be turning cold. I brought my arms in for warmth but didn't want to respond in any other way, giving the TV any power, if that makes sense. It took everything I had not to push the nurses' button. But I could just see their faces after I brought one of them away from an unstable post-op to adjust my TV.

I just set my mirror to cover the corridor, telling myself to simply wait and not to listen for anything in the shhhhhhhhh of the sand. An aide would pass by at any minute.

To kill time I took out my phone and did what I couldn't resist. I googled, "Witch of Indor" and hit the images option. I knew Grace looked stuff up about her in summers past. I never cared enough. And I didn't have the concentration to read much, but I wanted to see any images that surfaced.

The same drawing kept surfacing over and over. It was a pen-and-ink drawing of her as a very young woman. Sometimes the drawing showed up black, sometimes blue, and sometimes it was colorized. According to legend, there had never been any visual sightings. Even the Internet was faithful to that. There were a few other images here and there, but they had been drawn from people's imaginations, and none were claimed to be of sightings. The illustration I kept seeing may have been drawn of her while she was still alive or shortly thereafter.

She was wearing a cape with a hood, and in the colorized images, it was red. Her troubled eyes were blue. She looked around Grace's age. A teenage Little Red Riding Hood is the best way I could describe her but with a deeply troubled look. I tapped one that appeared to be a really old picture of the drawing. The ident said the image had been made from the black and white MISSING poster put up in the town of Indor after she disappeared.

I was coming to that standing position, and it occurred to me again that I hoped this *was* a haunting. I never wanted to believe in spooks more than that moment. I found myself listening through the *shhhhhhhh* of the sand on the TV, which made me feel suddenly ambushed when I sensed eyes behind me. I looked quickly with my mirror, knowing full well there was that blind spot. I thought I heard fabric or clothing rustling. And a growl that I could have mistaken for Trinity's wheezing. I thought I'd imagined that. But a moment later, I felt one of my socks pull off.

My left foot was cold, and the right one, warm. I knew this sensation of cold breath on my ankle was real. And I welcomed my terror, as much as I hated it. At least I did until the sensation changed to fingernails stroking down across my ankle. Then, the nails came back up. Fingernails sharpened to points.

I could wiggle my toes, but at the moment I was afraid to move them, afraid of what else I might feel.

The scratching sensation grew overwhelming as other pictures got in my head of what all this was leading to. *Is she going to bite me next? Why is she playing this game? Why not just finish what she started?*

I texted Rachel.

"Can you come in here? PLEASE?"

My screen clock read eleven-thirty-five. She'd been in bed since dinnertime just to avoid me—or my room. I tried to picture her coming back in here after whatever she saw following Mom and Grace in here. Fat chance. But one of the nails was stroking back down—

I sent another PLEASE, just so her phone would buzz twice more and wake her up if the first set hadn't.

I got a message back, "What's wrong?"

"I'm sorry but—" I accidentally hit SEND but didn't care because I got a new idea.

"MOM. CAN YOU COME BACK HERE??" I sent that, suddenly remembering she had my entire family in the hotel, and I could have just created a panic. I'd deal with that if Mom even woke up.

I half wondered if it was jagged teeth on my ankle and not fingernails. The scratching was accompanied by hotness, like hot breath that started and stopped. Half of me wanted to yell, *Get the hell out!* But she wouldn't, I knew, and I sensed she'd absorb my fear and grow more powerful from it.

I went back to Rachel, realizing I didn't exactly have a choice. "You have to help me. She's scratching my foot! I can feel it plain as day."

Don't pee yourself, became my biggest thought as I hit SEND, something I had managed not to do yet in this bed. I could always wait for the nurse with the key to get here, open the bed so I was lying flat, and pee in a jug. Maybe I should *just pee on her head.*

"Who is SHE?" appeared in my phone.

I hadn't spoken to Rachel at all about the Witch of Indor, except for Rachel identifying a fifth person at the well, and there had been no discussion about who the fifth person, the *abomination,* was.

"I don't know," I lied.

I listened for some sound, smelled for some smell to go with the sensation that was getting stronger, like she was now sticking a pin in my arch. My foot responded with little shudders. At one point, I thought I smelled oranges, which could have wafted from down the hall. What was real and what wasn't? I couldn't separate things. My foot shuddered again with another harsh pinprick.

My mom texted back. "What's going on?"

I wrote to Rachel first. "Nobody knows better than you that there is some stuff the nurses and doctors can't help with."

But by the time I hit SEND, a nurse was already going into Rachel's room like she'd responded to a call from her. It was Carly.

I typed to Mom, "Never mind—go back to sleep," and called to Carly as she walked quickly out again.

She didn't gasp or look surprised to see a presence in here with me. That meant either that she couldn't see whoever was scratching my foot or that there *was* nobody—because the scratching and pin sticking had stopped. Either that or I was losing feeling.

Because I could still feel cold on the foot, I went with something I thought we could both agree on.

"Come turn off that sand," I said tersely. "I know you're busy. Please don't ever leave that remote out of my reach again."

"Oh, wow." She disappeared behind the chair. Cartoons reappeared as she straightened up. "That's so weird. Has anyone else been in here?"

I rolled my eyes and held out my hand for the remote, snatching it from her.

"Toby, I'm so sorry," she said with compassion.

"Just unplug it, please."

She reached down again, and the screen went black. "I'm sure that gave you the willies. Damn. Last thing I wanted to do was give you more willies. I'll leave a note for the electrician. He'll see it first thing in the morning. Feels to me like the socket is loose."

"Now, can you please put my sock back on?"

She looked down, confused. "Does it feel to you like one of your socks is off?"

"Yes."

"Because it's not."

Surprise, surprise. Memories from my suspense class tore through my head including a great line from Alicia Simms, who one day noted, *the common thread with kids in horror films is how they will never get an adult to believe them.* My left foot was still cool, like some breeze was blowing it, and my right foot was warm and free of that sensation.

"Look," she said, kneeling down and pinching my toes on both feet. I could feel my socks between her fingers and my toes. "I'm sure there's a logical explanation—for the TV and everything else. But when it rains, it pours. I'm supposed to be helping with that post-op, and for some reason Rachel wants to get out of bed. I need another employee to help me—"

"Just go, thanks," I said, relieved to hear that Rachel was coming.

As soon as Carly left, I felt another pinprick, this time in my arch. I couldn't help it. I spoke up. *"Why don't you go pick on somebody who can fight you back? You're a coward, you loser—"*

A snapping sound came from the nightstand. Reluctantly, I took hold of the mirror and turned it. The umbrella was still there. Mom and Grace had spaced on taking it, though the puddle beneath it had dried up. I watched it move slightly, like someone had tapped it lightly by the handle.

It wobbled, then settled back still again. I watched it with so much intensity I didn't even blink. But it was still again.

It had happened on the other side of the room, as if she were taunting me, all, *ha! I'm over here now!*

I flipped the mirror to the door and just watched until Carly and an aide showed up across the hall, got Rachel back into her wheely thing, and left her in her room. She pretended she was about to go on her laptop, but after they were gone a few seconds, she turned and tossed the laptop on her bed.

For all she couldn't wait to get out of here last time, she came zooming in. I was almost completely face down, but didn't miss her wide eyes and heavy breathing as she zoomed past my mirror view. I could see her wheels right beside me.

"I told them I had a nightmare," she huffed, "but I don't think it was that. I think I was wide awake."

When I found her in the mirror, she gripped her throat. I'd seen Trinity do that so often that in spite of all my own anxiety, I put my hand out to her. She didn't seem to notice.

"Well. I can't avoid this by staying out of your room." She sniffed in a spastic way that implied tears.

"What happened?"

"I saw, um, something... someone... at the foot of my bed."

"Somebody not a nurse?" I guessed cautiously.

She just plowed on through with it. "No. She was dead. Definitely dead."

"You saw a dead person."

"Yeah." She sniffed some more. I remembered asking her today if she saw dead people. Her answer had sounded so petrified: *No, but it's coming like a fast train...I can feel it.*

"I do not want to *see*, um, dead people. Toby, I don't, I don't—" She sniffed up tears with shaky breaths.

"Okay," I said, putting on my calmest big-brother voice, not that I believed my own words. "Let's figure this out. We'll figure it out together. Let's eliminate possibilities. The first is that you were dreaming."

She thought about that for a moment. Then, "It happened right after you started texting. I was texting you back."

"Then you were awake," I reasoned. "So, like, what makes you think she was dead?"

"Because she disappeared right in front of me. But first, she did this..."

I watched her wave using only her pinkie finger. I remembered yesterday Rachel asking me if I'd ever seen that wave before. Now this alleged person was supposedly doing it at her. I just tried to push on without feeling confused.

"Did she say something that scared you?"

"She didn't say anything. She just did that wave thing looking, like, mad, or disgusted? How should I know? I've never seen anybody dead up and walking around."

"Was she old or young?"

"Couldn't really tell. I was afraid to stare at her face and only glanced— Can I just stay here with you?" she asked.

"Sure. Please just do me a favor. Keep an eye on my feet."

"Oh," she breathed after a moment. "I'm being selfish. I forgot you said that. What happened?"

"Somebody took off my sock and was scratching my foot with their sharp nails."

"That's horrible," she breathed. "Um... somebody you couldn't see?"

"Carly couldn't see them either. She said it never happened. Let's just say I know how you feel, being on the edge of your sanity."

The bed flipped. I was facing the ceiling. I squeezed my eyes shut, trying to keep my thoughts on what seemed sane. Could we *both* be hallucinating? *No.*

"What the hell is this? Some kind of a...a haunted hospital ward?" I asked, sarcastic yet numb. I added, "Have we been dropped into some grade-B horror flick? This can't be happening."

After time to reflect, she whispered, "Truthfully, I don't think this is any typical, horror-movie type of thing. I can't say what it *is*. But there's just not enough..." She trailed off, like something was distracting her, but her gaze was going in ten directions, not just one.

I finally asked, "Not enough what?"

"Emptiness. There's just too much live energy around here to attract a lot of permanent energy from the other side. Too many busy people, too much equipment, too much electricity."

"They like quieter places?" I asked, not even sure what *they* were. It felt weird talking about spooks like they were real. "Places that are generally deserted?"

"All the research I've seen would back that up. I think what's going on right now has to do with *me personally*. Or *you personally*. I don't know how they are related... I don't know what's coming next."

I thought of Rachel's comment about her gifts seeming like one of those fancy new dashboards when you've been driving an old pickup truck. New gifts make life better, but you have to spend some time figuring them out first. I knew I needed to say something wise and calming for us both.

"Look, let's work on finding you one of those camps for people with extra sensory perception, second sight, whatever. One that can turn your life around and keep it from being exhausting and confusing. Rachel, there's somebody somewhere who can help you make peace within yourself."

She sniffed but said nothing. I couldn't tell whether my promise was helping or not.

I rambled on, "My mom will help you. You know, she was orphaned herself." I felt more than saw Rachel look up at me. Her sniffing and shaky breathing suddenly stopped. "So therefore, she thinks of every kid in need as a personal project. If we tell her this, she will help you find someone. I know she will."

"Your mom, she's always so nice to me." She sniffed again but seemed to relax under the comforting suggestion. She was staring at the corner of the room like she had done last time but didn't seem upset by it.

"They left their umbrella," she mumbled, taking a tissue from the tray and blowing her nose.

I didn't mention what I just saw, but I didn't want to have to deal with the thing the whole night. "Do me a favor. Can you go close that thing? Put it on the nightstand?"

"You're not superstitious," she said. I wondered if that was one of her "newsflashes" or something she'd just known through common sense.

She spun herself, pushed her chair a few feet forward, then stopped cold. The umbrella wasn't rocking again. She wasn't blocking my view. I just saw her slowly move her chair in reverse and come back to where she'd been. This time her look was zombie-eyed.

"What's wrong?" I asked.

"She's back."

I tried to keep my heart from revving up, tried to keep my voice calm. "You can see her?"

"Mm-hm," she squeaked.

"This isn't just an aura," I murmured. "It's a whole, real—"

"Mm-hm."

I slowly turned the mirror again so the upside-down umbrella was squarely in the center. "Where is she? Is she near the umbrella?"

After a moment she whispered, "She's standing between the umbrella and the dresser."

All I could see was the wall behind it. Then the umbrella rocked just slightly. I swallowed. "Did she just do that?"

"Yes."

I turned the mirror away and simply studied the ceiling, not wanting to give it power, if that makes sense.

"What does she want with you?" I whispered.

"I don't know. She looks mad."

"Ask her."

"I can't," she said in an almost inaudible whisper.

"So you can't describe her for me?" I wanted her to look. I reasoned, not looking wouldn't make her go away.

She shook her head, sniffing, refusing still. I still had my phone in my hand and tapped it.

"Is that her?" I handed her the phone.

A yell roared up her throat that turned into a screech as she threw the phone and pulled her hands in. The phone landed on the floor, face up. But the force had shattered the screen. The witch stared back at us from a bunch of lines going out from the center.

"I'm sorry!" It came out like a yelp but was followed by a breathy exhale.

"That's the Witch of Indor," I said flatly. "I think she may have been the fifth person you saw at the well. I think she may have pushed me."

Rachel looked like she understood my meaning, though she didn't ask who the Witch of Indor was. She either got it when she gasped, or she was just too freaked out to understand anything. She merely said, "She's gone again."

I could almost believe her, having felt the energy in the room suddenly calm, like a glaring overhead light had become the soft, warm light of a beside lamp. Only it didn't have to do with the lighting.

"What does she want?" I asked, but figured I knew. She wanted to finish off what she'd started at the well. I didn't know why. *Do spooks need a reason to kill people?* This haunting involved two traumatized kids, two *immobilized* kids, and who but a sadistic demonic thing would come around to torment people like us?

"We'll figure it out...I'll figure it out..." Rachel said but amidst sniffs and hiccups that didn't give me much promise, and I muttered some apology for being this much trouble.

But it seems to me that no matter what kind of stress people are under, they will find some way to reach for a higher thought. Mine was that if the witch existed, Trinity was still sane and innocent.

Let her kill me, I thought, though it's hard to just lie peacefully when you can't see where the devil is.

Seventeen

The hand that managed to pick up my phone off the floor was Mom's. I hadn't heard the flipping and flopping of her sandals...until her fingers wrapped around it.

"We have AppleCare." She handed it back to me. "We'll get it replaced tomorrow. What's going on? Who's the girl on the cracked screen? She looks troubled."

The hundred cracks across her face probably weren't helping. A long silence followed. To just blurt, "Uh, yeah, that's the Witch of Indor, who just busted in on Rachel and has been tickling my foot," would have gotten the shrinks out of bed but done nothing productive.

I had no clue what to say.

"I was put on hold with the nurse's station, which was so unusual, I just ran the two blocks from the hotel," Mom said. She laid my phone gently on the rolling tray, being as it was useless to us.

Rachel cleared her throat. "The new post-op down the corridor just died. They're, um, a little tied up."

"I'm so sorry," Mom said respectfully.

I slowly turned the mirror until I found Rachel's eyes. They were red and bleary. She raised and lowered her eyebrows, watching me back. Nobody had told us the guy died.

I finally said, "Sorry, Mom. I didn't mean to get you out of bed."

"Oh, I wasn't asleep. I fell asleep at the pool today. You know what naps do to me. So, it's nothing medical. Can I ask what it is?"

I could hear it in her voice. She knew something scared the life out of us. She wanted to help. Memories returned to me of being afraid of the dark, once upon a time before Trinity was born and before Mom was increasingly distracted by all her needs. Mine actually started before Grandma Rose's death, but that was the event that got me scared enough to bawl about it. All us kids had actually passed through a brief period of being afraid of the dark—probably due to our old, chronically-creaking house.

Mom had had a common way of dealing with all our fears, though I did not feel like hearing it right now. The memory stood out from having heard similar versions passed on to Grace and Trin:

"Well, maybe he doesn't like being called the boogeyman. How'd you like it if somebody called you that? Maybe he's lonely! Let's give him a name. "Henry, would you like to come out and have a friend? I'll be friends with you!"

By the time I was nodding off to sleep, Invisible Henry had happily come out from my closet and sat on my bed, an angel who was happy to watch over me in exchange for having an actual friend.

Needless to say, our imaginary friends at the ages of four or five were epic. Not that the memory helped now.

"Scared Rachel more than me," I finally said, and decided to draw Mom to Rachel to keep her from talking babytalk right in my face. "Her mom was really supportive of her ability to see auras and know things. But her mom, you know, isn't here anymore, so..."

Mom sat down in the chair on the far side of Rachel, her silence reflecting a huge wave of sympathy. I thought maybe Mom was holding her hand. I didn't care. I was trying to figure out exactly how many hours I had left in this bed. Something like a hundred and thirty-six...*if I can manage to stay in one piece.*

Rachel was unwinding a bit and confessing stuff to mom—nothing about our thoughts that the witch had pushed me. She knew where to draw the line. It was that an exact likeness of the woman on my cracked screen had shown up here, harassing her and then harassing me, moving the umbrella.

I tried to give an account of the attack on my feet, which didn't sound plausible, though it had felt totally real.

Mom got up calmly, moved to the umbrella, snapped it closed, and laid it flat on the floor by the wall. She came back without the slightest hint of a shudder and sat down again. Here it came, her turning the *Witch of Indor* into Casper the Friendly Ghost. I just let her prattle on to Rachel, sensing some sort of juvenile truth, but it was a fact to me: *Kids get haunted more than adults. Mom just isn't getting it.*

"First of all, we need to stop calling her a witch," she was saying. "Back in her day, it was akin to calling someone a pedophile today. *We* know what it feels like to be orphaned and feel like nobody cares what we're *really* like."

From the corner of my eye in the mirror, I saw Mom scrounge through her handbag for her phone. The way she was scrolling, I supposed she was trolling Google. My adrenaline rush had sort of ended, even though I would still have jumped if that TV went back on. My eyes were getting heavy. I let this go on because it really did seem to help Rachel.

"She has a name, you know. Did you know that, Toby? Look here! Elizabeth. Her name was Elizabeth Ainsworth. Isn't that a nice name? Sounds like royalty!"

I rolled my eyes. *Yeah. And she's got nice, sharp teeth and nails. Mom. Wake up.*

She went on cheerily, "And so what if all the chickens died? Look, it says right here. Chickens still die around Lake Indoor in droves approximately every five years. Those bird flu tests are expensive, I'd suppose. It's easier to blame *her*. Poor thing."

Poor thing? She may have pushed me down a well. Stay in church where you belong, Mom.

But Rachel seemed interested, a little intrigued, maybe.

"Ew, what's that?" she croaked out. I had my eyes shut finally and didn't try to open them. But from their tone it seemed they were looking at the screen together. "What's in her hand?"

"Let's find out," Mom decided, then silence, like they were scrolling.

I took a guess. "It's a meat hook."

"*Ew,*" Rachel said more softly but emphatically. "Did she kill somebody?"

I thought Rachel would have suddenly *known* this story, pulling it from the greasy shadowlands like she pulled other facts about people. But her gifts really did seem unpredictable. You'd think she would have heard from her own mother at some point, or her dad, or some of the people her clients probably talked to her about.

"And so, what if she did kill someone?" Mom responded. "A bunch of grown men charged the girl, threatened to set her on fire or hang her, and there was no one to protect her. *I* would have grabbed for the nearest thing to protect *me*. Wouldn't you?"

I rolled my eyes, hearing Rachel say, very seriously, "Yes, totally."

But Mom the Calm had somehow finagled some peace into this room, and I could actually feel the energy shifting, the lights getting half a ray brighter, like the air was getting less heavy and easier to breathe. I wondered if phantom forces found cheery energy off-putting and ran away from it.

Mom went to the mirror against the closet and put Chapstick on her sunburned lips. "Rachel, I want you to promise me something."

"What?"

"You will not ever call her a witch. That had a terrible connotation when she was living. She has a name. Shall we call her Elizabeth? Or Liz?"

After a moment Rachel whispered, "Beth."

"When you think Beth is with you, speak to her nicely. Tell her you're very sorry about all the bad things people say about her, and you don't want any part of it."

Before pushing the mirror away again, I found Rachel taking my mom's cell phone and staring at the picture, which had just caused her to break my phone so she could get it away fast. She stared for the longest time, then let the phone flop over on top of the t-shirt that covered her cast, and she nodded off like that.

I was not so gullible. When Mom whispered to ask if I needed anything, I mumbled, "Yeah. Can you stay for a while and just watch my feet?"

Even though I saw her pull the chair around to the base of the bed, the good feeling didn't last. *Something had been in here—something that made me freak out--something that Rachel saw.*

With an awake person here with us, I was able to drop off to sleep. Not that it was easy. I had pictures in my head of some electric-gray aura standing between me and Grace, directly between, and yet I couldn't see or smell or hear anything of it.

Eighteen

The following morning Rachel and I paid the price for having told my well-intending mom what was going on. She had left sometime when I was not awake but made it back here by 7 a.m. when the doctors were still doing rounds. She may have told Rachel to speak nicely to a spook as if it were completely real, but then she told the doctors everything Rachel had told her—and about me thinking said spook was torturing my foot.

Rachel left my room around sunup. And by 7:30, both my surgeon and the orthopedic specialist were stooped beside my bed, brushing the bottom of my bare feet with a cold spoon, a hot washcloth, and tapping my arches with the stem of the spoon. They watched the reactions, noting differences between my left and right foot.

They stood up, and the surgeon started jabbering to Mom. "We're certain this is his nerves healing. It can feel like pinpricks, sensations moving up and down or from side to side. It makes sense it happened on his right foot first, as that extends from his fractured leg. That foot feeling cooler just means that his circulation is not as good yet. The blowing-on-it sensation means that it's getting there."

Mom nodded at me like I ought to agree.

"Right," I finally said to be polite and not sound like a nut-job. The umbrella was back, lying open, but there was barely a puddle this time as the weather was only drizzling. I kept glancing at it, knowing deep down that if it decided to do some possessed carousel spin, it wouldn't be in front of these witnesses.

I had so many unanswered questions, and I wasn't going to get answers from two doctors who are paid zillions of dollars *not* to believe the kind of stuff we experienced last night.

"Even after this bone heals and he's out walking around, he will feel new sensations," the surgeon said. He reached down and tapped my calf with the spoon, and a strange sensation ran down through my ankle again. I had to admit it felt very much like what I'd been feeling last night. So then, what turned the TV to sand? And how did Rachel recognize the image of the witch on my phone from what she had just seen—how, if it was all imagined?

Dr. Vapor was in Rachel's room now. My doctors joined them across the hall, and I couldn't imagine what they would pinch on her body. Her complaint had been seeing things, not feeling things.

"Maybe you shouldn't have told them about her, um, what she thought she was seeing," I said to Mom.

"Well, I always tell the truth," she said and plopped into the chair three feet from me. "The truth will set you free."

That was a biblical saying. Mom said it a lot. I grumbled, "Problem with the truth in this case is that the people making all the decisions won't believe it. Problem with that statement is that it's incomplete. The truth may set you free—but first, it can dice you into nine pieces."

"That...also is truth," she said with a leery laugh. "The staff, they need to work with *all* the information—everything you're feeling. They have to work with the whole truth."

"You're sounding like Dad," I quipped. I wondered when he'd be in here griping about his Facebook friends posting fake news like it was as bad as bank robbery.

"He wasn't in the greatest mood when I left the hotel," she added. "*Three hours,* he was on social media last night. I'm not kidding you. He was just turning out the light when I got back at two."

"Doing what?" I asked. "Does he have that many friends that he wouldn't start banging into last week's posts?"

"He's got three thousand followers."

"Whoa," I said. That was a lot for Facebook. His following had grown. It was like Dad not to brag. "I didn't know that."

One day a couple weeks back, Grace responded to my question of what she did that day with, "I watched Dad scuba dive in shit for a few hours." I actually thought they went scuba diving off a wreck or something, until she explained that Dad was spending like three hours a day looking up news articles. He wanted to see if the source was a gossip rag, and he spent time exposing how news photos were actually twelve years old and taken at unrelated events.

"*That* many people are passing lies around social media this summer?" I asked Mom in disbelief.

"Apparently so. By the time he sees some of them, they'll already have numbers like 1.6K shared."

"That's disgusting," I muttered.

A shadow filled the doorway, and I found Barry with the mirror. Barry was one of the techies who checked the motor on my bed just about every day.

"You ready for the Apocalypse?" he asked.

"Uh...this new hurricane?" I grinned. "Last I heard, it was going to strike near home, near Port Dingo."

"It's going to strike farther north, they're saying now, but not this far north." Barry looked content with this mystery.

"Your dad predicts Providence," Mom said. "He's rarely wrong."

That was in Rhode Island, maybe two hours south of here. Typical hurricane stuff, but it totally reminded me of my life. You never knew what terrifying things would show up when, or why.

Barry had a metal bar in one hand and a set of springs in the other, and he held them up.

"And that's not even what I'm talking about," he said. "The *Apocalypse*…I mean your *personal* Apocalypse. I mean the *Toby* Apocalypse. You're starting rehab."

I realized he had the push-bar for under my feet.

"Bring it on," I said.

He called for Ms. Gwen, who had the key to the bed. With an excited grin, she went through the steps so that I was facing the ceiling before hearing the clip-clap-clop of the engine turning off. She washed off my arms and legs as Barry installed the bar. I noticed I felt no pain as the washcloth ran over the spot where my compound fracture had broken through the skin. In the mirror I could see it was just a series of pink lines reaching outward in all directions. She'd told me many times the lines would actually turn white and then only be visible in certain lights. I would always know right where it was.

"Maybe it's time we throw out this bed," I mumbled as she closed all the clamps, from top to bottom as usual. "Can't I do rehab from a contraption like Rachel's?" I asked. "I feel like a sardine in a can."

"Your MRI is tomorrow," she said. "Good results, we're expecting. However you'll find you're more comfortable in here than in a stationed halo. That will take some getting used to."

I was supposed to wear a halo that attached to my shoulders for just a week after getting out of this mess. Then a collar for at least a month. It was at times like this that I'd been used to feeling my mind and body fill with fire, and I wanted to breathe it in Elijah Rune's face. But now, he wouldn't appear in my mind. Instead, it was a fog. A gray fog with red lines running through it. It was very frustrating, not knowing who to be mad at.

Barry spoke, straightening up. "You push down on the bar as often as you like to get your strength back. We can fix the tension tighter or looser. We'll start you off pretty loose, just ten pounds."

I could feel a flat metal piece under the balls of my feet, keeping them flat. I stayed still as Ms. Gwen finished re-clamping all my straps, as that part of this was routine. My feet were used to flopping, so just that bit of a change made the backs of my legs feel tight. As her keys jangled again and the bed engine was purring, Barry said to push on the bar, and it took me a couple moments to get my feet to move that way. I would have sworn there were forty pounds of weight on it, not ten.

"Can't believe how weak I got," I breathed, thinking how easily it had been to stand on my toes to reach in a high cabinet or climb stairs. I weighed one-sixty.

"Just push on it whenever you feel like it," Barry said. "We can add another pound every few hours if you're that motivated. Just be careful of the charlie horses. You'll get some. Just pull your toes up as hard as you can. The cramps can hurt like hell, but they won't injure you."

I'd had enough Charlie horses during football season that I knew what he was talking about. I was so busy concentrating on my next push that I didn't see the aid arrive who usually brought my breakfast tray. She had to stick it under my face, but then the smell of bacon and eggs wafted up my nose.

I chomped bacon hungrily as Rachel's door suddenly opened. Dr. Vapor wheeled Rachel into my room.

"Look," I said. "At my feet. Rehab."

It made her smile as she watched me push down and applauded when the bar sprung back up. But it was the polite type of smile that was for my sake only. When Vapor started talking, I could understand her anxiety.

"We'd like to talk to both of you because this apparently applies to both of you," he said, somewhat cheerily. "There is a condition called 'immobility psychosis.' People are designed to move around, come and go freely, and when suddenly they are constrained, their thinking can become temporarily skewed. They can even hallucinate. Visually, audibly or sensually."

Rachel and I exchanged glances. She looked away again quickly with a slight smile that could have been anything from sarcasm to hurt.

Dr. Vapor went on, "Once you get up and going, you will feel a release from that. In the meantime, we're going to prescribe you both the same medication, which should help with the sensory and visual hallucinations. It's called..."

I listened through the list of side effects and didn't decline the drug in spite of my distrust. One side effect was drowsiness, and I'd just recently felt like I was starting to conquer "the nods" after six weeks of them. I guess I thought that if anything would stop the sensations of being watched, or being touched, I was good with it.

Rachel said nothing.

"How's that writing going?" Dr. Vapor asked me, moving toward the door. Today, his voice sounded *loud.* Loud and invasive.

"Fine," I lied. I was thrilled when he backed away and didn't request to see a file. My hoagie hurling and Trinity's adventures in nocturnal cutting were not things I was looking forward to handing over.

We watched them file out, then Mom followed, saying, "I will go back to the hotel. When I come back, I'll have Trinity and Dad."

Trinity is coming. I looked at Rachel in the mirror and she must have picked up on the adrenaline wave the reminder gave me. She cleared her throat and spoke, but like she was being polite and distracted.

"How do you feel about that?"

"Not sure...." I said. "I totally miss her. I want whatever shot I have at making her feel better. But I have no idea what to say to her, especially now. I thought I had found the loophole—you know, the thing that really happened, which proved that Trinity didn't push me. Do you, uh, think we're having some…immobility psychosis?"

She finally said, "I lived through the death of my parents. Was it easy? No way. But it was pretty straightforward. Mom was always telling Dad not to drive so fast. It was the family joke. In the morning, he'd get beeped at for driving too slow. But driving home after work or driving anywhere at night?" I watched half a smile form on her face. It seemed she'd gotten used to her memories, and after a couple years, she could look back and smile. "Mom called it his 'evil night twin.' That night he missed the curb, skidded…"

Her smile disappeared. "I never passed out. The crunch of metal is really loud. And if your car flips three times, you hear it twelve times, once for each side. And then...you hear it every day. For years."

Raindrops pelted against the window. I let the small sound fill in the silence, until a small rumble of thunder seemed to urge me on. "So sorry, Rachel. That sucks."

"Well." She shifted around like I'd seen her do a few times, putting all her weight on her feet and elbows, moving an inch or two either way. "It is what it is. But it was simple. Daddy drove too fast. We skidded off the road and rolled down an embankment—cause, effect."

"Okay."

"All I'm trying to say is...life isn't meant to be this complicated." She wasn't watching me but staring at the raindrops, like maybe she could draw the same peace off a storm that I could. She shrugged and went on with more life in her voice. "So, I have some gifts that people would call psychic, even though I hate the word. It gets abused. But I'm *also* in a psychotic episode? Can a psychic *have* a psychosis? Some people would say it's *all* psychosis. I can't help what people say. I only know one thing."

"Tell me. I'd like to know something also."

She said quietly, but more evenly than I would have predicted, "Life is never as it appears. Alas, my new holy mantra."

I wasn't sure yet whether it would be okay to munch toast in all this heavy, respectful talk, but I chewed slowly with my mouth shut. She looked pensive but not sad. It put me in awe of all she probably had lived through.

I swallowed and tried, "So... you're saying the witch didn't push me down the well? Are we back to Trinity or a priest?"

She just raised and lowered her eyebrows. "Life is never as it appears, but it generally isn't all that complicated either. When extrasensory ability starts being construed as psychosis, and you're having strange experiences that aren't making you feel any better about what caused your accident...something is wrong. Most of the time, life is fairly simple. It's as if there's a piece missing—something easy, something we're not seeing. If we had that missing piece, everything would fall into place, a simpler place."

I took a bite of eggs, watching her in the mirror again. She looked a lot calmer than yesterday, but weak and tired. I'd been planning to ask her if she'd come in when Trinity was here, just to see if she had any insights, such as what went on inside my sister's head. But I couldn't forget she was traumatized. Maybe not psychotic—maybe not even having 'immobility psychosis' fit the bill—but I just couldn't ask her.

She went on, "I will be happy to take that medication if it's a little relaxing. Even though I'm convinced I wasn't hallucinating. *How could I hallucinate the very image I saw in your phone five minutes later?"*

"A shrink would have a field day," I muttered, pushing on the bar with my feet. I'd only done it a half-dozen times so far, and already I was using it as a tension reliever. My adrenaline built up over some frustration, and it could now shoot out my feet with a practical incentive involved.

"I think they just had their field day," she said. "Whatever. But I'll do anything to dull these experiences down. It's really unnerving, not knowing what's coming next while being this confined."

"Tell me about it." I reached my hand out to her, for comfort, and she took it. A few seconds later, she mumbled, "Sure."

"Sure, what?"

"You...you want me to meet Trinity."

I laughed a little. "If it won't hurt you."

"Everything hurts right now, so..." She stared at the window, lost in thought.

I quit chewing briefly then said, "I've got to write something in my journal."

She looked over at me. "You feel like you might have a breakthrough?"

I didn't know. I said, "It's not about who pushed me down the well, but I think it relates. I just can't see how yet. Can I give it to you when I'm done?"

"I'd love to read it. Go with your instincts," Rachel said. "You know where I am."

She squeezed my fingers, and before wheeling herself out, stopped to stare at the umbrella. "It was sunny out when your mom left. She must have thought it would last. Crazy weather..." She went right up to it, snapped it shut, then turned as something above and behind me caught her eye.

I turned my mirror slowly and looked, almost wincing, to avoid any sights that doctors would call a hallucination. All I saw was the security camera in the upper-left corner of the room. I hadn't noticed it too often. But Rachel kept staring as she laid the umbrella on its side by the wall, saying, "An open umbrella... It's like having a ball at a séance and expecting it not to roll, and security cameras don't hallucinate."

She tore her eyes from it as she turned her wheelchair. "You work on whatever it is you want to write. I'll work on getting you a copy of the security tape from last night, from when she was in here moving the umbrella. I don't see why they should object. It's your room."

Nineteen

WRITTEN ON: Tuesday, August 8, 8:30 am

SUBJECT: The Day Trinity Got Mauled

Your parents can spend days online picking the perfect place to stay on family vacations, then mapping out the perfect things to do. And then the weather can come along and dump all over you.

The year Trinity got mauled, my parents had already fallen in love with Lake Indor. But they had not yet fallen in love with the Chapel Rock Inn. We'd spent two June family weekends at the White Bird, a much smaller inn, a bed and breakfast, and there was a lot less to do when your whitewater rafting trip gets cancelled.

It wasn't about rain or hurricanes that year. It was mudslides from an overload of snow that winter. Lake Indor was exploding over its banks, and the river was considered too rough for tourists.

It made Grace and me think of what kind of water might be rumbling under the monkey bridge, a favorite hangout from the year before. Mom and Dad had told us not to go near the monkey bridge this year. What was three feet of still water last year could sweep us away and drown us this year.

A monkey bridge is three ropes that go across a stream—two higher and one lower. The lower one is to walk on, and other two are to hold onto. Crossing is a blast. Grace and I planned to race down there right after breakfast while the parents were still chatting it up with adult guests—just to have a look. I wasn't thinking about crossing it after the lecture, but Grace was used to taking dares because Wiley chronically double- and triple-dared her stuff. But I figured if she tried it, I could stop her.

I was in the lobby when Grace appeared trailing Trinity, pointing over her shoulder, and rolling her eyes. "She'll tell!" she whispered in disappointment. Obviously, the parents stuck her on us while they lingered with other guests over their morning coffee.

I even rolled my eyes, though it was hard to be mad at Trin lately, what with her not talking in school or much at home. Her lower lip was quivering like she was guilty of something. Grace had probably told her what a pain in the butt she was all the way down the stairs. She passed Grace and took my hand shyly, and I didn't want to see her cry.

"Let's just go down to the stables," I suggested, bending down so she'd see my attempt at a smile. "We get to see horses as much as farm kids get to see porpoises. You wanna see the horses, Trin?"

"I don't want to see the horses," Grace said between clenched teeth. "They smell, and remember that one that threw me off last year?"

I cracked up. The pony probably wouldn't have thrown Grace if she hadn't been all, "Ew! I saw a flea. Mom! It's got fleas!" She stood straight up in the saddle, and the pony, thinking she wanted it to run, took off. She ended up sitting on her butt in the dust. Mom and Dad called her Princess

Grace for a week over her flea conniption fit. Grace had always wanted a cat, but Mom said no, that Trinity would likely be allergic. Beyond that, she never much got into animals.

Trinity loved them. The White Bird was named after the owners' pet, a white macaw who sat on a perch in the lobby. The perch was eye-level with adults and too high for little kids to reach. Trinity tugged my hand as we approached. Every time we passed by I would have to hold her up so she could get closer to the thing.

There wasn't exactly a cage, but a fence made out of popsicle sticks around the perch and a sign that said, "Please don't touch Olive. She's a murderer." Interesting sign. My dad said a bird not in a cage was a lawsuit waiting to happen, and they probably put the sign up to keep guests from trying to touch the bird and getting bitten.

The bird said only one word, over and over: "Fine!"

I picked Trinity up to see if we could get a repeat of yesterday. The bird had said, "Fine!" to

Trin a couple dozen times, and then she started talking back to the bird, like she never talked at home anymore. I wasn't disappointed this morning either.

"Olive! What do you think about my new jacket?"

"Fine!"

"Olive! You wanna be my friend?"

"Fine!"

"You wanna come home with me?"

"Fine!"

Cracked me up. The day before, Grace asked one of the owners what the sign meant.

"About ten years ago, we tried to get Olive a mate. She killed him. The veterinarian says that classifies her as a rogue bird," he told us. "She's never bitten a person, but knowing that, we don't suggest people try to touch her."

I even let Trinity stick her fingers up. I was eleven. What did I know? She actually rubbed the bird's chest for about ten strokes, all excited, saying, "I love you! What do you think of me?"

"Fine! Fine!"

Grace took the opposite approach. She hid behind me, complaining that the bird was scary, that it would try to murder us. She was so scared of it after hearing about its murder rap that I don't know what all was coming out of her mouth except that it contained, "...probably has fleas, too, ew!"

I'd had to pick Trinity up to see the bird, and now I was all but picking up my other sister to get her past the perch. It was annoying, and I suspected drama. Grace could sometimes find ways to get more attention than Trinity. Before she got so good at ballet, friends had joked that getting attention was Grace's big talent.

Her hair was long and thick and blonde, and her ponytail called my name all too often back then. I ended up yanking her by it to get her all the way onto the porch.

"Owww!!" she whined. "Break my neck, why don't you? How'd you know that bird wouldn't attack us?"

"Sarah Heartburn," I countered, a favorite name from my parents, when my very tomboyish sister suddenly turned whiny and scared. They suspected drama also.

She jutted on ahead of me and Trin as we walked to the stables. The monkey bridge was just a stone's throw past there, and this year, you could hear the water rushing even before we smelled the horses. I heard the echoes of teenage voices down there as we passed the last of several vacation homes between the inn and the stables.

That sound of rushing water was almost irresistible. I gathered Grace felt the same way as she suddenly skipped in a big circle and came up beside me and Trin.

"Um, excuse me." She knocked Trin sideways with her hip and took hold of my arm with affection.

"Nobody's home," she whispered, pointing at the last house as we passed it.

"So?" I asked, not on her wavelength.

"There's a fence around the backyard. It's like a giant playpen! Let's just stick her in there for ten minutes."

It was a weird idea, full of dangers that I couldn't quite name at eleven. As the rushing water got louder, I turned to stare at the house. All the shades were drawn like it was a vacation home with no vacationers in it. The yard was hedged in fluffy summer brush against a hurricane fence protruding in several places.

"We'll only be gone ten minutes. C'm on. It's a built-in babysitter," she whispered, close to me.

Grace might be a ditz, but she always seemed to be able to "think outside the box" better than the rest of us. I would never have thought of this.

I picked Trinity up and said, "How'd you like to search for buried treasure? Did you know there's a treasure in that backyard?"

With that, Grace changed her tune. "Toby, don't."

I turned, completely irritated. I said something completely eleven-years-old like, "You can't think it up then take it back!"

"Can so. I can change my mind. I got a bad feeling."

I ignored her and dropped Trinity over the four-foot hurricane fence, and we told her to stay away from the edges, as I wasn't sure what might be poison ivy. And we told her to find buried treasure, and we would be back in a flash. Trinity never minded playing by herself, and Grace had a point: What could happen to her in ten minutes?

Ten turned into twenty when we got separated, galloping through the woods toward the bridge. There was a fork in the path. She took off to the right, whereas I remembered that the bridge was to the left. I went left and got to see two teenage girls almost fall in while crossing the monkey bridge. Two guys cheered from the banks. The water was only a foot higher than last year, and it only left a foot between the bottom walking rope of the monkey bridge and the water. The water was noisy and fast, and the girls' feet were slightly submerged on the rope when they got to the middle.

They didn't fall. I would have given just about anything to try it, except my neck. Living on a barrier island, I'd been raised seeing the flipside of water, when it wasn't friendly, when storm surges and rip tides turned it maniacal. And I weighed just shy of a hundred pounds. I kept my feet firmly planted.

Grace showed up on the other side, having run through a covered bridge I'd forgotten about, and she was really out of breath. It took her a couple minutes to catch her breath, and I thought the trail was likely longer than I remembered. Then I knew why she had gone that way.

From where I was, I couldn't stop her from trying to cross the bridge unless I crossed, which

I wasn't going to do. She had always planned on crossing it, I thought, little daredevil. She went up to the monkey ropes and stood on the far end, holding on with both hands.

Birds and animals were Grace's only big skeeve back then. She was less afraid of dangerous situations than I was. And I should have known her attention-getting buttons would have been pushed by big, strong boys watching her. Sarah Heartburn would be really tempted to need saving from these guys who, from our perspectives, were big as Hercules.

She took a few steps out, and the teenage boys took the bait like idiots. "Hey, little girl. Don't do that, man..." "Jeezus, she's nervy! Look at her go!"

One waded into the water to spot her. Just up to his thighs, this water would have been up to our waists. Dangerous for us, but not so much for him.

I actually left the bridge when she was only halfway across. It was all gut instinct. She'd make it. Though the water was drowning out the sounds of screams, I think my subconscious could hear them.

I hadn't seen the dog pen when we dropped Trinity inside, all the way up by the house, almost buried under a lilac bush. A hurricane gate was now swung open between the pen and the yard, making the pen noticeable. The dog was loose in the yard. It stood frozen in the center, its back haunches taut with pent-up energy, eyes on Trin, who was backed up against the fence across the yard from me.

"Trinity, don't run!" I shouted, my heart racing. The dog turned, barking and charging the fence in front of me, an oversized shepherd-husky mix of some sort. The clang of the fence sent my heart skidding into my throat. But the dog turned back.

At that point I noticed Trin had already been bitten. Blood ran out of this spot on the back of her hand. I've seen a couple of horror flicks with

stigmatas in them since, and they froze me with
flashbacks each time.

She moved only slightly to protect her face,
but it was enough of a movement to stir up the
dog. With her arm protecting her jugular, the dog
chomped down on her shoulder and underarm and
shook its massive head, sending her head over
heels like a ragdoll. The silence from her has
driven me crazy ever since. She didn't cry or even
make a sound.

I leaped for the fence but only got one leg
over. Grace was beside me, huffing and screaming.

"Don't!" she screamed, holding onto me for
dear life. "You'll get eaten too!"

Her fear of animals met up with her tomboy
strength. I couldn't pry her loose to jump the
fence. The dog approached Trin again, crouching,
ready to pounce a second time. Grace screamed. The
dog took one look at Grace and forgot Trinity as
it lunged at the fence in front of her. She let go
of me, and I scrambled far to the right. It barked

and snarled at her with so much outrage that I was able to climb over that fence and get to Trin.

There was torn flesh down her arm, a growing circle of blood that gurgled under her T-shirt. A sudden asthma attack was keeping her gulping, her mouth wide open.

"Hurry up!" Grace screamed, kicking the fence and further outraging the dog. Trin's eyes were open, but I didn't know how to pick her up without hurting her.

Grace had backed up behind a tree. The dog turned and locked eyes with me just as I stooped down. We were dead meat. No question.

I've seen what happened next in my head a thousand times. It was chaos aligned with intention, something that could make you believe in a good God if you were a doubter, or at least make you believe in some godlike instinct in his creatures. What saved Trinity was not me coming to the rescue. The dog was big enough and determined enough to take on both of us.

Down from the sky shot this white Macaw. It landed all over that dog, scratching and pecking and screeching like the bowels of hell. In this storm of feathers and fur and screeches and yelps, I gathered up Trinity and bolted for the fence.

The bird managed to drive this huge dog into its pen, which sounds insane, but it gets more so. I passed Trin over the top of the fence to Grace and leaped over in one massive thrust. But as Grace passed Trinity back to me, the bird was suddenly there in our faces, and it got its talons stuck in Grace's ponytail.

The attack of the animals was out of a nightmare, and there has never been any explaining it. There were repercussions. Grace fell to the ground screaming, and somehow, the bird freed itself, taking a clump full of blonde hair with it.

We ran Trinity back to the inn, her wheezing getting more and more scary. Hence, we barely noticed the couple more times the Macaw swooped down and ended up getting Grace, pulling a few more threads of thick blonde hair out each time.

We became that all-American family that was minus the dog, cat, or parakeet forevermore. No-family-pets was just something we all accepted would be our fate, save for my fish and Mom breaking down and getting Trinity a guinea pig, which she spent hours with in her room, but the rest of us forgot was there.

Here is something that hangs onto me—an internal scar. Maybe it's been as big as Trinity's external scars.

I never got my nerve up to tell my parents how Trinity got in that backyard. If Grace ever gave me up, I'd have retaliated by telling about the monkey bridge and a hundred things she'd done at home with Wiley Mathis, stuff like them breaking into summer homes in the dead of winter and hanging out inside.

But Trinity never gave us up, either. Maybe the homeowner had been too apologetic and taken on too much blame, saying she worked graveyard at the local hospital and slept with a fan on. She was sorry all the noise hadn't woken her up. The only bit of defensiveness she had was about the gate from the pen to the yard, which she said she hadn't opened in a year because the pen also opened right at the back door. She couldn't understand how it got opened.

Still not comfortable with this hotbed of issues to do with Trinity, my parents didn't want to say she was prone to doing weird things, loved animals, and could have done it herself. If there had been a lawsuit, I've always thought Grace and I would have come clean.

As it stands, my parents still think we got to the stables, turned around, and Trinity wasn't with us. They think the source of my guilt has always been that I let her tiptoe away to make friends with the wrong animal. Not even therapy brought the truth out, because my parents and the shrink were focused on what happened after Trin got in the yard—not how she got there. Grace had framed out the lie immediately because, in her eight-year-old mind, the parents finding out she'd been on the monkey bridge was about the worst thing that could add to this.

And Trinity couldn't seem to remember how she got in the yard. The fact that she was never mad at me gave me more reason to keep the secret.

Lies and cover-ups seem like small things, and how would it change anything for my parents to know that I stuck her in that backyard? Would they love me any less? Doubtful.

But lies are bothering me lately. Maybe it's my dad influencing me several times daily by phone. Lies have an undercurrent. They have a life of their own. If the truth is never told, the lie can shake, rattle and roll the person who told it. I'm wondering now about Dad's foreboding beliefs about us having turned into a nation of liars.

We pass on the lies of others without question, and that makes us liars, he says. Or we pretend that lies are true because something deep down tells us the lie will serve us better than the truth. It doesn't matter if that lie lives in

Madagascar or came to life beside an ambulance at the White Bird Inn. I don't have the answers. Right now, I just have a lot of confusion.

I'm feeling like this lie I just wrote about—the one that exonerated me and Grace from blame—is somehow connected to the Witch of Indor, but not in some churchy, retributive-God sort of way. God has nothing to do with this. It's like the lie came to life on its own. It reached down a well, awakened a witch, and raspberried her in the face.

Something like that. I really need Rachel now. I'm confused.

Twenty

I texted Rachel that I was done and glanced at my clock. The memory had poured out of me at a frantic pace for over an hour. Her door was closed, so I texted Mom from my laptop. She replied that Grace was taking forever in the bathroom. She asked if I was all right by myself. She said they wanted to take Dad's rental car to replace my phone before they came.

"I'm fine! I want my phone!" I replied. Texting from my laptop was slow and a pain.

Rachel couldn't wear regular clothes over her torso cast, so her door opened to reveal her in a clean oversized t-shirt with sweatpants—the type of stuff you knew this kind of girl would never wear if it weren't for the torso cast. Her hair was washed and shiny.

The nurse pushed her in. Rachel was trying to smile, but I was getting so I could tell her real smiles, when her whole face lit up, and ones that seemed to involve her mouth but nothing else.

"Listen, you two won't get your new medication until after dinner," the nurse said in a cautioning tone. "You take it at night. So in the meantime, don't be telling each other Halloween stories."

"Thank you!" Rachel said for the push in here, and her plastic-y smile all but cracked her face.

Her face straightened out into honest frustration once we were alone. "If you can believe it, the nurses said no, absolutely not, about us seeing the security tape."

"Why?" I asked. "It's just a tape. Who cares?"

"Policy," she said with rolling eyes. "They said the tape shows the corridor too, and you could see another patient passing by, and like, doing something weird. They said it could invade that patient's privacy."

"That sounds like bullshit," I said but was too fogged out from writing to argue. I carefully handed her the laptop.

"You mind?"

"Not at all."

She mumbled at one point, "You're a good writer." That was nice but I'd heard it from others. I really hoped the story might trigger her to "see something" about Trinity. But I realized that what I wrote featured more of Grace, whose actions were always easier for me to understand.

At one point, Rachel's eyes widened. She finished and lowered the screen, just to lie there blinking at the wall.

"The animals..." she breathed. "There's a message in this. It's from them."

"What do you mean?" I asked.

She pushed the top back up and gave a shudder, reading the final paragraph or so again. "Your opinion about lies is way interesting. It cuts deep. But the animals in your memory. Their behavior...I think that's a good place to focus. Animal choices are not complicated. Animals are highly instinctive. They simply react with their instincts to whatever the truth is."

"The truth is...Grace *thought* of the back yard. I *put Trinity in* the back yard, then *both* animals attacked us."

"Neither one attacked *you*..." she mused pensively, staring at the top of the wall, chewing the tip of her thumb.

True enough, though I didn't see any meaning in it. The dog attacked Trinity, and the bird attacked the dog and then Grace. The sound of raindrops, now heavy on the window, made me think of the hurricane about to hit land. It was just the type of mindless thought I needed to flip me back to the issue at hand with the right twist. "I just don't see what any of this has to do with me and the well."

"The dog attacked Trinity. The bird tried to save Trinity from the dog..." She seemed to be ignoring my need to push forward to the present.

I got one of my impatient adrenaline rushes and breathed out all over the place while pushing hard on the foot bar. "Look, I'm writing like mad. I don't know why, and I'm always stopping right before I get a really clear connection."

"It's your subconscious," she said. "If you're not ready to handle the answer you're looking for, your subconscious will create fog. It's a form of protection."

I finally inhaled, not liking the sound of that. "Listen, if Trin pushed me down the well, I think I am ready to hear it. Grace had a pretty good theory yesterday, one I hadn't thought of, but one I can live with— that it was an accident. Trinity did it, but she didn't mean to. If she spent years scratching her face because she couldn't fold the wash right, how is she supposed to admit to making a mistake like that?"

I remembered the holes in her memory with the dog attack. "Maybe she can't even remember it. I just have to leave off Grace's psychodrama about Trinity having two personalities or something. It's overkill. I just can't believe it. It smells of the type of complication that you're telling me is all wrong."

"Yeah…" Rachel's brows crinkled, as she had no clear idea of what I was talking about, as I hadn't told her, but she seemed to get the picture. "I really don't think Trinity pushed you."

I felt a flood of relief. She went on, "Animals attack good and bad people. Attacking has less to do with the person they're attacking and more to do with the people they are protecting. The dog had an owner. He may have thought he was protecting her, so he attacked. But as for animals who *save…* They only save *good* people. Think of it. When have you seen a dog save a bank robber or a sociopath? They attack that energy."

Interesting, I thought, though my mind was in a fog of confusion. "So then...what happened at the well? How does this relate to the well? Or does it, even?"

She had her own phone in her lap and did a one-handed swipe, watching the screen.

"What are you looking at?" I asked.

"The selfie you took of you and Trinity. It's flashing through my head again and again. That usually happens when something is meaningful."

I held out my hand and took the phone from her long enough to see Trin grinning shyly, and me smirking like usual in pictures. Then, I saw the red splotch over Trin's head before handing it back.

"You think that red blob is a spook?"

"Well...I don't like that word. There's all sorts of things it could be, including refracted light, including a manifestation."

"I laid my thumb on the button for that one," I said. "There's ten of them. It's there in everyone."

"Huh. Did it move or change?"

At that point I had to remember because my mom had my broken phone. "It was there in every photo but changed shape, sort of," I said, but added, "I *think*..."

She continued to stare, then put the phone down and gazed at the wall like she could do when she was gathering her sorts of info.

After a long minute, I asked, "What's up?"

"I'm seeing something that may be important. Did you know Trinity was at the well earlier the day of the accident?"

"No," I said.

I tried to remember earlier in that day. Those few hours after we arrived hadn't crossed my mind at all. "We got there around five. I fell down the well at eight-thirty."

"I'm seeing her at the well, sometime...it was still light outside," she said. I watched Rachel stare at the wall like it was some sort of movie screen, and only she could see the film on it.

"We had gone down to the restaurant for dinner around six-thirty," I said of me and Grace, and a memory slithered on out. *Trinity hadn't been with us in the elevator.* My parents had let her go wander the secure grounds, I suddenly remembered, keeping her favorite company—herself.

I said, "That *is* possible. Are you having, like, a vision or something?"

Rachel swallowed then shook her head slightly. "It's a lot of shadows. It's splotchy. More like one of my 'newsflashes.' Something I just know. Hard to explain..."

"Can you get what Trinity was doing at the well?"

"She wasn't alone."

"Was she with Grace?"

Rachel just continued staring into the nothingness of the wall. A memory surfaced, one of Mom and Dad asking Grace and me to look for Trinity, then changing their minds, saying that we would find something to distract us also, and the point of family weekends was to eat as a family.

"She was waiting for us in the lobby when we got off the elevator," I remembered. Rachel shushed me, still staring at the wall.

I couldn't shush. "Could she have run into another child?"

"Not an adult...but not a child." She shut her eyes.

I felt my stomach fall and muttered, "Tell me she wasn't with that... *abomination.*"

Rachel squeezed her sheet with one hand and pulled at it with the other while breathing funny. "I'm just hearing snatches...growling voice... threatening. Sounds almost demonic..."

I shivered with half a groan. "So much for Mom trying to make that witch into Casper the friendly Ghost."

"Shhhh..." Rachel put her hand up absently. "Let's not..."

"Let's not what? Was the Witch of Indor there?"

She kept her hand up for me to stop. It was hard, but I let her focus for what felt like ten minutes, though it was probably more like two. She relaxed her neck and exhaled in a "whew" sort of way, implying that whatever she'd seen was big.

She all but whispered her answer. "It seems that at the most important times, I can't ever see clearly. Wish I knew why that was."

"So...you couldn't see anything? In all of that?"

"I saw plenty, heard plenty, but not the...the answer to the question."

I felt myself leap to *maybe nobody was with her. Maybe she wasn't there. Maybe you've got a loose screw,* but being that I didn't exactly believe that anymore, I moved it along. "Why do you think that is?"

She muttered, "I think it's because it's important for people to see things for themselves."

"You mean me?" I asked.

"You may have noticed just from watching TV that psychics are rarely able to do things like give exact directions to where a murder victim is buried. They'll give landmarks...things they see near the site. I suppose a lot of people use the dimness of a sixth-sensory vision to call them fakes. I might have done so before my gifts started intensifying. But I think I'm at a place in my life to understand what that dimness, lack of clarity, really means."

"Which is?" I asked.

"People with extrasensory ability are here to *help*, definitely. However, it's important that people get their own epiphanies."

Epiphany... A big word I usually knew.

"Their own 'hel-lo' moments," she said.

"And, like, how would *I* know what happened with Trinity when I wasn't even there?"

Her voice was calming down again. "I do think Trinity was at the well earlier. From what I can see, somebody was trying to lure her past the sign, and she wouldn't go. I do think the Witch—Beth—was there..."

I got impatient. "You're telling me she was tormenting my sister for some reason. Now you're not wanting to call her an offensive name. I don't get it."

"I don't get it yet, either. Toby, I'm not good with telling people tough stuff," she said, swallowing. "I want everyone to be peaceful. I want to make everyone's lives better immediately. However, I'm strongly sensing something...something that's tough to say."

"Go for it," I said, hoping it wouldn't be *Trinity was possessed* or something off the hook like that.

"I think the abomination, the thing haunting Trinity, has actually haunted her for a lot of years. It's been following her for years."

It made my skin crawl. "You mean...like, something from my house?"

"Yes. Like that."

"And it, like, followed her up here?"

"Follows her everywhere. Have you ever heard her, well, talking to someone or something you couldn't, see?"

I thought about the *"Etwas böses kommt,"* thing Grace heard her say in the middle of the night when Trin had scratched the hell out of her face. *Something evil comes.* I hadn't heard it. I searched my head for other things.

One came to mind. "This one summer when Trin was seven and I was thirteen, things got weird in the middle of the night once. I wrote about that yesterday. She'd scratched her face in her sleep. But there was something during the days, also. We kept finding dead seagulls out in the yard on the path down to the beach. We must have found, like, eight of them that July."

Rachel watched me with interest but said nothing.

I went on. "Dead gulls on your property. On the barrier islands, that's considered bad karma. If you see one, it's supposed to mean, like, death is coming to your family. You have to bury it right away to break the spell. The first one, I remember best, because I was there when it died. It hit the window wall. It just flew down and hit it so hard, I thought the glass would have shattered. but it didn't. The gull just fell onto the deck and died."

I remembered picking it up with a bunch of paper towels.

"And Trinity was with you?"

"Yeah, she saw it. We were both in the family room. Grace was there, too."

And... what did Trinity do?"

"She went nuts. She loves animals, can't stand to see anything suffer. They were both screaming, but Grace's was more, 'does that mean someone's going to die?' Trinity's was more, 'a *bird* just suffered and is dying?'"

"Right," Rachel said quickly, like she might have the picture in her head. She asked, playing with her lip nervously, "Then, there were seven more that died?"

"Something like that. It was crazy. Like, I had to quit burying them right away."

"Did Trinity always see them?"

I thought for a moment but really didn't need to. "Actually, yes. She's the one who would see them first. I'd hear her screaming in the yard or on the dunes, and I'd be all, 'Not another one. Why couldn't somebody else find them?' Tell me, Rachel. Do you think, like, it was some sort of haunting?"

"I'd need to...to touch Trinity, to answer that, I think. I'd need to feel her energy."

She could do that soon enough. I just went on. "We've got two different theories going in our house, to this day. Mom thinks it was Grace's crazy friend, Wiley. He's a twit. He taught Grace how to pull the wings off of flies after he first moved here in third grade. And he pulls the claws off of blue crabs, then lets the things bang around the dock and laughs. Stuff like that. To Mom, that translates into psychopath."

She looked at me.

"I wouldn't put it past him. He's even got a bird trap. Or he *had* a bird trap. It turned up missing that summer. Or so he said. Then there's this theory Grace buys into. I think my dad does too. He won't say. He just gets really quiet when it's been brought up."

"Do you think it has to do with Trinity?" Rachel asked, in a knowing way I didn't like.

"Yeah." I stopped. I didn't even want to say it aloud.

She went on for me. "Is it that Trinity was killing the birds?"

After a moment I said, "Yeah."

She gulped. I sensed she didn't like where this was going any more than I did. She said warily, "And there was at least one other incident with a dead animal."

Not bad.

"It wasn't a dog or a cat—am I right?"

"A guinea pig," I confessed. "Mr. Stubbs. He was all black. Trinity used to hold him all the time when she was reading or doing schoolwork. It was like a best friend. She talked to him."

"Oh my God," Rachel whispered, this time sounding like she had some sympathy.

"Do you think *that* was a haunting?" I asked.

She stayed quiet.

"I have never sensed anything in my own house, Rachel. I haven't been spooked out since kindergarten. And those are the only stories I have."

"They're enough," she said.

"Enough for what?" I'd been pushing on the foot bar so much that my legs were tired, but ten pounds was no longer a problem. I grabbed the nurse's button and pushed it. I wanted eleven pounds. Or twelve. Or twenty.

"Because, Rachel, if it's not a haunting, then Grace is saying this right. Trinity would have to have, what? Some sort of schizophrenia?

Personality A kills the animals; Personality B gets equally hysterical about animals dying? That is lunacy. Trinity is problematic as hell, but there is nothing dangerous about her."

Twenty-one

Barry increased the tension on my foot bar to fifteen pounds, even though I'd only had it for three hours. I figured I'd have sore-as-hell feet tonight, but it would be worth it. There was a knock at the opened door. When I flipped the mirror, my dad was standing there with his knuckles on the frame, smiling.

"How's social media?" I asked.

"Well, that's a great hello." He sauntered in. "I'm happy to see you, too! These women primp, and they dawdle. After being exposed to all of that, I made the happy choice not to go with them to the Apple store."

I grinned back. He meant that he couldn't wait any longer to see me.

"You need a haircut," he said, tousling my hair above the halo.

Better to bust my stones, I supposed, than react to my condition. He'd seen it all, but not in a month.

"Yeah? Do I smell, too?"

"Smell like what?"

"Dunno. I'm always afraid I smell or something. Because bedridden people can smell, I guess. Dad, meet Rachel."

He reached over me and stuck out his hand. "You've got a beautiful girl in here. I don't suppose she'd be in here if you stank. Stunk? Which is it? Well, I don't think she'd be sitting right beside you. Does he smell, Rachel?"

"No," she laughed as she shook hands, then added her own humor nugget. "*Do I* smell*?*"

It amazed me how she could turn a subject and mood so quickly. I supposed it was a learned skill to hide her abilities from skeptical people.

Dad touched my hair again, then held his fingers about six inches from his nose. "Why does your hair smell like powder?"

"Because they wash it with spray," I said, "or it wouldn't get washed. Rachel, how do they wash your hair?"

I found her in the mirror. She was laughing awkwardly but with that same rich and sincere smile that I wished I'd see more often. It made me smile. "In the bathroom," she said. "This chair back folds down then backs right up to the sink, which has a shower head."

"Lucky you. At any rate, nobody smells." I flipped the mirror to Dad, who was dropping into Mom's chair on the other side of me. "So, you brought the dang hurricane with you? You leave Port Dingo to beat the evacuation throngs, and it's for no reason? Now you're predicting Providence?"

"I brought us up from Port Dingo to avoid putting evacuation throngs *between me and you*," he corrected me. "And the Who-Gets-To-Actually-Evacuate Award goes to...." Dad made a drumroll motion even though he had his phone in his hand. "Providence! Yes. When am I wrong?"

"Providence is evacuating?" I asked. "Really?"

"As we speak." He glanced over his shoulder. I hadn't noticed the sun coming out, but it lit up the side of his face. "Would you ever think there is some megalomaniac sky-troll waiting to devour yachts and businesses, just a day away and a couple hours south? Think of the unprepared people back in the 1800s. God rest their drenched and departed souls."

The spidercane's outer band that Mom walked through earlier was gone—probably over Vermont somewhere. Not that it mattered much to me in here. Watching the weather out the window was like watching a movie on a screen. I wondered if I would think of this later as "the summer that I watched on a screen but that never really happened."

"On a funny note, you know how people scatter when they think they'll need to evacuate. A dozen of our Port Dingo families went to Providence."

"Oh no," Rachel said but with her smile.

"Why's that funny?" I asked Dad. It happened in every hurricane I'd heard of. A smattering of people evacuates to somewhere that then needs to evacuate. It's a pain.

"Because of who was part of it—my, um, favorite islanders, Miles and Patty Mathis."

"Wiley's parents," I said and started to crack up. Dad disagreed with Mom that Wiley was a psychopath for pulling the claws off of crabs. Part of his reasoning was that both Mathis parents were pretty sweet. It's hard to figure how a kid can be such a troll with such sweet parents.

Dad said, "I'm just kind of hoping I won't get a call. 'Oh, Mr. Kellerman, we are so sorry to bother you, but would you mind taking Wiley, and we'll just go to a shelter?"

"Give me your phone," I chuckled, holding my hand out. "I'll block them for you."

Dad was already scrolling his phone with a furrowed brow, shaking his head, and otherwise ignoring me.

"You asked about my Facebook dilemmas when I first walked in, so I'm getting my review ready." Dad ignored my disgust, still married to the idea that I needed intellectual distractions for best health improvements.

"Need a laugh? You ready for this one? Here's the title: 'Muslim migrant beats up European boy on crutches.' What's this story trying to say?"

"Uh..." I got that much out, and Rachel beat me to the punchline.

"It's trying to say that Muslim people are bad?"

"Is it fake news?" I added.

"It was actually a dark-haired Dutch boy beating up a fair-haired Dutch boy. Neither practices Islam. The Dutch police tweeted the truth on record to correct the fake news that was already driving them crazy."

That kind of a lie is disgusting, but it didn't seem like a *huge* deal. "So, somebody taped two Dutch kids in a fight, one on crutches, and said the kid who started it was Islamic, to stir the discrimination cesspool."

"Yes. But I haven't gotten to the good part yet," Dad said, scrolling down. He said with a perfectly straight face, "It was just retweeted as an attack by a Muslim immigrant... by our local state senator."

"Senator Alton? Sarah's dad?" I felt my jaw drop. Sarah Alton, my ex-girlfriend. Her dad was our District 2 senator. One reason I broke up with Sarah is that she was an airhead. No fun to talk to. But I'd figured her dad would have been smarter. "Senator Alton believes that?"

"Enough to expose his forty-six-thousand Twitter followers," Dad said, still managing not to crack a smile in spite of Rachel's laughter. "Yes, our very own senator did, this morning, retweet fake news. And Mrs. Alton defended him. She says it doesn't matter that the story is fake."

"Why would she not care that her husband is lying in public?" I wondered. Looked like Sarah had been doomed to be an airhead, having collected it genetically from both sides.

"Something about…the principle of it being true. Which it's not. I'm not done yet," he said. Dad knew how to not laugh to get *you* to laugh. Rachel was still cackling.

"I followed a share to another friend's page. She believed it and thought it would be nice to pass along how 'bad all the Muslims are.' It had already been shared some nine thousand times. Since this morning."

"Nine thousand times?"

He only stared at me, which meant 'yes.'

"Jeezus. Did you post your 'unreliable source' notice on *that* friend's page?" I asked. "And did the person unfollow you?"

"I did, and she wrote me a reply. She said that if the medium declaring it fake was the *New York Times*, then the declaration is fake, because Ted Turner is an anti-Christ, and Ted Turner owns the *Times*."

"Dad…" I laughed again in awe. "Just get *rid* of these people. They could make you nuts."

"I can't. I need to know how people respond to my 'unreliable source' notices. In this case, my Karen-friend has not deleted her fake news. Seriously. She just left it for fifteen more feebs to gobble down and projectile vomit."

He placed his phone upside down on his knee and laced his hands behind his head proudly. He'd gross you out to make his point anytime. "We've become a culture of liars," he said again, like I hadn't just been thinking about this. I didn't need it. But he went on anyway. "So, guys. Which is worse: Passing on somebody else's lie or making one up from scratch?"

"They're both lies," I said after a moment. "A lie is a lie. They're equal."

Rachel asked a pretty good question. "Well...does the person spreading the lie *know* it's a lie?"

"Ah," Dad said. "We get away with so much these days by telling ourselves we didn't know! 'I didn't know it was a lie! I thought it was the truth!' It's as if we think it's okay to be deceived. Is it *okay to be deceived?* Did you know the very first sin was due to deception?"

Rachel's smile looked cautious but still interested. "You mean the Bible story? With the snake and the fruit?"

"Snake deceives Person One by telling a purposeful lie. Deceived Person One passes the lie on. Person Two either believes the lie or believes it will serve him better than the truth. So, he bites." Dad sighed. He held up his phone, stared at the screen, then turned it back over on his knee. "Do some things never change?"

"But Dad. How are you supposed to know if you're deceived? I mean... *you're deceived.*"

He watched my feet, flexing on the bar again and putting that slight scraping sound in the air as the springs tightened and relaxed. "A lot of people who helped facilitate our current mess may suddenly be saying, 'Oops. I didn't know. I was *deceived.'* Will I be less inclined to want to punch those people in the face when our country goes to hell?"

"I didn't tell you, Rachel, my dad's intense."

"I got that," she giggled.

With his phone back in his pocket, he turned his neck slowly to her. "So, I understand you are trying to help Toby solve the mystery of how he got to the bottom of the well."

BA-am. The man could switch tracks like that and leave you in the dust. I figured Mom must have told him everything she told the doctors.

"I'm trying to help," Rachel replied, her cheeks suddenly blazing. "Most of my gifts are pretty new." Hesitantly, she gave him the analogy of the new car with the fancy dashboard.

He merely pinched his lips and said, "Interesting."

Dad wasn't one of those intellectuals who likes to stomp on others. He always said he learned a lot by listening to others, and I'd even watched him listen with interest to island butt wads like Wiley Mathis, when he managed to get out more than "Ayee." But I couldn't recall actually discussing the supernatural with him, beyond the standard Protestant God is real/Jesus is real. I didn't know his feelings.

He said, "Just be careful, please. I understand we have the Witch of Indor involved."

So, Mom had told him.

He turned to me and exchanged stares in the mirror. Completely blank, but this was like him. He processed behind his eyes, not with his eyes. I thought he liked to process things before showing his feelings.

The witch being involved was not an argument I could win with one sentence. Yet I blurted, "Dad, Rachel saw her last night. Twice. I was there. I know she is not lying."

It took him a minute to say softly, "I would not accuse her of lying, but, um, aren't we supposed to be taking a medication for this?"

"We are taking the medication, but not because we think we're hallucinating. It's so maybe we can sleep through something we can't figure out how to cope with. Besides, I didn't hallucinate my TV turning to sand *twice* last night when nobody had kicked the plug. The nurse saw it, too. I didn't hallucinate Mom's umbrella flying the hell around the room. That's probably on the security tape..." I pointed behind me and above as best I could. "If we can manage to get it somehow. How much cash you got on you?"

He honked a little laugh. "I'm sure the HIPAA Laws will prevent us from seeing the tapes."

HIPAA: Privacy. It occurred to me he wasn't going to argue hard about anything, being that I was racked up in this bed, and he wouldn't want his words to create more stress. It gave me a slight advantage that I moved on.

"Before that, Rachel was seeing auras. Just auras, no bodies to go with them."

He stared kind of wide-eyed out the window, and I wondered if he was sorry that he came early, if watching girls primp might have been a better deal.

"Auras," he finally said diplomatically. "They are a light around the body that appears to some gifted people, in different colors, depending on the amalgamation of one's life events, if I recall?"

I looked at Rachel. She said, "Close enough."

I could sense him grabbing for a choice, polite question to ask, though he may have wanted to throw up. "So, what color was this, er, aura?"

"Two colors," Rachel replied. "Gray and red. Very much like this."

She passed him her phone, where the image of me and Trin showed the red splotch over Trin's head. I hadn't noticed before that there had been a smokiness behind the red.

I passed Dad the phone. He touched it and spread his fingers, making the splotch bigger, barely blinking.

"That certainly is...very red and gray," was all he said. I couldn't stand to see him looking so torn up. He probably thought his conspiracy-theory friends had jumped out of the screen and possessed his son.

"Look, Dad. If you want to believe that that photo—and the ten others on my phone showing the thing in different shapes—are a trick of the lights, I can understand that. I'd like to believe that, too."

"Please," he said, "let's not accuse *me* of picking my truths like melons at SuperFresh. I am the truth police, don't forget. I don't dismiss the supernatural, if it's proven to me in means I find plausible. I have no idea what that light is. Ignorance confessed." He passed the phone back to me, and I handed it to Rachel with one more glance.

He went on after slumping. "I just don't want to negate the idea, however painful, that one of my daughters might have done this."

I cringed. He really *was* being just as determined as ever in seeing the honest truth about this. This wasn't about him defending a simple belief against ghosts.

"I know what you're thinking, Dad. You're thinking I'm bringing a witch into this because I can't stand that thought either."

He had his hands folded, his pointer fingers on his lip and flipped them into the air in a shrugging way, continuing to stare off. "I'll tell you this. To consider that your sibling or your child is capable of attempted murder...this is so hard to even contemplate that it's like keeping your eyes open when you see fireballs zooming straight at them. To leap into denial would be a thousand times easier. If you've managed to even attempt that, Toby, I commend you, especially in your condition."

I wanted to prove to him that I had considered my sisters. I cleared my throat, then let it rip. "Dad, did you hear anything about Trinity being at the well earlier in the day, on the day we got to the Chapel Rock Inn?"

He turned to look me directly in the eye. I was on my way to facing the floor but could still see him. I pushed the mirror away.

"Because Rachel says Trinity was at the well earlier. She could, you know, see shadows of it."

It was his turn to clear his throat. "Rachel would be...correct."

I glanced over at Rachel, who just raised and lowered her eyebrows with humility. "Did Trin tell you that?" I asked.

 "Trinity did not tell me that. Grace told me that."

I shut my eyes with a sigh. I wished Trinity would *be more open, damn it.* It looked bad, really bad, when we found this stuff out from other people.

"Did Grace say what Trinity was up to?" I felt confused and off-center. I added, "And how did Grace know this?"

He cleared his throat again. "She took video from her balcony. I saw it. Trinity was standing by the rope and staring at the well. At one point Trinity waved at nobody. I mean, waved at somebody Grace couldn't see. Trinity can, you know, do some mysterious things."

I sighed. "Why didn't Grace tell me Trinity had been there and acting weird before she and I climbed over that rope and started sticking our heads down?"

"Your mother and I surely would have appreciated a heads-up also," he said. "But as Grace explained it—whining as usual about how she gets blamed for everything—the accident hadn't happened yet. So, it didn't mean anything to her except that Trinity was, well, being Trinity. Grace forgot about it. Until I started picking her brain after she recovered."

"And she showed you her video."

He just stared at me. That meant "yes."

"So, then, did you ask Trinity what she was doing at the well?" I asked.

"No." Dad shifted, rolling his shoulders.

"Why in hell not?"

"And risk a face-scratching session so soon after her cornea healed?"

I brought the mirror around to check out the window once I realized the room had darkened. The sky was dark gray again. The shining sun was gone again that fast.

Grace stood in the doorway huffing. "It's raining. Trinity's with Mom. Mom didn't want her to run. They're coming—hey. You're Rachel, right?"

She moved right over to Rachel who by now had bags under her eyes. I wondered if listening to my dad's weird, sometimes unfollowable thoughts, could take it out of her, or if I'd worn her out with too many issues at once.

Twenty-two

Rachel was as polite as possible, but she seemed nervous and distracted, talking with Grace about her surgeries and this place. Grace sensed enough not to make it personal—like asking about her family or her school. She kept it in the present. But it made me wonder if Rachel was seeing something. *Was that abomination standing between me and Grace again?* That probably would have made her scramble out of here.

I interrupted with, "You look tired, Rachel. You don't have to be in here, if, you know, you want to catch a nap or something."

"I'm good." She smiled, but I knew she had promised to meet Trinity, and I hoped she wasn't holding herself to that if something weird was happening. Finally, Mom was at the door complaining about having left the umbrella here last night. Her hair and t-shirt were shiny with sprinkles but she wasn't drenched.

Trinity came in behind her. She looked at the floor, her mouth a thin line. But my heart flipped upon seeing her, and some sort of relief flooded through me that she was walking and breathing and looking like her old self.

Maybe it was a good thing that Grace came in first. She started motor mouthing about my bed to her, and maybe it made Trin less nervous.

"You gotta see this cool thing," she said, moving around Rachel and back to me. "Look, it's got weights on the back. There's these pins that hold it in place. Look at all these cool clips to hold his stuff. This back here is a generator in case of a power outage. This is a receiver..."

Trin's eyes got big and went everywhere Grace pointed, though her mouth stayed a thin line. She had an iPhone box gripped in her hand. I held my hand out and watched her from the bottom corner of my eye.

"Did you download my playlists?" I asked, nonchalantly. That brought her eyes to mine in the mirror. She nodded, pulled the phone out of the box, and handed it to me. It was in an even bigger drop-proof Otter case.

"How'd you do that without my passwords?"

She grinned, biting her lower lip, and her face turned red. I didn't know if she hacked or just watched me enough when I wasn't aware to know the passwords. I touched her hand when I took it, and for whatever reason, it brought a tear to my eye, which I tried to ignore as I scanned all my apps. "Look, I even got all my Netflix favorites back. Thanks, Trin."

The tear in my eye would not go away, so I pointed to the other side of me. "This is my new friend, Rachel. She had a surgery on her back. Cool cast, huh?"

Trinity nodded and went over reluctantly as Rachel held out her hand. She actually shook her hand but then recoiled after Rachel asked her a question she didn't answer, something like, "So you're homeschooled, huh?" Trin just came back to me.

"Trinity, answer people! That's not nice," Grace pointed out flagrantly, then turned to Rachel. "She *can* talk. She's got this, like, stratospheric IQ. She actually motor mouths at times. I, of course, will talk your ear off any time."

Rachel laughed along with Mom and Dad. I watched her hand, though, the right one, which she shook when meeting Trinity. She kept flexing it and glancing at it now and again.

Mom asked, "How's your PT going?"

I pushed down on the bar twice, watching Trin, who just wanted to stand a few feet off and study every last piece of my bed with her hands curled to her chest. She wouldn't make eye contact with me, but that was typical. She'd always been more interested in a good gadget than in people, and I was just glad her asthma wasn't showing up. No signs of it.

Rachel was telling Grace she would take her on a tour of the ward, show her the yoga room and all this stuff. I just wanted to get Trinity alone, if such a thing were even possible.

"Why don't you go too?" Mom asked Dad. "It's a fantastic facility. Last time you were here, we were way too distracted to see anything except Toby's eyes open..."

Grace moved over to the mirror, making sure her hair was perfect, the usual. "He can come if he doesn't piss and moan about politics," she said, looking past her reflection to role her eyes at Rachel. "Negative Ned! That's my nickname for him this summer."

"Politics will not surface. On my life," he said. He seemed happy enough to go, and he and Grace went out in front of Rachel, who stopped to look at Trinity one more time. She did something strange, looking visibly upset, though I couldn't tell which person in my family was upsetting her—or whether it was something she was seeing in the room. I couldn't ask.

Her voice shook as she said, "Trinity, I'll see you later." And she gave Trin that little wave that she'd claimed to see the witch doing with just using her pinky finger.

Trinity slowly raised her hand and did the same wave back. Then, Rachel quickly left. Did it mean Trinity had seen the witch? Was it all a coincidence? Rachel had gotten some sort of a jolt on touching Trinity's hand, and it made me wonder if she were glad to scram out of here. She hadn't seemed to be. I just wanted to enjoy my sister for a few minutes— my sister, I felt certain, was innocent.

I was in my straight-up position, and it was as good a time as any. I said to Trin. "Come here. I need a hug."

She'd been left between me and the door like a lost puppy. She came slowly toward me but didn't hesitate in the way Mom and I had been afraid of. Surprisingly, she put out her arms and hugged the whole damn bed. Mom laughed. I got to touch her hair and rub her back, though she was so far below me that her head was at my ribs.

"I miss you, kid. I can't wait to come home. We're gonna hang out. Okay?"

Trinity nodded but didn't move away. It was unusual. Trin never showed any affection unless we were absolutely alone, which was rarely. I figured my injuries had upset her more than she let on. My mom moved toward the dresser and mirror maybe to hide the happy tear in her eye that I also had. I talked while I rubbed her back and her hair.

"One good thing about all of this is that I realized I don't spend enough time with my sisters. I'm going to spend more time. Okay?"

I could barely feel her head move. Was she happy? Wouldn't most girls be happy to spend more time with their big brother? You just never knew with her. She might just be thinking about the wind velocity in fucking Egypt.

"What do you want to do with your big brother?" I kept it up. "I could name a hundred things I would like to do with you, but I want to know what *you* would want to do."

I wasn't sure I would get an answer. Fifteen seconds in, I decided she had just been thinking long and hard, because I did get an answer. It shocked the hell out of me.

"Go on Daddy's ship."

"That sounds cool," I said, hiding my surprise, watching my mother turn slowly to stare also.

Dad thought it would be a good idea to finally take the girls on a trip to Norway when he was delivering a couple houses last August. He'd never taken either on an overseas trip before. Dad got the eighth grade to agree to let Grace off for the first two weeks of school so long as she emailed all her assignments. Nobody even asked me, tied down as I was with high school life.

But I did go with Mom to see them off in Philadelphia. Trinity had long loved beeping the horn, but this time Dad had said he would let her steer over the open water, and she was as excited as I'd ever seen her, seated in the captain's chair and seeming to understand every gadget he explained to her on the dash. All looked grand.

But a day later, when they were in Boston, Dad called Mom saying Trinity was homesick and asking to come home. Mom tried telling him to be firm with her. He called again from Nova Scotia, Canada, and the last stop before open seas, saying she was *really* homesick and all but refusing to come out of her room. Grace and I were against it, though Grace told me she had made herself beyond crazy trying to get Trinity interested in the stuff on board. There was a game room for the crew with a pool table suspended on springs so that your balls wouldn't roll with the waves no matter how rough the seas were. Who wouldn't want to play on that, or in

Trinity's case, figure out the wave height by watching the springs' behavior?

Mom flew to Nova Scotia to get her, and after Grace returned from Norway, I don't think she even spoke to Trinity for months.

"Hey, I'm supposed to go on Dad's boat anyway, once I get out of here," I told Trinity. "It's supposed to be my gap-year big plan. You wanna come too? At least for one trek across the Atlantic?"

Mom kept watching as Trin nodded, but she only nodded slightly. Was she serious or trying to make up for having upset the whole family over the last trip? My mom had given a reason for going to get her but made me swear I wouldn't tell Dad. I never had, but her reason was that the crew of fourteen was all men this time, and how did we know one of them hadn't tried to molest a ten-year-old? Dad had had most of his crew since I was born. *But had one of the crew scared her in some way? Is that what caused Trinity to want to get off?*

Who in hell knew.

I mouthed to Mom over her head, "Leave us alone."

She put her finger to her lips, meaning "don't mention the accident," but then went easily out the door.

I rubbed Trinity's hair some. She was still hugging the whole bed.

"If you don't move soon, your back will get broken." I was starting to tilt farther forward. She giggled but didn't move. It turned into a game of her leaning backwards, spreading her feet a little more, and bending her back a little every time the bed inched forward, but she didn't let go of me. After a while I found some questions to ask.

"What are you studying in homeschooling?" I asked.

"Mm... Mm-mm."

She was afraid I would make fun of her, so she didn't want to tell me. That much I got because I made the mistake before.

"I won't laugh, I promise. Grace and I used to laugh just because we were jealous. We wish we were smart like you."

"Mmmmm..." she finally said, "theoretical physics."

"Wow. Sounds cool. What is that?"

A laugh squirted out her nose. "It's theoretical physics!"

I was just glad to hear her laugh, even if we weren't entirely connecting. "I know that, but I'm not Einstein, so I don't know what it *involves*. You have to explain it to me."

"Mm...." She leaned back farther and spread her feet more rather than let go. The top of her head was kind of up to my nose. I could smell her hair. Shampoo. Shampoo and...little girl. I can't exactly describe the smell, but Trinity was not nerdy. Mom never let her miss a shower, and her shorts and tops always matched.

"There's this set of equations. They prove that there are ten dimensions," she said.

"Okay," I said, kind of frozen. That was more words than I usually got out of her. "You mean that there are seven dimensions beyond length, width, and depth."

She nodded and pulled her head away to look up at me for a moment. "I got the equations."

She put her cheek back down on the front of the bed.

"You mean you...were able to solve the equations."

"Just four of them so far," she said. "It's actually nine equations. I saw what the first three were and then figured out what the fourth one would be. They're like sentences. Only numbers instead of letters."

"Wow," I said, with about as much interest as I had in the tides of Spain. But if she wanted to talk about it, then I wanted to talk about it. "So...what does that tell you about real life, Trinity? What good are all those extra dimensions?"

She shrugged, giggling as the bed tipped forward again. I was looking into her forehead, giggling myself. I didn't suppose Trinity needed an equation to tell her something. It was fun just because it was, maybe.

I was surprised when she said, "I think that's where God lives."

"What, in those other dimensions?" I asked. "What's God got to do with science?"

"Um, he invented it." She didn't sound sarcastic, just delivering a fact. That's when I remembered she spent a lot of her math lessons with

Uncle Todd. Now our youth pastor, he had been an aerospace engineering major for three years in college before he changed his mind. In his free time, he wrote one of the first software programs that generated online Sudoku.

"Okay so...if he's God, why doesn't he just come out and show himself?"

She giggled as the bed tilted forward one more time. Her feet were about two feet apart. This time she was looking into my eyes. She didn't look away. She just giggled right into them.

"Mm... You know a playing card? Like, the queen of hearts?"

"Yeah," I said.

"Well, if she were alive, she couldn't see you. Because she only would see in two dimensions. She would just see a line. So that's like her saying, while you're holding her in your hand, 'Why doesn't Toby come out? Why won't Toby let me see him?' It's like that."

"Okay..." I laughed because she was giggling again, really enjoying the fact that she was now looking me in the eye. I wanted to tell her not to pull on the bed. I wanted to tell her it could mess up the settings or even pull me forward. But it was so rare to hear her say this much and even rarer for her to look me in the eye. I didn't want to ruin it.

Our eye lashes were sort of brushing. She thought that was funny. She laughed and blinked a few times. I had not been this close to my sister in years, maybe not since I used to pretend to chomp her fat neck when she was a baby. I had tried to hug her sometimes, but she liked it about as much as she liked being held down as a baby, only her older dislike was quieter. She didn't yell. She just would politely wiggle away after a few seconds. Trinity was polite. That was for sure.

I thought I would take advantage of a great situation. I said, "You are my bestest sister. And I. Love. You."

I heard this little "ping" sound coming from the corner of the room. Trinity turned her neck, still giggling but hearing it too. I adjusted the mirror and looked first for the umbrella, which was still closed and lying on the floor next to the wall. But something shiny was rolling back and forth between the dresser and the wall.

Trin's wide eyes turned back around to me, and our eyelashes locked again. She giggled out, "You've got screws falling from your ceiling!"

If I hadn't been unnerved by disturbances in that corner, I would have laughed too. Trin's behavior was so free of wheezing and throat grabbing and full of kid fun. She was unpredictable, and that was for sure, but I wanted to enjoy this. However I could barely see that screw-or-whatever was still rocking back and forth.

After seeing my face freeze, she looked back again, her arms still wrapped around the bed. I adjusted the mirror. It looked longer than a screw, but I couldn't tell what it was.

She left me, walked slowly toward it. When she was a couple feet away, the thing got sucked backwards, right before our eyes, like something invisible had pulled it, like it was on an invisible string, and flung it against the wall.

Trinity stopped, froze, staring at it rocking by the baseboard.

"Trinity. Don't go back in that corner," I heard myself say, and felt my arm reaching out. "Trin, come here. Come to me. Don't look at it, Trin."

She backed up slowly, but kept staring at the thing, which looked like a nail, except shinier, rocking back and forth after its bounce off the baseboard. I fumbled for the nurse's button, with no clue what I would say, except I had to get Trin out of here.

She banged into my arm and jumped slightly as my arm went around her waist. Her hand went to her throat and gripped.

"Trinity, listen to me. Go get Rachel," I said to her. "Just ask the nurse where she is. Then go to where she says."

She shook her head and gripped onto my hand that went around her. "Then go find Mom," I said. "She's closer by."

She shook her head again, slowly turning toward me, while continuing to stare over her shoulder. I was almost facing the floor. Her arm slid across the bed, across my forehead and the halo. She didn't want to leave me alone with whatever it was. She was trying to protect me.

The shiny thing suddenly flew off the baseboard, came sailing across the room and hit the hard plastic coating on the front of the bed with a loud crack. I watched it clang on the floor right in my direct view.

Trinity saw it, too. She reached down cautiously, picked it up, and seemed to recognize it. She gasped.

"Trinity, what is that thing?" I asked in a whisper.

She looked behind me, sort of down by my left hip and rushed to it.

I could hear some rattling after she moved down toward my feet, and I realized the metal piece was some sort of large pin. It held the bed to the motor. I heard it clatter to the floor. She swiped it up again, but her breath had grown wheezy, and I could see that her hands were shaking too. I grabbed for the nurse's button, but in my sudden case of the nerves, I knocked it to the floor. Its cord was attached to my arm with tape, but it was hard to get the coordination together to reel it back up.

"Trinity, maybe you shouldn't touch it," I said. "Go get the nurse."

"I'm not leaving you alone!" She stepped underneath the bed again, now on her knees and put a hand on the bed on either side of my head.

But something was off, something I could feel back before the pin came flying at my head. The motor had been making a funny noise. It usually "purred" but suddenly it had "whirred."

It was like slow motion. I heard a sliding sound, felt movement I'd never felt before, and I heard a noise like explosions going off. I felt upside down. And then I realized my neck halo was pressed into Trinity's stomach, and I was staring at her shorts, seeing floor tiles from the corners of my eyes. I couldn't think of what to do except not move. Surely the nurses heard the clatter.

"Trinity, are you okay?" I said. I only heard wheezing and could only see her the tips of her sneakers pointed up while spread apart.

She would never scream. I just knew she wouldn't, or maybe she couldn't.

"Hello! Nurse!" I shouted with a flash thought that if I could figure out how to land feet first going into the well, I could certainly find the nurses' button again in this mess. I was only in a slight bit of pain above my eyebrows where the halo screwed into my scull. I just felt gingerly with my fingers because I didn't want the pain to get worse. I finally hit the button over and over and over, hoping it would flash at their station each time I did it, or we could be here for three minutes.

I heard a croak from Trin that sounded dangerous, like maybe her windpipe had closed. She could be passed out in a minute and a half, dead in four. Within seconds the room was filled with the sounds of rubber-soled shoes and calm yet loud voices.

"Toby, does anything hurt?"

"Toby, can you hear us?"

I was wrapped in an armored truck and felt annoyed, shouting, "It fell on top of my sister! Get her out!"

"She's okay, Toby. We don't want to move you without a doctor if we don't have to." I heard the practical sound of Ms. Gwenn, who was being too practical.

"She can't breathe," I said, panicking as the croaking sound spilled out again. I knew what it meant, but maybe they wouldn't. "Get her the hell out!"

I heard girl-screeches, and realized my family was back. It was a bit of *deja vu* of the well, where the loudest yet most reasonable voice at the top came from my own father.

"I can hold him up until you lower the back part down," Dad said. He had one knee on either side of Trinity. I could feel less pressure on my temples but wasn't aware of having moved much.

"Pull her out, Lara!" he said. I could hear my mom yelling, and suddenly Trinity's legs disappeared between Dad's.

"What the hell happened?" Grace's shaky voice croaked out the question.

My mom said to a nurse, "It's her asthma. Grab that wheelchair in the hall for her to sit in."

Then there was a huge argument among the nurses as they were trying to get the bed part off the stand part to lay it flat on the floor, I gathered.

"How did it tip over?" one asked.

"Look, we only work with these about once a year, but one has never tipped over before," another said defensively.

"Was your sister pulling on it? Hanging on it, Toby?"

"Uh...yeah," I said. "But not when it happened. A pin had come loose. She was trying to put the pin back in—"

"She tipped him the hell over?" I heard Grace exclaim quietly to Dad.

"No, she didn't!" I said. "She didn't cause this!"

I knew if I said, "a witch did it!" I'd end up doing six weeks in a psyche ward when I was done with this bed. Instead I pointed out, "She probably just saved my life!"

Grace rubbed my arm, which made me realize I had hit the floor with my elbow and I'd have a bitchin bruise. I tried to ignore the pain, being as it was the only pain I currently had. I could feel Grace shaking and realized I was calmer than she was.

I got very quiet, now that my elbow hurt like crazy, praying that there was no other damage I was about to feel.

Please. God. We've all been through enough, I prayed. *Does it never end??*

I heard Grace's voice break as she said to Dad, "Why in hell did Mom leave her alone with him? She's alone with him for ten minutes, and all this happens?"

Twenty-three

I can only remember a blur of new scenes and faces for the rest of the day. Mom stayed with Trinity, who had to be sedated so she wouldn't freak out further inside the MRI tube so they could make sure her abdominal bruises weren't internal bleeding. She was already on some slow-working IV version of the EpiPen.

My dad stayed with me much of the time. He actually got the call from Mr. and Mrs. Mathis, but the sickening-sweet part was the opposite of what he expected. They wanted to know if they could help us out by hosting Grace at their evacuation hotel, about a mile down the road.

For once, Dad was all, "Yes. Please take her."

I wasn't just out of the bed; I was out of the room. It was a huge relief. We tend to think of spooks as attached to places.

Inside the MRI tube was where I felt the first pains in my back and my halo screws, and it was nearly impossible to stay calm. I was freezing, having been stuffed between mattresses for weeks and suddenly feeling the cold air right on a hospital gown. They told me I had to keep my teeth from chattering in the tube and gave me one blanket.

My neck showed some swelling but hadn't moved, hadn't re-broken. My hip showed swelling, though my thigh bone on the other leg showed as being completely healed already. I was glad to hear about my leg but couldn't follow their argument on what caused the swelling. The arguing wasn't about Trinity and the bed falling as much as about whether or not I could finish my jail sentence in a regular bed.

They had no choice that day, though they didn't take me back to my own room. I couldn't follow why not and didn't ask. They sat me up on a gurney about as high as Rachel sat up, with a stationary piece added to the halo that felt like my neck was stretched up six inches taller. I finished out the night in front of the nurse's station, not comfortably.

While sitting up like that, I tried to pretend my hip didn't hurt like hell. In fact, I didn't let go entirely of my physical therapy. I tried joking with myself that I must have grown a couple more inches while wedged in that bed because I could push on the bottom of it without stretching my legs. Ignoring the pain in my hip I pushed one foot against it, then the other, with what strength I could muster.

Dad distracted me after dinner. I had the nods back, and maybe the third time I came out of it, I noticed he was sitting in a chair facing me but not in the middle of the corridor. People could still walk back and forth behind him, though one way you can tell it's night around here is that the traffic slows way down. He was scrolling on his phone. His family could be falling apart, but Dad could still play defender of the universe as a sidebar.

"Do you believe in ghosts?" I finally asked him. His head stayed down, but his eyes came up, and he just stared.

"Well?"

He cleared his throat and crossed his arms, which meant hiding his phone almost in his armpit. "I'm a sea captain. We're ensconced in lore. I try to be, um, a respectful skeptic."

"So, then you don't."

He snapped his hand up, fingers in the air, then rested them under his chin. "I don't think there are any sea captains who are atheists. Out in the middle of the Atlantic, when a good wind is whipping up…you want to be respectful of whatever is out there. You want to believe there is a God who's on your side. As for ghosts? I don't know. I don't know what kind of a God would let people hang out around here just to make mischief. Seems they'd have better places to be, better things to do."

It was a say-nothing answer, or maybe a say-little answer. But I didn't know what I was looking for.

He went on with a shrug. "I suppose I do believe that some spirits get stuck, or have a reason to come back." Bringing his phone out from under his arm, he scrolled again while saying clearly, "However, I don't think one pushed you at the well."

He could go from say-nothing to say-everything fast enough to spin your head. I was feeling dizzy anyway. The *lack* of constant movement was making me dizzy, maybe. And this new drug had brought the nods back ferociously. I'd gotten my first dose with dinner a couple hours earlier.

But I don't think I nodded off before saying, "You think it was Trinity. I know you do."

He watched me for a moment with that blank expression that wouldn't let me see what was going on behind his eyes. He said, "There are other options without involving the supernatural."

"Which are?"

"There's the idea that somebody *else* came up behind you and pushed you…before Father Rune got there and ran away again."

I had not considered that. But Dad was looking funny, like for some reason that was not feasible.

"You don't believe that," I guessed.

He shrugged, shaking his head. "No motive."

"Well, *nobody* had a motive," I said. "*Anybody* who could have pushed me would be just some psychopath looking for a cheap thrill. Does it need to be more complicated?"

"It's already complicated," he said. "For one, what are the chances of a psychopath looking for a cheap thrill just happening to stumble upon three kids fooling around at a well?"

I said nothing, only swallowed. Maybe one in a million? Couple hundred thousand?

"And if one cheap thrill wasn't good enough, why not drop *two* kids down there? Grace had passed out. It would have been a piece of cake. Trinity was already trying to jump in after you. Why not three?"

"I don't know, Dad." I became aware that I had a headache. I felt sure it was from my new immobilizer stretching my neck, but these conundrum-type thoughts weren't helping.

Open-minded as ever, Dad said, "You've been fixated on Trinity. I think you're projecting."

That was a shrink-word that meant accusing other people of having your thoughts so you don't have to say that you yourself have them.

"What other choice is there?" I asked.

"There's Grace. Let's take a look at Grace."

I groaned. "Let's not and say we did. We've got all Trinity's problems. If we make Grace into some sort of… of *secret sociopath*? On top of everything weird about Trinity, that is too much weirdness for one family. We would have to set the entire reboot program. You and Mom would have to get divorced. We kids would have to look for different parents. We were just never meant to be together, if that's the case. Re-*boot.*"

"Well, if you're looking for ghosts, you'd do better to talk to your mother," he said. "She's actually seen one. I've never had the privilege. And thank God, being that my mother was paranoid and schizophrenic. I'd have to sign myself into a hospital."

"Mom saw a ghost?" I asked. She'd never mentioned it.

"It was back in her previous life."

Mom never talked much about her life before the Downeys adopted her as a teenager. She always said getting invited into a nice family was such a huge miracle that it cancelled out most of what happened before. It made her believe in miracles.

"You know her mom died when she was ten years old, and until her dad got arrested, she lived with him. It happened during those four years."

I had heard these details but little more. Might explain why I never heard about any ghostly encounter.

"Her dad used to beat the crap out of her. You knew that, right?"

I did know about that. "He was some sort of drug lord in west Texas. He got arrested for drug running."

"Actually he got arrested for murder," Dad said.

I stared at him. No, I hadn't known that. "I thought it was for running drugs."

"It's all tied in. He murdered a guy who owed him money. That sort of thing. Got killed in jail by friends of the other guy. It was one of those big messes where one thing led to another."

I felt myself shudder. I'd have to process *murder* later. *Mom's dad was a murderer.* I thought it was enough to have Grandma Rose in with my grandparents.

"So, what about her…encounter?"

"I'm not sure she'd want me telling you."

"Why not?"

Dad had looked down at his phone, sniffing, but he laid it in his lap. "Right now? Well, it was also a water encounter."

"What do you mean?"

He just stared at me until I realized he was comparing Mom's encounter to me falling down a well into the water.

"Tell me," I said.

His eyes rolled sideways as he shrugged. "I don't see the hurt. Her father was…very high and very angry, and she ran from him. There was a big lake about a block away. She ran into the water, thinking he would not look there. When she saw him drawing near, she dropped down and held her breath. And she could tell by the water vibrations he had seen her and was coming out after her. So, she dove deeper and tried to swim away, not a bad swimmer, back then. Much better dancer, but this wasn't the first time she swam to get away from him. But she was running out of air this time. She knew if she surfaced, he would see her and likely drown her."

"So…what did she see down there?" I asked.

"A phantom of some sort. A woman in white, with all these white, floaty things billowing around her. She figured she just jumped from the frying pan into the fire. She said the thing wrapped itself around her. She just let herself go limp."

"Well…obviously, Mom didn't die. She's *sure* about what she saw?"

"I think the brain will do funny things when it lacks oxygen," he said with a shrug. "I've told her as much. She just goes, '*Yeah, but it was so real…*' "

"I'm surprised I'm not giving her morbid flashbacks," I breathed, "talking about the witch at the well. Sometimes it felt like that witch was *in* the well with me. Somebody screamed. It sure as hell sounded close to my ears."

"I think the brain will do funny things when it's just dropped ninety feet and its body sustained injuries," he said.

I ignored that. He hadn't been through any trauma experiences. His mother was never even bad enough to get locked up until Dad was already married to Mom, and they'd moved to the coast so he could join the Coast Guard.

"So…how did Mom get away?"

He shrugged. "She says she passed out, and when she came to she was on the beach, and her father was gone."

"So it didn't do anything to her."

He sighed, like his patience was being tested. "No, it didn't do anything to her. Just like this alleged witch didn't do anything to you. I think it's a very…romantic and simplistic way of dealing with a shock. I hope you don't mind if I say."

"I don't mind," I mumbled, not wanting to pound on the question of how my face ended up planted on the floor and my bed was being fixed by a technician they had to fly in from somewhere.

I must have gotten the nods because when I woke up, Dad's seat was empty. I hadn't even heard him get up. The new drug made me stupid enough that I could watch the nurse's station like it was television and see what the conditions of other patients were. It was a blur, however. A lot of strange casts bounced in and quickly out of my view, and strange pieces of equipment similar to Rachel's wheelie thing were visible now and then.

The rain continued, beating on the plate glass windows behind the nurses' station, and high winds roared past. The sounds finally put me in an in-and-out state of sleep.

The next morning, I wanted to curse a blue streak, realizing I'd have to go back in the revolving bed. My butt was on fire from being unable to move. I'd tried to get my feet under me and push up to move a little, but my knees wouldn't bend that far.

It was about the swelling in my neck, which they decided was caused by the fall, and even though nothing broke, they wanted the safest place for me possible. Fortunately, they didn't take away Friday as Freedom Day. *Two days to go.*

I glared at the ceiling, hearing the shell casing click around me as they locked it, and Nurse Gwen turned the key. I mumbled a few more good curses, which she looked sympathetic to. Somehow, the mirror hadn't cracked, and I brought it close, thinking I looked worse than I ever had. I made a face at myself.

The technician started talking. "Just don't let any kids near him who are going to hang off the thing like it's a jungle gym. It's obviously not meant for that." He was functioning on zero sleep and not in a very good mood, I gathered. He went on, "Lesson for all of you. You too, Toby."

I watched as Ms. Gwen and five other staff members drew close to him as he stood on my left side. Dad and Grace were leaning against the wall out of the way, but it was like a convention when the only person I really wanted to see was Rachel. I hadn't seen hide nor hair of her since she went to show Dad and Grace the yoga room yesterday.

"These beds are a miracle of balance and precise mathematics," the technician went on in a loud, lecturing voice. "When we say nobody should lean on it while he's in it, here's why." He held up the metal pin, the same one that terrorized Trinity and me, bouncing all the hell all over the place. As he pushed on one end, the other end separated into a four-prong fan with a click. As he let go, it snapped into place.

"This is all that's needed to hold him, two of these pins, one on the left and one on the right."

He was in my blind spot, but I heard the pin go out and into the frame and the same clatter as when the four ends opened. I supposed there was one on the other side. He stood back and held up his hands. "That ought to be enough to hold him in place in anything except a ten-scale earthquake, unless somebody pulls one out. *Why* somebody would pull one out, I don't know. Curious kids, inattentive technicians, or incompetent staff... I'm a technician. That is for you to decide."

There were no "vindictive spooks," among his options. I got a sickening chill. I was seeing it in my mind, the pin flying across the room, thanks to someone only Rachel would have been able to see. Someone who tried to fling it at my head. Someone who had stood between me and Grace two days ago. Someone who wanted to hurt me and my sisters.

"I understand, there were a lot of people in here," the technician went on. "Who would do this?"

I rolled my eyes.

Ms. Gwen spoke up. "The youngest girl was sort of hanging off the bed. She was happy to see Toby, you know. Just foolin around."

He looked directly down at me. "Toby, did you see your sister pull this pin out? Maybe, not knowing what it would do?"

"She didn't pull it out," I said. "I swear. It was already out. She picked it up off the floor and was trying to put it back in."

There was an uncomfortable silence. I could feel the less experienced staff wanting to blame a kid quickly so none of them would get blamed.

"She didn't pull it out," I insisted. "She wouldn't do that." I pointed over my head to where I couldn't see. "If you really need to prove that to yourselves, look on the security tape."

The technician grunted in a way that let me know he was done with that subject. "Any questions?"

The nurses were shaking their heads, but Grace raised her hand, which was shaking a bit. As usual, she was falling through the cracks between me and Trinity, so it hadn't really dawned on me how upsetting all this might have been to her.

Her voice was hoarse, almost like laryngitis, which made me wonder if she'd finally been crying. She almost whispered. "My brother…

he scared me when he told us yesterday that this bed will just open if it stops, like, if it loses electricity?"

A nurse moved next to her and touched her arm in sympathy, and you could hear a chorus of poo-pooing noises. The technician explained about the key. He even talked about a second keyhole in the electrical outlet that I hadn't even known about.

"Your brother will not swing from his halo, I promise you," he said.

She wasn't satisfied. "I mean there's a storm! What if all the lights go out in the whole hospital?"

I thought that was a pretty good question. I'd never thought of it. My little sister with the big mouth and self-centered view of life was growing older. Even the technician seemed touched. "We put everyone who is on equipment on private generators if there's even a hint of a blackout. I promise you." He crossed his chest with his pinkie. "Toby will go on his own private generator before that hurricane gets anywhere close. If we lose power, he won't lose any power. Who's in charge of that?"

Ms. Gwen raised her hand and waved it at Grace. "In fact, I'll stay late tonight. I'll do overtime just in case he needs me."

Grace nodded thanks, and Dad mumbled maybe they should go get some fresh air, just the two of them. I know that made her feel better—one parent all to herself.

"Thanks, Ms. Gwen. You're the best," I said, then I started to text Rachel. Her hand reached in front of my phone as she was probably reading my mind.

She said in a nice voice, "Rachel's sleeping. She's on that new medication, and she needs sleep—hasn't had much the past few nights as I understand it."

I stopped texting, pretty wiped out, the brunt of the new medication still felt.

"How is Trinity?" I asked as she moved to the bathroom and returned with a washcloth for my face.

"Don't you be worrying about her. She's upstairs."

"She had to stay over?" I asked.

"Oh...Harvard Medical School to the rescue," she said vaguely. "They're trying a new course of medication on her that was just approved by the FDA this summer but only for use at research hospitals. It could significantly improve her asthma. But the first course is intravenous and takes a couple of days."

But she looked troubled, I thought, and I asked what was wrong. She wiped off my face, neck, and even went around behind each ear before speaking.

"Well, you know the pin the technician was talking about."

I didn't tell her it had made its way around the room without any help from us. "Yeah?"

"Your sister. When we got her out in the corridor, she had it gripped in her hand."

Ms. Gwen watched me. I watched her, until I shut my eyes in frustration. *The abomination pulled the pin out, not my sister.*

"Ms. Gwen. How'd you like to make an extra *thousand dollars* this week?" I asked.

I was only joking about the bribe, but I really think if she had been the type to say yes, I would have gone for it. You'll say anything when you think you could easily wind up dead in two days.

"My sister is going to be blamed for this. It wasn't her. I can prove it. I'll give you *a thousand dollars* if you can get me a copy of the security tapes from this room for the past three days."

She flinched, then took my hand, using the washcloth on it briskly. "What on earth makes you think I'd take money for helping you out?"

I knew, from all the nurses telling me, how attached they get to their patients on these long-term wards. I'd been coming up, so that now, I was just about eye to eye with her. I stared intensely into hers, hoping she would recognize my desperation.

She grabbed my other hand and wiped it, staring back. "To get the tape would be illegal. But to let a little girl get blamed for something an aide could have done is unspeakable."

"Right," I agreed, keeping the stare.

"I'll speak to Barry and see what we can do. No promises, though."

With that, she left. I could even hear the wind blowing outside. It was cutting through the early afternoon rain and whispering against the large pane. But I kind of loved this new drug. It's almost like I could go to sleep on command.

Twenty-four

When the hurricane hit Providence seventy-five miles south of here, it was a slow storm, but a massive one. A furious Atlantic washed over docks and into streets, slammed against taped windows, and punched sideways off of roofs. I was there, above it, in a dream maybe, or maybe it was one of those immobility trances you hear about, where you can leave your body and zoom off to wherever you want.

I wanted to be outside with real weather zooming into my face and all over my body, hurricane or no.

I saw telephone poles come down in clusters of sparks and stormwater pouring down streets and into basement windows. But a confidence surrounded me which, I sensed, was coming from the people. These people were seasoned, nobody's fool, and a slow storm, however big, had given them time to get boats and trucks and cars under their canvas wraps. They'd had years of practice.

Lights all over Providence went out with a dull boom and it left me in shadows—shadows of rooftops I flew over and between, and X-shapes that glowed from the hurricane tape placed across so many windows. I could hear generators flipping on, and I felt the confidence of people who have been surviving storms for generations and passing down the stories for grandchildren to awe over.

It was a shame to wake up, but my bed was acting a little funny—just funny enough to wake me. It was shuddering ever so slightly. And there was a strange noise in here. Another whirring noise, but one that didn't sound unstable, like when the bed toppled.

I opened my eyes and found I was tilted slightly forward from straight up. Rachel was on her laptop below and off to the side, with extreme bags under her eyes. I could hear the rain and the angry wind outside the window. Providence was closer to Salem than it was to Port Dingo but still a couple hours south of us. If it took the eye, we'd still get a big storm.

"What's that sound?" I croaked.

"Barry was just in here again about fifteen minutes ago," she said, watching her screen. "They put your bed on the generator in case the hospital loses power. They do that in advance sometimes."

"Is that why the lights are kind of weird?" I guessed. The room had a dim, orange glow to it. I lived in here twenty-four-seven with one overhead on, I realized. I followed Rachel's pointed finger with the mirror. There were two small lights built into the wall, so that if this were ever used as a two-patient room, there would be a light behind each bed. Like nightlights. They were on.

"Barry said the whole setup is a little more primitive. But not to worry, it's just as safe. He switched the overhead to the bed lights but said if it's not working out for you, you can put the overhead on. It's just that they use a lot of generator juice if the big generators go on."

"It's okay," I said with a yawn.

"I'm your nurse's button for the next half hour or so, speaking of primitive. They have a different set that works with the generators. Your bed kit came with a special one for its own generator. They just can't find what they did with it yet. So, I'm here to give a shout-out for what you want."

"You look really tired. 'Bout as tired as I feel." It sounded slurry. I felt for my phone.

"I wish I had toothpicks to prop my eyelids open," she said. "That anti-hallucinogenic drug? Stay awake for a while and see if you don't feel like you have cooked cabbage between your ears. I'm getting off of it— probably tomorrow. Told my aunt today I couldn't stand it." She yawned but looked alert in a funny sort of way, like her instincts were to defy the drug.

The time read 8:01 PM. Still Wednesday. I didn't blurt my disappointment, but I had hoped I'd slept enough that it was Friday.

I muttered quietly, "And obviously, what you're not saying, and what I'm thinking, is, *what if the abomination shows up*?" Perfect weather for a haunting, I couldn't help but think.

But it's like my adrenaline would not rush. I pushed on the push bar. The muscles on top of my ankles hurt like a bitch. I likely overdid it on the regular bed. But my mind was going, *who cares?*

Rachel was watching me, an anxious flash in her eyes. All she said was, "I may not be in great shape, but I can scream. I'm not moving from here."

I turned the mirror and gazed into the active corner, though nothing was moving.

"I totally owe you," I said, though I wasn't sure what she'd do against a dead person trying to do evil on us.

"I don't mind at all. Second, Barry had come by earlier with a copy of the security tape on a flash drive. Right around dinner time. He said since he was breaking the rules anyway, it shouldn't matter which of us he gave it to. I've got it on my hard drive. It's two nights ago until three a.m. and yesterday around noon, but I was able to isolate the times when we had manifestations and cut them into individual segments."

"Yeah? Do I want to see this? You see anything weird?" I asked.

"I... did. It's pretty shocking."

"You saw the stuff moving by itself on the tape?"

She seemed distracted by her screen but finally said, "You mean the umbrella wobbling and the pin flying across the room that was supposed to hold your bed to the frame?" She made a face. Not a very enthused one. "It's grainy. Security tapes aren't meant to pick up fine details like that, and of course, everything _I_ was seeing is not visible. Beth isn't showing up. You can barely see the umbrella moving. _If_ that's what you're looking for."

"In spite of Mom, you really don't have to give her a warm-fuzzy name," I muttered with annoyance. Sounded like a fear-prevention tactic. "So, you _can_ see the umbrella moving," I persisted.

"I'm not sure it would get us off of a hallucination rap. But you can see it. It'll be good enough for _us_ to know we weren't hallucinating."

"What about the pin that was supposed to be holding this bed in place? It came flying at my head."

"It looks like a small pixilation," she said, shaking her head a bit. "It's the same color as the floor, almost. The tape pixilates, and then Trinity ducks and picks it up. The pixilation is a manifestation, but nobody will believe that. The good news is that the tape will prove that Trinity didn't pull the pin out."

I was forward, halfway to the floor so we could both watch.

"First, the umbrella," she said. "This is short."

The camera was way above us, so it was easy to catch Rachel's face as she gripped that sheet, petrified, wide-eyed. She kept glancing into the corner, but the tape matched my memory. No visible Witch of Indor.

The tape showed a little of my profile and my looking in the mirror to see the corner.

"Right there," she said, and put her finger on the screen beside the umbrella. Because her finger was still, it was easy to see the handle of the umbrella disappear under her finger and then roll back again.

"Let me see it without your hand there," I said, and we watched it again. It was very obvious to me, and yet, I knew another person seeing this would make it out to be a flaw on the tape.

I sighed in frustration. "Let's look at the other one."

At that point, I was coming close to being flat on my stomach, the bed getting ready to flip. I took the laptop from her, but before I could get it snapped into the tray, the nurse came in with my dinner tray. She needed the tray holder.

Of course, the food was something sloppy with gravy—turkey and mashed potatoes—and not a sandwich that I could hold in my hand. She was also holding a cup out to me and a glass of water. The dreaded pill. Or at least Rachel dreaded it. I kind of liked sleeping to pass the time instead of watching the corner and waiting for things to come flying at me.

Rachel nodded at me silently and made a muscle with her arm. In other words, she was pretty alert, so take it.

I thanked the nurse for the food but rolled my eyes when she turned to leave.

"I'm starved or I'd have told her to let it get cold," I said, shoveling food into my mouth.

"Don't choke," Rachel said absently, returning the laptop to her own little desktop. "You're watching a *tape*. Tapes don't change. It'll be here when you get done."

I'd been told never to eat flat on my back because I'd choke. So, I was stuffing food in my face before the bed made the whirring warning it would soon flip, or I'd have to wait about ten minutes until my neck was a foot higher than my feet. I wanted that laptop back. I watched her in the mirror as the slight tapping sounds from her mousepad implied she was watching the same piece of a clip over and over.

"What's got you so focused?" I asked between a couple swallows. "You already said you can barely see that pin fly across the room."

"Right. It looks like a tiny pixilation. That's what they'll say. But the rest is unbelievable."

"What is it?" I asked in frustration.

"You need your own epiphanies," she said mysteriously.

"Take this," I said, unsnapping the dinner tray and gently holding it out. I'd eaten enough to take the hunger pangs away. She wheeled up to me and took it, laying it on the floor out of the way.

"Just let the bed flip, and then I'll give you the laptop. I don't want you to drop it."

The thirty seconds until the flip felt like ten minutes. When I finally flipped and snapped the laptop in the clamps, I was looking at a stilled image of Mom coming into my room with Trinity. I hit play and watched Trin give me my phone. After shaking hands with Rachel, she held her hands to her chest, one of her shy moves, gripping my new phone in one hand. Grace was pointing and explaining, between her and the camera for about twenty seconds. Trinity was nowhere near the bed, so the blocked view didn't bother me.

I kept my eyes on her the whole time, and she came nowhere near the bed until after Grace went to check herself out in the mirror before leaving the room with Dad and Rachel. That's when I asked Trin for a hug, and she hugged the whole bed. But her hand never came down to where the pin would be.

As we played that game, the clip showed she was not "hanging off" the bed like the Minneapolis technician had implied. She was a ballet student—strong and flexible. In fact her hands dangled off her wrists, high enough off the bed that her fingers weren't touching it. It was a good acting job of pretending to be hugging the bed since she couldn't hug me.

I looked down where I thought the pin would go on the side of the bed. I wanted to see if it was still in at that point. But the camera wasn't that good. There was a little gray dot there, which could have either been the pin or the shadow of a hole.

But I kept watching Trin like a hawk, my eyes moving from the hand I could see clearly to the fingers on the other side of the bed. Suddenly she jerked her head sideways, laughed, then went back eyeball to eyeball with me. That's when she had heard the sound and said we had nails falling out of the ceiling.

"There's no audio on this?" I mumbled. Rachel said no, but to keep watching.

Trinity moved to the center of the room. Only her profile showed, but she had stopped, the smile faded, and she froze.

"I can see the pin on the floor because it just rocked," I muttered, my heart revving a little just with the memory. It did look like a gray square and not a thin nail on the film because it was rolling slightly back and forth. But as Trinity stepped forward, the little square moved backward, all by itself, until it was against the wall. She stopped cold, then slowly started backing up toward me, like she knew something was horribly wrong over there. Like maybe—

"Rachel. Can Trinity *see* the witch, like you can?"

"I think she sees little flashes," she said. "Not as much as someone like me, but enough to register an image."

I stopped the tape, continuing to stare. "How do you know?"

"*I* saw the whole thing happening. I was down by the yoga room with Grace and your dad. It's like I was in everybody's head at once.

Trinity's. Yours. Beth's even. I can't explain it. I couldn't scream, couldn't move, but I knew at that point there was nothing I could do, so I just managed to say to your dad, 'You need to get back there.' He ran. Grace followed."

"Trinity can *see* her?" I asked again.

"Your dad and Grace were talking in the yoga room. You remember Grace had said Trinity waved at something by the well that afternoon? And it looked like she waved at something invisible?"

"Grace taped it from the balcony," I remembered, though the drug was starting to kick in. I wasn't feeling sloppy-drowsy. Only that I didn't have any urges to go off like a rocket and screech as she went on:

"I asked to see that tape. One of my unexplainable hunches. Trinity *was* waving at something invisible. Like this." She did that wave that uses only your pinkie.

My mind went somewhere like *what in hell did she see when the pin flew across the room? A flash of the witch? What had she seen that made her refuse to leave me?* I wished I could pry Trinity's mind open and have all her little secrets laid out like car parts in an auto body shop. I needed answers. We were drowning in questions.

I finally blurted something slightly more positive. "Do you realize you're saying that you can see, and my sister can see, an entity that nobody else has seen? Ever? Isn't that a huge part of her legend?"

"So the story goes," Rachel said.

"So how is that possible? I can understand *you* seeing her, maybe. I mean, maybe a few especially-gifted people like you could see her, but why Trinity? Does she have sixth sense too?"

"I don't think so." Rachel's tone sounded unsure. "I mean, I think she's hypersensitive. I think she can see into the fourth dimension a bit. That's not completely unusual. People—"

"The fourth dimension?" I interrupted, having lost her for a moment in the mirror, and tapped it impatiently to find her again. "Trinity was talking about the dimensions today. Ten dimensions. She's been studying theoretical physics with my uncle Todd."

"Science, spirituality, they're not opposing forces. That's just people's ignorance. I can't tell you what gives her that ability. Could be the weird…. what do you call it…"

I couldn't follow her to that point, so I let her find her own missing word, the drug making her voice sound farther away and like nothing really mattered.

"*Synapses*. The synapses in her brain are wired a bit differently— you guys have known that for years."

"Synapses, spirits, science…I'm not confused," I managed some sarcasm in my laugh.

"Let' s not get too sidetracked with what we're not going to understand. Here is something I'm sure of: *This...*this is a manifestation. Beth was here. Trinity had a momentary sighting, probably." She pointed at the laptop for me to return to it.

If the Witch of Indor was getting closer, or stronger, or able to pull the pin on my bed in front of my little sister, I thought Rachel ought to not look so chill. And what was up with the cutesy little name? It was annoying.

I let the tape roll rather than say anything else. I'd seen the innocence of my sister plainly enough in this latest adventure.

I watched the little square pixilation come flying at my head. It bounced off the bed and hit the floor. Trinity slowly reached for it. Her jaw dropped, and her eyes went right for the pinhole. Complicated as it was, the bed would have been a piece of cake for her to remember. She recognized the pin.

"There's another thing," I said quickly. "Did you see the shocked look on her face?"

"Yes," Rachel said.

"She'd had no idea the pin was out." I watched as Trinity tried to get the pin back where it belonged, but the bed was slipping forward already. I got a tear in my eye, watching her all but dive under the bed on her knees, trying to hold me up.

She was under me sideways, and she turned herself without lowering her arms, to get a better grip, so she was looking all the way down to my feet. And that's when the bed slid forward, and I landed with my halo gouging her in the stomach.

The film was all pixilated during and after the fall, all around me and then up behind my dad.

I took a deep breath and pointed at the screen. Rachel was below me now, below the tray, so there was no chance of her seeing this. But I knew she had the thing pretty much memorized.

I pointed at that large pixilation. "Please tell me that's not the Witch of Indor. That blob of gray squares right next to my dad. Please don't tell me she got that close to me and him."

Rachel only sighed. I supposed that was a "yes."

It was one thing to hear her tell me the witch had been between Grace and me one day. It's another thing to *see* her starting to manifest on a tape, right over my dad's shoulder.

"That's so disgusting," I said loudly.

"Toby, you're not seeing what you need to see. You're only seeing what you think you're going to see. Watch the whole thing again."

She had just repeated that people need their own epiphanies, and I figured I was supposed to be having mine. I ran the tape back and watched all fifteen minutes, watching Trinity like a hawk, looking around for anything to pixelate that I didn't see.

"What do you see?" she demanded as I tapped the pad to stop it at the end.

"I see...my sister is innocent, stuff is flying around, and some disturbing presence that I can't see got almost right in my face!"

Her sigh sounded frustrated as I pushed the still image of the blob behind my dad away in horror. I shuddered.

She finally said, "Your dad is really disturbed by people's behavior right now...how they could believe lies and spread them and be totally convinced lies are true. You are *seeing* how that happens, Toby. People come into something with a preconceived notion or two, and even what they see doesn't matter. They will miss all the fine details that would disprove their theory *because they don't want to see them.* Or they're not looking. And even if an expert pointed them out, they would say the expert was wrong."

"Look, I am ready to see just about anything," I said to her. "If you think I'm blind, then make me see."

By that point, I was about halfway to facing the floor, the perfect position to get right up close to her again and watch the footage together.

We watched until she and Grace and Dad had left the room. At that point, Rachel stopped the tape and rolled it back to the beginning. "You missed it," she said.

"Can you just tell me what I'm missing? I know you know the whole thing—"

"That's not my job. You're looking in all the wrong places. You're watching Trinity. You're looking for manifestations."

I watched the beginning again. Mom was too busy watching Trinity's reaction to everything to notice me. At one point, from the camera's point of view, I was looking Grace in the eye. It had been weird, seeing it the first couple of times, because I was sneak-watching, from a camera's perspective, and if somebody looks you in the eye, you feel exposed or something.

I shrugged while muttering, "Grace looked directly at the camera."

"Keep watching."

Grace pointed to this or that and got Trinity to look around the side of the bed to see the generator. But Trinity didn't come close to the bed.

"Trinity just peeked around. She didn't come close to where Grace pointed, or even to me and the bed."

"What did Grace just do?" she asked, raising her voice impatiently.

"She pointed," I said.

"You are so gullible. You'd be one of the people your dad is talking about—"

"I would not," I snapped back.

This time she slowed the clip after running it back so that there were standstill frames, one after the other. She got to the one where Grace was pointing, and Trinity was peering.

She said, "Look at Grace's *other* hand."

The frame stopped a total of four times with fairly good stills as I watched my perfectly normal sister reach where the pin was, then drop her hand with her ring finger up and the other three down. Like a sleight-of-hand move. The hole looked slightly different now—darker.

Rachel fast-fowarded to Grace at the mirror, reaching down to scratch her ankle. That's when the first pixilation showed up, but it was quickly under her foot and then she quickly walked away, leaving it revealed but unmoving, so you would never notice it—unless you were absolutely looking for it. She had reached down to scratch her ankle... *to keep us from hearing a clang?*

Rachel had a point. I could not compute what I was seeing. I could, but I couldn't. My brain got it right, but out of my mouth came, "Grace would *not* do that. *No way...*"

Twenty-five

I watched the clip two more times, feeling myself get more numb yet more amped up. The second time the screen was practically up to my nose. I was almost facing the floor again which meant Rachel could watch, but she had backed off to give me some space.

As I finally pushed the arm of the computer holder away, it was like my life flashed before my eyes, but not in order. It was more like a strobe light, every moving dot being a piece of a puzzle that was clear one second and gone the next. The pink and purple lights were the memories, and the yellow lights were my case of the yeah-buts.

I remembered long ago, the shock of hearing a seagull smash against a window wall. I remembered Trinity sobbing. *"Toby! Don't let the birdie die—"* And I remembered Grace, too, all, "Ew! Does that mean somebody's going to *die?"* But that was *after* something I hadn't thought of again, maybe because it didn't fit into any reality I could have made sense of. First I had turned and saw how Grace watched from across the room, watched the back of Trinity's head, watched like her wheels were cranking...

Yeah-but... Grace would not, could not, kill birds. She can't even stand to be around birds. How is she supposed to catch them?

I saw a dead Milo the guinea pig, slumped in my hand, his neck extra-long and falling at odd angles. I saw us dropping Grace at the mall hours earlier. We hadn't picked her up. How did she get home? More importantly, *when* did she get home?

Yeah-but... how is a normal 15-year-old girl supposed to put her hands around a guinea pig's neck and just fucking wring it? And why? That's impossible--

I saw Trinity all covered with blood in the middle of one night. Grace said Trinity had been chanting something in German. *Something evil comes...* I had totally believed Grace heard it and that Trinity had been upsetting herself--without help from anyone else.

Yeah-but... why wouldn't I believe Grace? She'd been crying real tears--

It was a little like peeling back the layers of an onion. My eyes were watering. But I was not ready to bawl. My first feeling was extreme anger, but misdirected, going all over the place. For one, I wanted to punch the laptop. I just pushed it farther away as the bed flipped so it was at an odd angle, shedding a weird light on the ceiling.

Rachel finally spoke slowly and cautiously. "Everyone knows that Trinity was traumatized from the dog bite. It just seems like the issues were being clouded. I mean, any kid who got forty stitches would be traumatized for, what? A few years? She might be afraid of dogs her whole life but otherwise would move slowly back to being functional?"

Rachel was saying Trinity should not have been as traumatized as she's been—I got that. I said nothing. The strobe light flashed. I saw Grace come out of the woods on the far side of the monkey bridge. She'd taken the longer route to the other side. She'd been running. She should have been out of breath. *But not as out of breath as she had been.* Where did she go, and what else did she do?

Yeah-but... how is an eight-year-old girl supposed to get a gate open between a pen and a yard without getting bitten by the dog herself? Without her little sister seeing her? Surely, Trinity would have told.

Rachel was speaking again. "...and then there was her IQ. Your mom told me the doctors said to be prepared for anything. Right?"

"Right," I grunted absently.

"In their minds, 'anything' could include having strange speech patterns, or reading complicated books... Right?"

I saw Trinity on a playground in kindergarten and instead of playing on the monkey bars, she's reading *To Kill a Mockingbird.* It was probably our most famous family story, showing Trinity's ability with languages, and it was one good thing my parents could wave around so that all the darker mysteries didn't defeat them. But I relived what I'd felt each of the dozens of times I heard it—something I almost didn't remember feeling, like an invisible hand was pinching my stomach, then letting go.

Listening to the wind rise outside and the rain patter harder, I felt it again, this time along with what it actually meant. Something I'd never let myself examine, because it would have been inconvenient.

I'd always had the thought: *what a really weird thing for a little kid to be doing*. Reading *To Kill a Mockingbird?* That was *so* weird. Was that the spring when all her problems started? Did Grace start doing things to her?

Yeah-but... what could an eight-year-old do to a five-year-old that would make her quit talking, and want to disappear into the other worlds books can provide, and get stress-related asthma?

Nothing. That's what.

I'd gotten used to thinking of Trinity as being odd. It's just part of life—life in your family. It's a life you rely on to be, if not completely normal, at least predictable. So long as whatever makes you sad is unchanging and predictable, you can live with it. Even Trinity being unpredictable was predictable.

The strobe light stopped flashing in my head. I just lay there. I finally was hearing nothing more than a strengthening hurricane flinging fistfuls of water at the window. The world returned to what I'd been used to. My family was my family. A little weird, but whose isn't. There was no such thing as ghosts. There were no new, convoluted, twisted views of things.

I completely relaxed, this sleepy drug perhaps allowing me to be calm enough to realize I loved Grace as much as Trinity. It just was not something I thought about much. She didn't need a lot from me. Except that we had an unspoken alliance, so normal it almost went unnoticed. We were the strong ones—Trinity was weak. We didn't always see eye to eye on what ailed her. I thought Grace was kind of heartless at times, but she thought I was snowed by my guilt over sticking Trin in that backyard, especially after she told me not to put her in there.

Master manipulator!

The thought shot through my head, seeing clearly a habit of Grace's, of suggesting then withdrawing the suggestion so she could put an idea in my head and then not get any blame. But the thought dissolved into sand dust with my more important need to see things familiarly. It had been our job to keep each other stable when anything got crazy—whether it was Trinity being weird in the middle of the night, or not talking during the day, or telling me the Witch of Indor was at the well.

As much as I loved Trinity, it hadn't dawned on me before how much of my predictable life relied on Trinity being weird and Grace being normal.

I pinched my eyes shut and heard myself speaking. "Could it be that, you know, Grace had found the bed so interesting, and maybe the pin was coming out already, and she just..."

Rachel sighed with some galling combination of patience and impatience. "Do you need to watch that tape again?"

I pulled the mechanical arm toward me, then pushed it back, realizing it felt easier to watch the weird light on the ceiling. "Ya know, in school, Grace loves to make people laugh. She pulls pranks. Maybe she thought she could pull one, but she didn't realize how major it would be. Maybe she just thought the bed would just stop or something. Or rattle a bit."

Rachel's silence was thick and nauseating.

"What I just said is an explanation, isn't it?" I asked impatiently. "I mean, you're the one who says life is never as it appears. What about this tape?"

"Oh. So now you've got the what-abouts."

I'd hear my dad use that term recently but couldn't remember what it meant. A social media version of the *yeah-buts,* I decided impatiently. "Look, take your laptop. Thank you for all your attempts to help. But I just need to think about this."

"I'm not leaving. I'm not taking my laptop. You're not getting any time to form one excuse after the other. You've got a little sister who's likely been horribly abused. There is no time for you to relax in your denial and take days to show this tape to your mom. Trinity is back in the hospital. How many times has she been hospitalized for stress-related asthma? How many times has she scratched her face hard enough to draw blood?"

"Okay, okay," I said, pulling at my hair. The answers respectively were *four* and *a couple dozen,* though I didn't say them aloud. I just felt myself getting angrier, more backed into a corner. "If there's something wrong with Grace, why did my parents never notice anything?"

Excellent question, I thought.

"They probably did," was all she said.

Too simple. "Uh-uh. I can see where you're going with this, Rachel. You think, because a pin came out of the bed--okay, by Grace's hand--that means she would push me down a well and wanted to see her big brother dead."

Instead of answering, Rachel inched up to me and took my hand, holding it in both of hers. I thought she was offering comfort until I felt that slight chill wandering from her hands up my arm, and she was looking at me super intently.

The scene I envisioned was a lot like a dream or a memory, only super clear, which made it more like a movie. I didn't have time to think.

"I don't want you to go over there...Don't go near the well. She will push you."

"Are you talking about the Witch of Indor?"

"She wants to push you. She's at the well. She's telling ME *to push you."*

I swallowed hard, and though Trin's words sent a chill through me, I was breaking into a sweat.

"Go on," Rachel whispered. "Say what was *really* happening that night..."

This mental TV screen showed Trinity's wide-eye gaze with the pause button pushed. I muttered, "Trinity never said the Witch of Indoor was at the well. I just took it for granted Trin was talking about her..."

"Who was she speaking of?"

A different scene came clear like a change of channels. Grace was standing beside Trinity, four feet back from the well. It was daylight.

"Grace was with Trinity that afternoon at the well," I said. "Shot the video later. Earlier, she was there, too."

"Listen to her," Rachel whispered, gripping my hand tighter.

The whipping wind outside was replaced with a soft voice tuning in louder. It sounded like Grace at first, though the words were horrific.

"...Nobody will miss you. You're just a big pain to Mom, and why do you think Dad travels so much? You think he has that much business, really?? It's you he's trying to stay away from. Do you want them to finally, finally, be grateful to you for something?"

"No way." I stuck my free palm up to my ear, as if that would keep the sound away. "She's telling Trinity to jump. It's like a... like a bullying routine on steroids..."

It grew even more intense, Grace's voice morphing into something gravelly and seething. "Jump, or guess what?"

The rest is unspeakable. I've never quoted what I saw in that vision. Doing it would take unspeakable concepts and reduce them, and there really are no words big enough for the thoughts she brought forth. It had to do with hurting me—or Mom. It put an idea to an eleven-year-old about who could live or die depending on the eleven-year-old's choices. It was jaw-dropping in its manipulation. Grace was my younger sister. I wondered what it would be like to hear this from an older sister, when I was younger, how everything wrong in our family was my fault, and these choices were my own doing, my own creation, and my big sister was just another victim, sadly stating the options.

"Stop!" I said, twisting my hand away and putting my palm over mt ear. "How could anybody think that way?"

The strobe light turned off. I was back to hearing the rain against the windows and, eventually, Rachel's answer. "I'm not a shrink. I only have a spark of it. Extreme jealousy. Jealousy morphed into hatred. Hatred turned to violence—"

It didn't sound big enough. It sounded too simple and yet too monumental, all at once. Trinity's selective muteness was rolling through me.

Rachel went on, "Look, I don't have any second sight about your parents. I'm just using my logic. They probably noticed but couldn't prove anything. That's a real dilemma. That's a real sleep-snatcher. Didn't you tell me your mom used to wake up at the drop of a hat?"

I thought of Mom spending half her nights sleeping in Trinity's room. *Protecting her, not coddling her?*

But Trinity had slept in Grace's room the very night before we left on vacation, as Mom hadn't finished repapering the walls. She had booked Trin and Grace into the same room at the Chapel Rock Inn! If Mom knew, how could she let Trinity fall into the vulnerable state of sleep in the very room with someone this dangerous?

As if reading my mind, Rachel cleared up her thought. "It probably ran in phases…or moons, seasons, whether or not Grace was bothered by something and needing a scapegoat. At that point, your parents probably thought it was over, *hoped* it was over…"

I still couldn't walk in my parents' shoes, but the word 'scapegoat' floated around my head. "Grace was in a great mood all last month. Trying out for cheer. She got to miss ballet to go to the practices for tryouts. I bet there were only three, while she was saying they were every day for a month. Bet she got to do whatever she wanted until eight o'clock every night when Mom got home."

"Which was?" Rachel asked.

I'd no idea. I just didn't imagine it was anything good. Out of my mouth flew, "Catch birds with Wiley, pretend you are delivering them back to the bird sanctuary, and pluck their feathers out instead, while they're still alive?"

Hearing my own words made me queasier, though Rachel didn't shudder. I admired her humble vulnerability wrapped up in strength.

"I think...I think my mom had a clue," I finally whispered. As for recent stuff, I remembered how long it took her to leave my room yesterday when Grace asked to be alone with me. Mom only went down the hall. *Was she afraid to leave us?* And yet when Trinity was here today and I asked her to leave, she went without hesitating at all.

"I'm sure she suspected, Toby. To me, the most chilling thing on that tape—it was the move she made was *so* casual. You saw her look right at the camera. She knew it was there. She did everything possible to make her actions not show... You'd think that you're just not that stupid. If evil were going on right under your nose, you'd think surely you'd see it. You'd swear that you'd notice."

"What about Dad?" I asked. "Does he suspect that Grace is the cause of Trinity's problems?"

I also liked being able to ask Rachel a question when the answer from anyone else would be, *God only knows.* Or, *that's too weird for me.* She could take a stab at an answer.

"I'd say he does. But don't be too rough on him if he couldn't stop it. I'll tell you something, Toby. I pass by people every day who are psychopaths, sociopaths. I can spot them before I touch them. Do you realize there is one doctor and a couple nurses on this very ward who are sociopaths?"

"No," I said, more fixated on my own family.

"They're the ones who can deal with all the blood and guts without losing it, and in the calmest way, walk out to the family and tell them their loved one died. They're very charming. They can fake emotions they don't have. They just don't feel things, at least not like the rest of us do. They're walking around all over the planet. They own businesses. They run banks. They sit next to you in English class. Most are non-violent, but hey. They'll lie to your face, feel justified, remember their lie as the truth, and walk away without feeling any guilt. That has been the hardest thing about my second sight. Bumping into someone or shaking someone's hand whose conscience is...a void, a vacuum."

She was calling my sister a psychopath or sociopath. I was an inch beyond feeling shocked by the concept.

"All I'm saying is that this is not your parents' fault. Your sister is, I'll be honest—probably the worst I've ever touched."

"An *abomination...?*" I wondered out loud. Rachel had called the presence at the well an *abomination.* Had she been talking about Trinity and Grace, and not Father Elijah Rune and the Witch of Indor?

She said, "I would doubt your parents have ever seen this side of her. She keeps it hidden. Her friend Riley probably knows. Birds of a feather flock together..." She picked her weight up by her ankles and elbows, shifting a bit to find comfort before going on. "She learned at a really young age to direct it toward Trinity. It's become a pattern. Grace sucks energy off Trinity because Trinity doesn't know how to fight. It morphed..."

Another chill passed through me as Grace's voice chimed out during our walk to the well. "*Ya know...why do I have a target on my back? I'll tell you why... Because it's easier. It's easier for you and Mom to think I did something to her than to think of what she's capable of dreaming up in that...that very locked little mind of hers... Blame me! I'll bounce back. I always do.*"

"Rachel, how does somebody do horrible things, only to accuse others of those horrible things, and not feel guilty? It's like a lie, wrapped in a lie, wrapped in...I don't know what."

I was tempted to just blurt the word "evil." But it's a word like "abomination." It doesn't work anymore. It's too old. Maybe it's just too honest—

The word she came up with was, "Gaslighting. I think that's what they call it."

I remembered the word and that it had something to do with an old black and white movie my dad had liked.

"I'm sorry," she whispered sincerely. "I feel like you just lost your innocence. Like I did when my parents passed over."

It took me a moment to answer, as my throat closed, the way I suddenly imagined Trinity's having done a thousand times a year. It finally came out breathy and shaky. "Well, maybe I needed to. Trinity obviously lost her innocence a long time ago. My God..." My mind was lurching all over. "You said my parents don't know about this tape yet."

"Your dad took your mom out to dinner. She wants to stay tonight with Trinity, but he wanted her to eat something decent first. You need to tell her. As soon as she gets back, she needs to see this tape."

I glanced at the window with the rain blasting against it in torrents. It's not easy, like it is in suspense films, to turn your whole worldview around on a dime. In suspense tales, the good guy finds out who the bad guy actually is, and his eyes flash. There's this moment of alertness, a single Ah-HA! moment. *Solved! Let's go make our arrest!* There's no struggle, there's no grief. There's no remembering all the fun times you had with that murderer and wondering how in hell it could be true. I felt like I needed to cry. I needed to go to a funeral and say goodbye to someone forever.

My instincts stopped me from getting all emotional, maybe because my feelings had always been stronger for Trinity. She was upstairs, all alone, which she probably didn't mind.

"So then, what does the Witch of Indor have to do with all of this? Could Grace be possessed?" I didn't get an answer from Rachel. I got an adrenaline rush so strong that Rachel picked up on it in the silence.

"What's wrong?" she asked.

I said so loudly it even startled me. "Where *is* Grace?"

Twenty-six

Rachel stared at me, rigid, yet her back deflated the pillow like her mood switched from alarm to relaxation and mere thoughtfulness. She said, "If she were in this hospital, I would feel it. *I think.* Wow. I need to find some sort of genuine extrasensory school when I get out of here."

"We'll get you there," I said absently, and flipped back into my normal thinking mode for a moment.

"Where are you?" I started to text Grace, and Rachel put her hand between my eyes and my phone.

"Don't do it." She stared at the wall like she did when she was having second sight.

I backed out of the text, watching her in the mirror and waiting. I waited so long that I had to move the mirror to get her back in the center.

She finally went on. "Some of these people who come off as so charming but are so pathological…there's one thing they fear, and it's not hurting others. It's getting caught."

The silence hung. My sister *was going to get caught.* I didn't see the big deal.

"Here's a newsflash," she said, meaning that thing where she just knows something. "Your sister didn't have to come up here. She could have stayed in New Jersey, could have gotten out of it. She came because she's afraid. She's afraid you're going to 'remember.' She wanted to be here in case you 'remembered.'"

Part of that made sense. In fact, it gave me chills. "But…she could have called me on the phone to find that out," I argued, over the part that didn't make sense.

The wind rose up, and Rachel's eyes went from the wall to the window and we listened to rain clatter on the pane. "Yeah, but then, she couldn't do anything about it."

I listened as the wind pelted some raindrops against the window. I went with my gut instinct. "She's not going to do anything to me."

I realized I was still thinking of the airhead Grace I was accustomed to. It was confusing.

Rachel looked directly at me. "Honey. She pushed you down a well."

I wanted that to register, but it just didn't. I couldn't picture it.

"It's important that, until this is put in your parents' laps, you need be very careful. We're in a bad-weather situation. You don't really know if your parents will make it back here. What if she comes here and they don't? It's just important that you don't let on, don't give a single clue that you *know*. She came here to find out if you knew, and if you do, she'll see no way out for herself except to finish what she started."

"We still don't have much of an idea of *why* this started," I reminded her. "I can see she's jealous of Trinity. What did *I* ever do?"

"I don't think it has to do with you or Trinity as much as it has to do with *her*," Rachel replied. "That's more a question for a shrink. But think how hard it's been to see anything provable. She will do anything to continue on in that. Anything."

I thought of Grace's panicked reaction to Mom and Dad finding out she'd been on the monkey bridge all those years ago. It seemed no big deal to me after what happened to Trinity. The details came flooding back of *how quickly* and *how vehemently* she cooked up the lie about us looking around at the stables and realizing Trinity was gone. If she felt that adamant about something stupid, to what lengths would she go to now?

I remembered something important. "Grace is with Wiley. His parents took her to their evacuation hotel. I think we're just getting carried away."

I flipped the mirror to look at the window. The raindrops ran down the glass in streams, glowing orange and making more pelting sounds as the wind drove them against it.

"Maybe you're right," Rachel said, scratching her chin and letting her arm flop in frustration. "I was upstairs with Trinity for a couple hours today. I was starting to put all this together, and I made sure Grace didn't get a second alone with her until she left the hospital."

"Nice of you," I said. "So, is Trinity, uh, sane and rational?"

She chuckled without smiling. "She's reading a book on trauma, one I recommended. She downloaded it to her phone. I left after she hadn't looked up from the pages for twenty minutes, but dang, the girl reads fast. Swipe, swipe, swipe..."

"That's Trin," I said and yawned. The anti-spook drug was really fighting with my adrenaline. My arms felt heavy, and I pulled them in beside me between the mattresses after finding Rachel in the mirror again.

I was just relaxed enough that thoughts could flow through my head, without me pushing at them to come or pulling at them to leave. It was almost like a dream state in which I'd been having flashbacks.

I saw Grace standing here beside me saying her reasonable explanation for my fall: "It was an accident," blaming Trinity without exactly blaming her. Every time Trinity allegedly did something, there was blame from Grace. But always with this feel-sorry-for-her attitude. *"I think you're afraid that if you admit she's got a screw lose, that means you can't love her as much. For me? It means I love her more—"* Her accusations never sounded hateful. Hateful would have been over the top, putting me on alert that something was off.

Yeah-but...how can any person be that *manipulative? Did Grace believe herself? How could a person utter such a hateful lie, knowing there's no truth in it? Is that even possible?*

I felt a thump. Or maybe I heard it. When I opened my eyes, the orange lights seemed slightly duller. I tapped on the mirror and saw that the glass outside was completely black, whereas before, raindrops glowed orange while running down.

"Power just went out in this part of the city," Rachel said, and I found her gazing at the window, too... "But you're already on your generator. There's nothing to worry about...nothing to..." She stopped mid-sentence and slowly rubbed her arm like she had goose flesh.

"You okay?" I asked.

"Yes." She rubbed her other arm as well, glancing at the ceiling and down. "I wish I knew what electricity has to do with how my abilities, like, *shift*. All that electric just cut out, and I swear I... feel so different."

"Better or worse?" I asked. But she didn't answer at first, as if the question were not important. However, she looked more anxious.

I thought it might be that she sensed or saw the Witch of Indor. But she was still fixated on Grace. "I think it is safe to say she is probably the one who killed the animals. But she's *only* killed animals. This whole business with pushing a sibling down a well is a new level."

I could not picture Grace killing animals. Yet, it was starting to make sense, to become that "missing piece" that Rachel said would simplify what had looked so complicated. Replace Trinity with Grace. Instead of our injuries and Trinity's many issues looking like a bunch of convoluted and unrelated messes, it was one person causing all of it. I knew it would take a long, long time to reckon with the idea that Trinity's selective mutism and stress-related asthma could have been caused by a loved one. *What had Grace said to her, done to her, all these years?* I had a clue now and at least the ability to see the big picture, except for the Witch of Indor.

I thought of a connection and asked Rachel again, because she hadn't answered me before. "Do you believe in possession?"

"Oh, sure," she breathed, studying the ceiling. "It's not easy, though. A dark spirit has to find a willing host. Or a host that has a certain open door. Most people do not have that door opened."

"You said you thought Trinity had been haunted by something for years. Are we now sure it wasn't Grace who was haunted?" I asked, glad for this drug that made my mind feel screwy, but relaxed enough to consider totally stressful options without freaking.

"Oh, I think Grace *was* the haunting..." she murmured.

"I like the idea that something could have possessed Grace. That makes her less responsible."

"Yeah, but we're not looking for what we like," she said, still rubbing her arms.

Good answer, I supposed, but I couldn't shake the feeling that this room was shifting, filling with something. I tried to tell myself it was the different lighting.

"Is she here? Is she coming here?" I asked anyway, this time meaning the witch.

Rachel just shut her eyes like she was either trying to escape a thought or focus in on it. All she said was, "Trinity...I keep getting flashes of Trinity alone in her room upstairs. Wish I knew what it meant."

I texted Trin as that comment hung in the air. "Hey. How you feeling?"

The wait of two minutes felt like ten. No response.

"She could be asleep. Under sedation," Rachel finally said.

Yeah, or she could be dead. "Can we call the nurse's station up there?"

"And say what?" Rachel swapped gazes with me, and I tried to think of something to say, other than, *Can you check and make sure my sister is all right?* They'd get around to it in half an hour and call me back in an hour. What else do I tell them—*that we're afraid my other sister could come here and try to kill her?"* We were already on medication for weird-ass thoughts.

"I think Grace is with Wiley, and we are getting paranoid," I repeated. But it wasn't long before I had to add, "So then…why am I still worried about her showing up here?"

Rachel breathed in deeply through her nose and exhaled through her mouth before nodding. We're both on the edge of our seats here, trying to figure out the secrets of the universe. And yet, she started yawning.

"I hate this drug," she said. "It's messing up my, uh, gifts. I feel like I'm on a Ferris wheel while trying to finish some exhausting homework assignment."

I suggested we both give into the nods as there was nothing else to do. But as soon as I shut my eyes, I opened them again wide. *Never mind where Grace is. Where is the Witch of Indor?*

Whatever she had to do with this, if this haunting was spatial, Trinity was in the same building. *Why wasn't she answering her phone?*

"Would you mind going to check on Trinity?" I asked.

Despite that her eyes looked so heavy, Rachel only hesitated a moment before grabbing both wheels. She'd really taken on my family's garbage, and I'd no idea how to make it up to her.

She stared in some confused but trancelike way. "I'll be back."

And she was gone. I listened to rain and wind outside, which always put me to sleep, and being this groggy, there was nothing I would have liked better. But I wanted to give my dad a nod, what with all he'd gone through to see truths clearly. I wondered if he had had any suspicions of Grace over the years, or even just suddenly this summer.

I almost speed-dialed him but stopped myself. *Let them have one final decent meal together before this news I have changes their lives forever. There's no rush, no immediate threat.*

I gave the mirror a tap and stared into the corner of the room by the mirror, where all the activity happens. It was all in shadows. Something was giving me chills. What did this haunting have to do with Grace? We obviously had two problems.

Still, it dawned on me that if Rachel were right and Grace had pushed me down the well, I was probably in more danger than Trinity. I was immobilized, whereas Trinity could run.

I texted my mom: "What's your login and password to FindMyPhone?"

She had downloaded the app after Grace came in blotto the first time. I had the app but had never set up any phones or anything. I didn't have the brain power.

Mom finally responded with, "Why?"

"Because I'm bored," I lied and opened the app to the login. I figured the Wi-Fi wasn't on the generator when she took so long to reply.

I finally heard the ding and saw, "You'll hate me when you see who else's phone is listed in there."

She wanted forgiveness for creeping on me before giving me the info. *Let her creep.* Compared to my sisters I was this boring, responsible-oldest, three-beer Charlie.

"You're barking up the wrong tree, Mom. What is the LPC?"

I looked into the corner again while waiting. All I could say was that the air felt dense—like when you're dreaming you're underwater, but you can still breathe. It's like my adrenaline, trying to rush, was squeaking out like the energy from rusty train brakes. I felt intensely watched.

"Whatever you have to do with Grace, you troll... *leave me alone!*" I growled between grit teeth.

Rachel and I had forgotten she was supposed to be my nurses' button, I realized, not that I wouldn't have sent her to Trinity anyway. And, of course, Mom would have to have a blather fest with Dad before I could pry what I needed out of her with a crowbar. I pulled my arms in and gave in to the nods while waiting for a reply.

Finally, LARA226 and Stubbs0609 showed. The 0609 was Trinity's birthday. Stubbs had been her guinea pig. After entering that, I had to wait for my phone to find a tower instead of the Wi-Fi before dropping down a map. I saw my dad's phone was in there too. I touched

FIND ALL. It was the biggest button, and I had cabbage brains. It took almost a whole minute of watching that little circle go round and round.

A noise came from the corner after around thirty seconds. It sounded like a ping again. I reached down quickly, felt the pin on one side of my bed, then switched hands. It was not a pin this time.

I turned the mirror slowly and saw a ballpoint pen, with the name of my mom's ballet school on it, in the middle of the floor. It was rolling back and forth like it had just landed. It had been in the drawer. Now, the drawer was open.

I quickly clicked on my camera and took images of it—just on instinct. I kept my thumb on the button until I had, like, ten shots. Sure enough, the same red blotch, over Trinity's head from the pictures on the Chapel Rock Inn porch, were there.

I couldn't even call a nurse.

I seethed aloud, "Look, if you possessed my sister, don't think you are going to get me that way. There are no open doors over here, lady."

The pen on the floor suddenly came whizzing over, landing right about where the bed pin had been, twirling a circle like the spinner on a game. It finally slowed to a standstill. I was just past the standing position. A few seconds later, I could see it without the mirror by looking way down, the name of my mom's dance school reflecting the light.

My phone vibrated. There was finally a map of Salem. Dad's phone was way out in the upper left corner. My phone, Grace's phone, and Trinity's phone were three dots, right on top of each other.

"No…" I whispered. The pen on the floor kept rocking a little. "What in hell do you want? You will *not* take over my sister; you will not hurt me further. Do you hear?"

I thought I heard a whispered laugh, or maybe it was a cry. *Too much.*

I texted Rachel quickly, though I had no idea how long it would take to get to her. "YOUR DEAR FRIEND BETH IS HERE."

Twenty-seven

While this drug was exhausting, I was still too amped up to fall asleep while watching every corner of the room with the mirror. I was going around and around and around, from one corner to another, fully expecting to see something move, or some crazed blue eyes staring at me.

I finally brought my arms in beside me and surrendered, falling into something like an exhausted trance. I wouldn't call it sleep, at least not at first, but suddenly I was waking up. I realized the room looked different. I was too busy being amazed at my ability to knock off while stressed to the max. I couldn't figure what had changed.

Was it the lights? I could see the night lights glowing at their place on the wall where beds would normally be. As I was unaccustomed to them, I couldn't tell if the room was actually darker or just felt that way. I closed my eyes to take more advantage of this almost sleep-on-command thing, when my mind tossed up the image of what I'd just seen that was different in here. I opened my eyes to verify. *The door was shut.*

Without the bright lights from the corridor, the wall lamps looked even more dim. The alcove where all the activity happened was almost black. I slowly reached my hand up to circle the room again. The mirror's handle had bent slightly in the fall yesterday, and I realized if I tugged on it a little, I could even see into my blind spot. Nothing was there. *Not Grace, unless she could make herself invisible.*

Without a nurse's button, I felt cut off, like I was living on the other side of the Looking Glass. Especially since the shadowy corner kept drawing my mirror back to it. The drawer was still out, as if to remind me that if she could open a drawer, she could close a door. I couldn't help but seek out shadows to see if they were moving or morphing.

Rachel had left me news that I hadn't even come out of the nods for. "Trinity is asleep. I have to find one of the two elevators that are on a generator. One is outside of surgery and the other outside the ER. Do you have the number for the nurse's station in your phone? Use it if needed!"

She had sent it eight minutes ago. I didn't have that number in my phone. I could find it on google. But I didn't want to waste a call and end up being the boy who cried wolf.

That's when I thought I heard breathing behind me. I listened for the sounds of an exhale after what sounded like a gravelly inhale. *Rain and wind,* I told myself.

I texted Rachel instead, "Any signs of u know who?"

I didn't put Grace's name in there. The move was as irrational as being quiet with my phone, but my sense of being watched was off the hook. My heart revved up and sent a crusty version of my adrenaline into my arms and legs.

Rachel texted again. "I was getting tired and found an orderly to push me to the elevator."

The text told me nothing about how long she would be.

I heard an inhale, this time followed by an exhale.

"Grace?" Could she be behind the curtain? Was it bulging slightly or was it my imagination?

Only the wind rose as a gust that sounded like a giant gasp.

"Beth?"

I turned the mirror back to see my own tight, alert face. Beth? Grace? Was there a difference? Were they connected, one taking energy from the other? I suddenly knew without any rush of memories that the Witch of Indor had never been the big problem.

"Grace. I know you're in here."

I pushed the mirror all the way to show the floor and realized then I'd always had a second blind spot, on the floor at the back of the bed near the generator. But I'd no reason to ever need it.

I pulled on the handle of the mirror, creating pressure, afraid it would snap. There in the denseness of the night light, her light skin took on an orange hue, and her eyes never blinked.

Grace said, "Boo."

Twenty-eight

My adrenaline beat out the drug and rushed so hard I could feel my face flush. I went on autopilot with Rachel's warning: *Don't let on you know.*

She laughed. "We were wondering how long it would take you to wake up!" She scooted forward until she was under my face, then rolled sideways into the middle of the room. She stopped by a pair of docksiders and legs with hardly any hair, which I recognized as Wiley's after he stepped out from behind the curtain.

"We're in the middle of a hurricane." I faked a laugh pretty good. "What are you doing here?"

"That's great," Grace said. "We pay fifty-two bucks of our own money to an Uber to visit you, risking our lives to keep you from being lonely and miserable, and we get corrected on our behavior? Great gratitude, Tobes. Great compassion for our soaking wet asses."

I laughed again, hoping it didn't sound choppy. *Don't give a single clue that you know.* I hoped to gain something…time, sanity, a grip on what was going on here.

The closed door made me think of a huge rock rolled in front of a cave opening. I just turned the mirror and glanced into the active corner. The drawer was still open, but the energy didn't feel so electric, now that I knew who shut the door.

Grace was sucking up all the energy in the room. As for her intentions, I was able to grasp the situation with so much insight Rachel would have been proud. It was just my instincts, but I knew I was right: *This is a fact-finding mission.*

Grace swooped up the pen off the floor and held it out to me. "Drop something?"

"No... just put it back in the, uh, drawer."

Grace walked to the dresser, dropped the pen in and shut it without a twitch, then plopped into Mom's chair. Wiley came close, looking me up and down with a smile that didn't bother hiding its mocking look.

"Dude. You look like a pig on a spit. Like, remember those pig roasts we used to go to up in the dunes?"

Before I could answer, he added, "With that halo attached to that bar over your head…you look like you're in the electric chair."

Grace sucked her teeth. "Don't tell my brother he looks like a burning pig or an electric chair victim," she sounded like her usual self. "Is that polite? God."

"How do you take a shit in that thing?" he persisted.

I would have said, "not easily," but Grace stopped him again. "Wiley. Maybe he doesn't take a shit. Maybe they got him hooked to one of those...those bag things. Mind your own business. God."

It all sounded so usual, so *normal.* And I was supposed to apologize to Grace for implying she was stupid to come out and visit me—after she just scared me to death. And came out in a hurricane for what was stupid, no matter how hard she tried to gaslight me.

It started to dawn on me how many times I had thought her actions were just weird enough to give me a pause, but not weird enough to make me want to say anything. *That's just Grace,* I'd always thought. Every family had its weirdnesses. But because it's your family, your flesh and blood, you just see through it.

"Is your TV on a generator?" she asked, picking the remote control off my cover. "Can we watch something?"

"Only one way to find out," I said.

Stuff like this. Wouldn't most visitors have asked, "May I take the remote off of you?" Or even, "I'm taking your remote." The bed was sort of a part of me. Most people wouldn't just pick things off of you, but was it all *that* weird? Was I just paying attention to every last thing, for once?

She had the TV on before I finished the sentence about the cable, speeding through the dials, the changing screen lighting up with different versions of sand. Yeah, I was supposed to think this was just a normal visit. My sister had come to hang out.

She'd found two working channels. I turned my mirror to see a rerun of *Little Big Shots* playing, which they were arguing about.

"I don't want to watch these brats," Wiley was saying.

"There's nothing on!" Grace harped on him. "There's no cable, hello."

She had breezed past some repeat of *NCIS* he wanted her to switch to, but she won. They were always arguing, it occurred to me, like two squabbling siblings. They were as close as siblings, but I never got it. I never heard them talk about much. I'd always supposed they did when they were alone.

And why was I finally seeing clearly all this annoying stuff now, when it had been going on for years? It was like that video of her—you're not watching like you should be. You're looking for what you think you're going to see, maybe need to see, to keep with your belief system that everything in Downtown America is good and normal.

No questions were being asked like, "how are you feeling?" No concern showed about the guy in the bed with the halo and his feet hanging out the bottom. And no questions were asked about Trinity and how she was. Is that *weird? Fact-finding mission.* And I was seeing that something was going on beneath the surface here—something I would have missed last week or even yesterday. It's like their whole focus was to argue between each other about TV shows. Yet I sensed their keen awareness of me. Like they were secretly focused on me, yet not a word of it passed between them. It *felt* weird. But it wasn't weird enough to comment on.

I started to come clear on what I'd been used to, how often Grace had given me brain bumps over the years. She never looked anybody in the eye. When you talked to her, it was a matter of principle that she never let you feel like you had more than half her attention. I figured Wiley got her full attention. But the truth is, I'd never seen her look him in the eye either.

I remembered Mom, back when the two of them first met in third grade. Mom had tried to be nice, but she never liked Wiley and had made no bones about it to me. Grace had always defended her friendship with him by saying almost the exact same thing every time: "He's really sweet. You just have to get to know him. Not many people really know him."

We just believed her, or at least I tried. But after one of the first times Grace said that and walked away, Mom rolled her eyes and whispered to me, "They're not like other kids, playing together. They seem to play *around* each other, but never *with* each other."

And then there was the well. I felt my heart race over what I couldn't bear to think of. But I finally did. Everything happened exactly how I remember it. Except for one important detail.

It's before the footsteps… after the mushroom of light burst up. *We're looking down the well shaft again, more warily than before. It stinks of lantern fluid. I glance to my left. There's no Grace. She's not there….* THEN the running footsteps.

The footsteps had been Grace's.

She'd been right there to catch my legs and somehow pretend she'd been there all along and was trying to save me—

As calmly as possible, I turned the mirror away from my face so she wouldn't look into it and see my expression. I didn't think I could hide my outrage or to-the-core betrayal. She would know if I looked her in the eye—*I had remembered...*

I needed to get them out of the room. *Fast.* I was afraid to text Rachel again for fear it would draw attention to my phone, Grace would see my first text and realize I felt threatened, knew of the danger. I could yell for Carly, but if she didn't hear through that closed door, what would they do?

It was impossible just to lie there, listening to Wiley make snide remarks about the kids on the show.

I decided to take a risk. If I could get Gwen or Carly in here, I could get them to make Grace and Wiley leave. I could say I didn't want visitors right now, and she'd have sent them to whatever Uber had braved the rain to get them here. Then, I could tell her not to let them back in the building, *anywhere* near me and Trin. And I'd tell Mom and Dad everything when they got back.

I cleared my throat and said as casually as I could, "Grace, can you go get Gwen? The nurse?"

"Why?" she asked. It sounded like a demand.

I didn't even have to lie, though I got another adrenaline rush. "The bed is vibrating or something. The generator is making it act funny."

Terrible judgment call. I knew it was a risk when I said it. Only as it happened, I realized how badly I set myself up.

"Oh! Let me see if I can help you. I know this bed pretty well..."

She came up beside me and started touching things. "Grace, don't touch the bed," I said, trying to sound calm.

"Wiley, see if the plug is all the way in on that generator."

Rachel's words: The setup is more primitive... Did the generator plug need a key like the wall plug did?

"Grace! Don't touch the bed!" I yelled, giving up any pretense of not wanting Carly to hear me.

The bed suddenly stopped. She gasped, "Oh God. That's not it!"

The bed slowly unlocked. I heard the snap, then the familiar clip-clap-clops of thirty straps, felt everything loosen around me.

I opened my mouth to scream but the sudden pain above my eyes was so shocking that I swung there stunned, afraid to move. I was swinging by my halo, by four bolts on either side of my skull. My feet hit the ground as the bar bent. But the pain didn't stop. The bar was bending slowly. Two pounds of weight on my feet became five pounds, became ten pounds...I was up to holding fourteen pounds in therapy, but suddenly it felt like sixty. I'd lose my balance…

Grace was backing away and "panicking" and jumping up and down and screaming without making much noise, all so the security tape would show it was a blunder, a panic, a klutzy maneuver, all while "trying to help." *More than anything, she feared getting caught...*

My head was about to split into a canoe. I could feel it starting to happen, the top of my skull cracking. I shut my eyes to ward against the ringing in my ears.

People say that when you're dying, you see a white light. I saw silver. With splotches of red. The ringing came clear as a scream so loud that I felt like I was back in the well. The scream was filled with outrage that filled the room and probably the whole ward.

It hadn't come from one of my sisters, both now in this room, one just having thrown open the door and leaping across the floor to tackle the other. Grace had been *laughing*—I heard her. Trinity couldn't scream, not while using all her strength to scratch Grace in the face and punch her over and over.

Rachel came zooming in next but instead of rushing to me to try to get weight under me, she simply stared.

"Come! Help me!" I tried to yell, but I'd been disconnected from my voice. Rachel had backed out and yelled down the corridor. But I couldn't hold my weight up any longer. My weakened knees gave way, and I twisted sideways, the pain in my head hitting me like a sledgehammer.

Only I was no longer swinging free. I had become weightless.

It happened in a split second that became suspended in time so that I've been able to live in it for twenty minutes at a shot ever since. I could feel strong arms, strong muscles, around me. I could see the color red right in front of my eyes. My face was in a shoulder. Wool has a smell to it. I smelled wool, wet wool, which has been stamped in my brain. I'm not a jewelry person, so I'd no idea what these purple and gold gems were around this person's collar, but they flashed, and I knew I wasn't hallucinating, because I cut my left cheek on the purple one while she was holding me up. I remember how it stung because it was the worst pain I had felt, which is saying a lot in these circumstances.

The nurses came flying in the room, but somehow Trinity got to us first. She looked the woman in the face and said, "Thank you—we're here now."

I saw the woman's face, golden hair, blue eyes. Outrage is not a good enough word—not enough density, or truth, or concern, or reality. I looked straight into her outraged blue eyes, and an encyclopedia was written there, a history of outrages. Of course, she was outraged. She was outraged *for* me. She was outraged *with* me—

And then Trinity passed me off to Carly, who took over the screaming with only one-tenth the density. She said to hang on to her until a techie arrived, but I couldn't stop staring at this figure. Her face changed as her expression took note that I was saved again. Her lit eyes dimmed, from flashlight beams to candles, and the lines in her face melted. She blinked with satisfaction down to my feet and back. She never looked me in the eye, or even the face, but took in the whole package. With a silent sigh, she turned and moved out of sight. I could see from the corner of my eye a change from a swirl of red and silver to normalcy, and a sound sort of like a giant zipper, zipping shut.

Twenty-nine

I sat in a regular chair beside the regular hospital bed I'd used my final two weeks here. A duffle bag and a small wheelie suitcase sat bulging beside the bed. I'd done most of my own packing—sitting down, but still. I was leaving in the afternoon, flying back to Port Dingo, where I could breathe real salt air and begin my journey to jogging, rowing, and whatever waited beyond that.

I now had in my lap the final thing to pack—my sailing jacket, the one that saved me by inflating at the bottom of the well. They'd had to cut it off of me. Now it lay in several pieces before me, the deflated hood dangling like wings. I was surprised that they'd kept track of stuff like this. But when Ms. Gwen brought it to me today, she said some people like to keep stuff like this as memorabilia. I was just really curious about what became of the joint I'd been wanting to smoke, back when I was with Trinity on the porch of the Chapel Rock Inn.

I opened the front pouch, and it fell out into my hand, stiff from having been wet once.

Rachel sat under the window, giggling at the thing, giving a cautious glance over to Trinity, who was sitting Indian style on the bed, using my tray table to play on her laptop.

"You're not thinking about sparking that in here, are you?" she whispered.

"I'm going to have to memorialize this for having gone through so much," I said, tucking it back in the pouch and zipping it carefully. "I'm giving it back to Casen, along with a great story."

After I folded the jacket pieces and found room for them in the top of my backpack, I sat there beside Rachel, gazing at Trinity while waiting for the parents. I watched her a lot lately. The little changes were entertaining.

Her face seemed different. Her lips had always been one tense line, like her mouth had been zipped shut. Behind them had lived whatever secrets Grace had threatened her life over if she ever told. She'd spent half her life at least with that zipped expression, realizing early on what was true about her sister. It took my being pushed down a well for the rest of us to see. Now her face was relaxed. Her lips now formed the shape of lips, and her chin dipped down, relaxed. It made her face look a bit longer.

And she had started humming. She rarely made noise before. Now she hummed when she was playing, like most little girls can do when they are fixing up a Barbie or painting a picture. Only, my sister was writing code. Humming while writing code.

"Trinity, why don't you do something *fun* while we're waiting?" The parents were at Grace's hearing—the last thing we had to do before leaving for home. They'd said it would be over by noon at the latest. It was half past eleven. "Why don't you play a video game or something?"

She crinkled her nose but didn't look up. "That's not fun. *This* is fun."

"I'd have been a basket case around here for the first six weeks without video games." I rolled my eyes, already wanting to block out those days. "I thought all kids were supposed to love video games."

Rachel's sincere smile showed up all the time now, and she wore it while watching Trinity. She took Trin's side with, "A lot of kids do, but, obviously, some don't."

I just loved to see Trinity react—to anything. At least now, there were reactions, though I didn't think she'd ever be the type to talk your ear off. I had to prod her but generally, I came up with something worth the prodding.

"Trinity, what are you working on, and why don't you like video games?" I asked. She looked up into my smile but with a frown.

"Well?"

"That was two entirely different questions. Which do you want me to answer?"

I resisted the urge to look at Rachel. I wanted Trin to know I enjoyed teasing her, but I didn't want her to think we would laugh at her. It was a thin line.

"Which ever one you feel like answering," I said.

I thought she would tell us what she was creating. But she went for the second question, while staring at her screen with a scrunchy brow. "When I play video games, I can see all the code in my head that's behind it. It's distracting. It just starts spilling out of my brain, so that I can almost see it."

She didn't talk much about her feelings. Most people would have followed up a statement like hers with something like, "It's annoying as hell," or "It drives me crazy."

She just left it. I was going to ask about what she was creating, I think. But I opened my mouth and out flew, "Trinity. You saw her too. Right?"

Rachel and I had talked endlessly about the manifestation and what we saw and heard and felt. I found out Rachel saw her clearly and knew I'd be okay, and that is why she backed up to call the nurses. But we didn't bring it up too often around Trinity. She'd make a comment or two if we did, but grudgingly. I thought it probably came too close to talking about Grace, and we'd found out, from her one-word responses and calmly walking away, that Trinity did not want to discuss Grace—at all.

I figured I would let her bring it up, but it had been two weeks now. She'd only given a couple grudging answers—nothing too telling. But now the question was out there. *How much had she seen?*

She kept staring at her screen while chewing the side of her pinkie nail. She pulled her hand away just long enough to ask, "Saw who?"

I could feel Rachel staring at her along with me. Trinity *had* to know who we meant.

I ignored the question. "Because you said 'thank you' to her. So, I take it you must have been able to, you know, see her."

None of the nurses and aides who rushed in had registered any such sight. They claimed to see me standing on the very tips of my toes. The only thing they mentioned being thankful for was all my physical therapy, which they thought had managed to keep my feet under me.

Trinity nodded. "I saw her." And she was back to typing.

Rachel drew her chair up in front of me. "Did you see her at the well, too?"

Trinity looked up and started chewing her pinkie nail again. She nodded. "I saw her at the well. I saw her in here. I saw her when she kicked the pin out so we would know it was a problem. I saw her when she saved my brother."

As she typed out another line, I let out a sound that was kind of a laugh mixed with   "thluh… "

"Well, don't you think that's extraordinary?" I finally got out. "We're talking about having seen a… a… "

"A what?" Trinity blinked at me, then waited patiently. The question resonated. Was she an angel? I'd never heard of an angel touching people, let alone holding up all their body weight. I'd never heard of one screaming. Was she a ghost? Weren't ghosts supposed to be, like, translucent and not in full body, such that they couldn't carry your weight even if they wanted to?

"A what?" she repeated like maybe I hadn't heard her.

"Well, it's not like a regular doctor or nurse. You're acting like she falls in the same category as a normal person."

Trinity thought on that while chewing her nail and finally said. "She *is* normal. For where she comes from."

"And where is that?" I asked in astonishment.

"Fourth dimension. There and beyond."

Rachel slowly pulled her chair up even closer, so that I could see both her and Trinity. She leaned her neck forward, kind of twirling her ruler between her fingers. The ruler went everywhere with her lately. With one week left in her body-cast sentence, Rachel had started to itch. She was always sticking the ruler down her back or up her front. Her neck craned forward.

"What did she look like to you?" Rachel asked carefully. I think she had just moved forward to get in Trin's energy field so she could determine if a question was upsetting her. I take it she didn't sense anything negative or she would not have asked.

Trin finished whatever line she was working on and said, "She had a long red coat. Blondish hair. The cape had jewels on it around the shoulders and neck. Toby cut his face on one."

She pointed at my left cheek, which I reached up and felt. The scab was gone, but there was a bump. I'd have a half-inch-long scar, unless I had plastic surgery. I'd already decided I wanted the scar.

"She was *real,*" I said. "You don't cut your face on somebody's clothing if it isn't real."

"Right," Trinity agreed but absently. She typed out another line. It started dawning on me that the manifestation might not be like a doctor or nurse to Trinity, but it was factual. Factual things don't shock us.

"Well, *I* thought it was amazing," I said.

My big regret was having been afraid of her when she'd been on some sort of a mission all along to protect me. *Why me?* When I was in danger, she'd throw something, like the pin when the bed was breaking. Or the pen when she knew Grace was coming back here. Rachel, of course, felt worse than I did. Trinity caught us talking about this last week and just backed out of the room after looking confused. I still had no idea what thoughts were behind her actions.

So, I said to Rachel more than Trinity, "I wish I could write her a thank you note. I wish I hadn't said all those horrible things about her and thought all those horrible things. You know what I think?"

Trinity just shook her head and Rachel asked, "What?"

"I think we're surrounded by spirits that want to protect us. And we're all busy calling them names and being scared of them. I think we watch too many horror movies, that's what."

Trinity shrugged, I think even more perplexed about my reactions to her than the manifestations. She said, "Then, just write her a note. Leave it on the bed. She'll get it."

Rachel and I cracked up. I supposed she would. "How do I start? Uh…Dear Witch of Indor? That sounds all wrong. I associate that name with what I *thought* she was."

"Witch of Indor? That is… like Daddy's unreliable sources," Trinity added, not even looking up. "She doesn't exist. At least not as that meat-hook person everyone thinks is trying to kill them."

I agreed, and it made me wonder how that whole myth came about. I had no doubt a young girl died trying to defend herself from a bunch of angry, horny old men. And maybe in despair, she threw herself down a well. But I'd seen a spirit, which implies that there's a good God (or where does she get her goodness from, but I don't want to get distracted). The whole business about her swinging a meat hook for three-hundred-plus years and scalping people and stinking up the woods…it wasn't real. I don't know what Carly smelled. Maybe she fake-newsed herself. It is possible. People believe what seems like the most useful explanation unless they search for the truth relentlessly.

I wondered how relentless a search for truth can be if you can't believe your eyes. I asked, "Why should Rachel see her clearly several times, whereas I just saw a piece of her that was very strong and so real, it left me a piece of memorabilia so I could never doubt—an actual scar."

Trinity smiled and let out a "kk-kk" laugh, like she thought it was funny, like she thought this being had a sense of humor.

"I only saw pieces of her," Trinity added. Finally, a contribution I didn't pry out. "She was foggy. Like something was around her. Like smoke or steam, only not smoke or steam."

While Rachel claimed to see her as clearly as one of the staff, she encouraged Trin along with all she'd seen, until they hit on the northern lights and decided Trin's smoke or steam had more of that look, only red and silver instead of green.

"I still don't get why the same thing would look different to three different people," I kept it up, thinking Rachel would have more to say on that.

Trinity took that on with yet another shrug. "That could just be the way our eyes are wired. Rachel's missing a membrane or two, or something. Dogs can't see in two dimensions, right? They can't see a photograph. Doesn't mean the photograph isn't, like, *clear*."

"Interesting," I said, watching her chin dip way down as she typed out another line before coming back to it. Her face looked much longer today.

She went on, "Supposedly the common house fly can see a person, but they see prismatically. That means they see nine images of it instead of one. Doesn't mean there's actually *nine* of that one person."

Trinity sat up straighter and her eyes got wide. "Hey! Do you think Mom and Dad would let me have a cat or a dog or a bird now?"

"I think Mom and Dad would let you have a zoo now, if that's what you wanted," I laughed, awed that a pet would make her wide-eyed, but a manifestation wouldn't.

I did an exercise they'd taught me for when my neck got tired. I'd been reduced to a hard collar, and when that came off, I'd have to be able to keep the weight of my head on top of my neck. I pulled *down* with my shoulders and counted to ten before relaxing them again. Sometimes a few rounds of that could eliminate neck tiredness for another few minutes.

Then I stood up straight. Slowly, of course, but I was back on my feet for short bursts almost immediately. To wear normal clothes, to be able to sit in the shower, to stand up for the first time and walk—all of that was starting to make up for everything that came before it, though I had a long way to go to feel anything like normal.

I stared out the window at the blue sky, then reached to the side for the walker on wheels that the doctors insisted that I use. But I kind of pushed it along with one finger over to the window to look out at the beautiful and calm day. My doctors were calling me a miracle, even though I was earning every step in physical therapy the old-fashioned way—with sweat.

I knew what the miracle was, or who it was, even though I didn't know what the who was. Sorry if that doesn't make sense.

But while it didn't seem at all jaw-dropping to Trinity, she brought a lot of smiles to Rachel—the big, genuine kind that rarely showed up at first. I decided that the rocket scientist and extrasensory folk had a lot more in common than you'd ever dream. Both thought that a spiritual realm was factual. Trinity had been insistent that the girl who died at the well had not turned into an angel, just like cats don't turn into dogs. And Rachel went along with that fully, though I don't know their sources. It was something each had studied. And they agreed with me that ghosts were sort of disembodied and couldn't hold up a hundred-and-sixty-pound guy.

Rather than risk upsetting Dad with half-truths about what saved his son, Rachel and I just decided *not* to give our visitation a definition—

angel, ghost, or even "human existing in bigger dimensions after death," and we stopped calling her by name. Elizabeth…Beth… didn't seem huge enough. A being like that ought to have a name that sounded like a waterfall or something. We just decided to be grateful.

And I didn't share any of those conversations with the big-gun doctors, torn between my mom's and dad's favorite sayings about sharing your greater truths. Mom: *Shout it from the rooftops.* Dad: *Don't cast your pearls before swine lest they devour you.* I figured all the staff around here would process what happened in their own ways when they heard it, but their responses would never, ever feel like enough to me.

The only example I could think of was Dr. Vapor, who might say, "Oh! That was your higher self holding you up! And you scratched your own face without realizing."

Whatever. He'd liked my writing, especially the twenty pages I worked on all last week, which was the actual truths in my life I'd always failed to see… Grace standing over Trinity's bed in the night, whispering horrible things like what she'd said at their afternoon visit to the well. Whispering, until Trinity, unable to scream, scratched the hell out of her face. Then Grace made it all up about something she would have loved…*something evil comes.* Grace running back from the monkey bridge to open a dog pen she knew was there. I still didn't know how she did it without getting bit herself, what with how the bird reacted to her. All I can say is that the damn dog was probably scared of her, too.

"What time are your parents coming?" Rachel asked, bringing me back to registering the pains in my leg and neck. I wondered if I'd always have pain of some sort. I wondered how often it would make me think of Grace.

"That's why I'm standing here, to see if they're walking up the street yet. I really want to hear about…my sister."

I knew better than to even mention Grace's name. Still, Trinity slowly got up, and without taking her eyes off the screen, carried my laptop into Rachel's room and sat down on her bed. When I say Trin *did not* want to talk about Grace, I'm not exaggerating.

Rachel just swallowed, trading in the smile for a far-off gaze. She knew we'd be leaving shortly after my parents got here. We'd talked about it this week because she'd start to feel anxious. She hadn't seen any more supernatural beings, but now she thought of that realm as containing protectors and helpers. She knew if it happened, they would no longer scare her.

The big problem was that she'd be lonely. So I went over it all again. "Look, you'll be out of that cast in a week, out of here in eleven days. We can talk on the phone whenever. Facetime me anytime you want. It's not like I'll have a ton of stuff to do. And I definitely want you to see me jog for the first time."

"I will," she said, but without as much enthusiasm in her voice as I'd hoped for.

So, I made a prediction. "If Trinity and I both go to sea with Dad in October, Mom will have an empty nest. I don't think she will be able to stand it, not even for six weeks."

Rachel grinned sincerely. "She invited me yesterday."

"Yeah? You should come a week or two before we leave, and we can hang out. I think it would be a great place for you to recover. Not nearly as many people are around in the winter. You could take long walks on the beach without seeing anyone, and when you're ready to do big crowds, Mom can take you to the mall."

I sat down beside her again—slowly. Getting down was harder than getting up. For sitting I needed the leg muscles that got severed in the fracture. I ignored the pain, watching her face.

"I'm only seeing one problem, though it's big," she said.

I thought she might be talking about back pain. But she went on, "Grace's room. I can feel it already. Just being in the same house with years of bad energy accumulating...I'm not sure what it would do to me."

"We'll sage it," I said. "Mom already said she would paint that room."

I'd call her smile brave but unconvinced.

I told her, "Father Rune offered to come down personally and ...I don't know what Anglican priests do. Maybe exorcise the place?"

"When was he here?" She stared, interested.

"This morning. He came to visit me while you were in yoga. I was too embarrassed to bring it up, I guess."

Her broad, sincere smile showed up like that satisfied her. When Elijah Rune showed up this morning, I didn't recognize him. I didn't know how I was supposed to, but when he said his name and shook my hand, I wanted to scoot out under the door. I apologized over and again for having accused him, but he was such a nice guy that it only heaped hot coals on my head. He'd be taking a trip to visit his sister in Virginia in September, he'd said. We'd gotten to talking about things that had happened at home that should have been red flags, but we'd been more into the fake news of our own narratives. He offered to stop in and pray over our house to help stabilize it. I thought that was pretty amazing and felt like I owed him all over again.

"He's testifying this morning," I mentioned. "He's going to tell the judge that when Grace was allegedly passed out after I fell, he saw her eyes open and shut a few times, like she was faking. Pretending to be passed out meant she wouldn't have to answer any questions. It was just an extra layer of being manipulative. Keeping herself out of trouble."

I felt myself tense up with more of my usual line of questions about Grace lately. "Who could think that clearly with a broken nose? I just don't get it."

"Maybe you shouldn't try." She let out a long breath. "She can't hurt anyone now." She sounded convinced, so I took that to be a truth she was seeing, that today's hearing would get Grace placed in a permanent facility somewhere.

It still was a bit of a roller coaster around here. I'd just gotten Rachel feeling better, and in walked my parents. I heard their footsteps but couldn't spin my neck.

"Pull up chairs, you guys," I said, telling myself I was almost to the end of my daily annoyances, but a big one now was still not being able to look up when people were speaking over top of me. "Please don't stand over me and hover and shuffle."

I heard chairs sliding across the floor. They faced me, beside Rachel. Mom looked tired. Dad's energy was angry or frustrated—and wide-eyed.

"You tape it?" I asked.

"Nobody tried to stop me," my mom shrugged, slowly pulling her phone out of her bag. "Maybe because I'm a parent? But Toby, I don't think you want to watch this, hon."

"I want," I snapped, holding out my hand. "Am I really supposed to let you guys suffer alone? Let's split the suffering pie three ways. Besides, it was my life that could have ended. Did she confess?"

Mom handed me the phone. Grace had agreed to confess in front of the judge and admit she was guilty, thereby sidestepping a lengthy trial that would be expensive to the state and cause pain to her family.

It wasn't a courtroom in the video. It looked like a conference room, though Grace was wearing a tan outfit. Grace *hated* tan. Everything she wore had been white or pink, sometimes blue to match her eyes. Feeling another jab in my neck, I figured wearing tan for years was a part of justice.

I recognized the lawyer seated on her left as the guy who'd come to me to see if I had anything to add to the police statement I'd given in early July. I'd had plenty of suspicions, going back years, though Trinity had a lot more to tell than I ever did. I wasn't there to hear what all she told the investigators. I only know she went into that three-hour meeting with selective mutism and came out without it, and it hadn't shown up since.

One of the biggest contributions from my own meeting was to tell them to ask Trinity why she came back from sea when she was on Dad's ship with Grace. If Grace hadn't been afraid to push me down a well, had she scared Trinity into believing she'd be pushed over and lost at sea?

I stared at her face as she sat blankly in this conference room. On her other side was Dr. Vapor. I supposed it was a lady judge at the head of the table beside him and my parents on the other side of this table but not visible.

The judge said, "The defendant, minor child Grace Lara Kellerman, has chosen to make a confession and avoid a trial. Grace, you may start. Your doctor and attorney are here to help you."

There were no cameras in the room that I could see except Mom's. So, Grace turned her face directly to it, so that she was looking me in the eye. A part of me wanted to toss the phone, but I gripped it tighter, thinking of how my mom must have felt. My parents just listened. My dad's wide eyes gazed into the corridor, his hand loosely over his mouth.

"I did say that I would make a confession today," Grace started. She still had a swollen bottom lip, though the fifty-or-so scratches Trinity put there were gone.

"But, so...here's the thing. I can't confess to something I didn't do. That wouldn't be right."

Her lawyer spun his head to stare. Dr. Vapors said, "Grace, you already confessed on tape in my office."

"Well, that was coerced. You can see it plainly on the tape."

Strangely, the lawyer and doctor didn't look upset. They scribbled some notes, and I saw the lawyer roll his eyes.

Grace looked down, licking the open sore on her lip, then looked up again, staring back at the camera. I realized how hard it was to look at, when Grace hardly ever looked you in the eye. It was overwhelming. It was scary, like she was feeling some sort of great conviction for once in her life.

She went on, "The tapes *clearly* show that I did not pull the pin out of the bed, and what happened when Toby fell out of the bed...am I some sort of electronic genius that I was supposed to *solve* it? And whatever it is that my sister and Wiley Mathis think I did...or said...over the years, I can't help that. I can't control other people. I mean, I feel *sorry* for them. I'll tell you who I feel *really* sorry for, and that's my parents. They've had to live all these years with two kids who don't deserve them. Kids who've threatened me over the years, scared the life out of me, blamed things on me..." Her eyes were huge, still staring.

I said, "Jesus, God, and Mother Mary."

Dad twitched in his seat. Grace's eyes darted upward. You could hear Dr. Vapor's voice beside her.

"Grace, we've watched the tape of you pulling the pin out of your brother's bed several times together now. And before that, we watched the tape that the Chapel Rock Inn was recently able to secure—from the guests who realized what they had in the corner of their video. You were wearing a white, long-sleeved T-shirt. We can clearly see you run up behind your brother and push."

"What you can clearly *see* is *me trying to save my brother,*" she said with some sort of extra diction. I'd seen the tape already. In spite of the moon being behind a cloud, you could see that white shirt glowing in the dark. It did clearly show she pushed me. And then it showed some half-assed attempt to hold onto my legs. It's where I kicked her in the face. But that part was an act, in case there was a passerby." It was the first version of what she'd try to pull off in my room by making it look like the bed opening was a freak accident.

"And if you look, *clearly* it was my sister who pushed my brother. It was her hand. Not mine." It was like she thought if she spoke with authority and some sort of extra diction, that it would make what she said true.

Dr. Vapor said, "Grace, that is false. Do you need to look at the tapes again?"

"No," she said emphatically. "Look, people. I have always gotten blamed for the things my sister did. Nothing has changed. I'm here because...I love her...because she's weak and I'm strong...because she will never confess. She will never, *ever* confess."

The tape went to black.

"Mom, what in hell *was* that?" I breathed.

"I don't know." Mom covered her mouth with a shaky hand. "I'm just wondering, does she believe herself? The doctor isn't sure."

My parents looked like two versions of "speak no evil" with their hands dangling over their mouths in horror, but Dad finally dropped his.

"It's not great news, either way," he said. "She either believes herself, or she doesn't care that she's lying—that she's put Trinity through hell for years and you through a summer of unspeakable horror. Here's what I'd like to know. How did we end up with something like this...in *our* family? You know I would take a bank robber over a liar any day of the week."

"Very true," I said, though I didn't know how to make him less haunted.

"It *has* to have something to do with us," he went on. "Was I gone too much? Did we let Trinity's gifts eclipse Grace?"

"Stop, Dad." We'd been through this yesterday. I was sure we'd go through it more times. "Don't forget about your mom, Grandma Rose. Maybe it's all genetic."

He said, "It would be so *easy* to let myself off the hook and blame genetics. I'm not going there yet."

I thought of something to say. "Do you know what the word *abomination* means?" I glanced sideways at Rachel, who'd come out with the term.

"Abomination..." Dad got all technical without breaking his stare. "It's a word, which, in the 1800s, described something akin to a dark spirit or demon or walking dead. Please don't patronize me with superstition, Toby."

"I wouldn't dream of it. Here's the modern-day meaning of *abomination,* in a day when the walking dead win Emmy Awards and stuff."

He looked at me.

"It's a compulsive liar who stops compulsively lying only long enough to accuse others of lying compulsively."

His eyebrows flew up. He put his finger in the air, dancing it one way, then another. "The accusing-others part...that's actually a compulsive lie also. But keep working on that. Not bad."

Dr. Vapor had not been allowed to use words like "psychopath" to diagnose Grace because you had to be eighteen to get that kind of label. But he had said, quietly, to Mom and Dad, he felt confident it would lead to that, and, based on the crimes themselves, she would be locked up for at least ten years. I'd been looking forward to this confession, to some truth coming out of her.

"Does this mean we now all have to go through a trial?" I asked.

Mom shook her head. "There's too much evidence. There's the tape the Chapel Rock Inn secured last week that shows her pushing you. There's the taped confession the doctor got in his office. There's Trinity's interview, and another really compelling one was Wiley Mathis spilling his guts. I wouldn't say the kid has any sort of high moral compass. He enjoyed whatever she suggested. But because she loved attention so much, she actually let him tape her doing some things, and he was happy to share."

She shuffled in her seat anxiously and looked me in the eye. "He actually taped her killing a trapped bird."

When I almost choked over that she quickly went on, putting a hand on my knee. "She'd been telling the police Wiley killed the birds. Wiley did this or that. But he gave the police tapes, and she had nothing to give them. They checked all her photos back to fifth grade, when she got her phone. She had nothing. *She* was the bad influence, I hate to say. Anyway, her performance today just means they will add delusional to the diagnosis."

A few days back, the parents had shown me the confession tape that Dr. Vapor made of her in her evaluation. It is true...he got her to have a semi-lucid moment, one where she actually cried and said, "I'm like a demon. I feel like I'm possessed." And out spilled, not a reason for why she pushed me, but some general feelings she associated with Trinity and Mom and me, like feeling squashed or unable to breathe when we were around. She made the metaphor that it was as if we were standing on her chest and the only way to breathe was to think of ways to "get rid" of us. She didn't mention my father. She didn't come clear on her meaning of "get rid," but having spent seven weeks in traction, I took it as the obvious one.

I call this only a *semi*-lucid moment because she was still blaming someone, the devil. She wasn't owning up.

Mom went on, "Toby, we just couldn't catch her."

Then Dad told me something I'd known nothing of. "Three years ago when you were a sophomore, we were so suspicious we had the house wired. We taped everything in every room downstairs and the upstairs corridor between Labor Day and Christmas, video *and* audio. Grace was twelve. Your mom or I watched those tapes every night. I watched them from the ship when I was gone. *Nothing* showed up. "

They went on to tell me that they'd asked me questions over the years, but I had only vague memories of it. They were careful, they said, because to falsely accuse one child of torturing another could do a lot of damage if it wasn't true.

"What was making you suspect?" I asked.

"I couldn't get passed the dead birds of two summers earlier. The idea of dead animals kept haunting me," Dad said. "I believe in the supernatural, the God-angels-forces-of-darkness bit, but I'm rational, too. The birds' necks were wrung. That takes a *person,* not a phantom. I found Wiley's missing bird trap in the back yard of some summer people who lived on his street and who hadn't come down that summer. I took it apart and took it to the dump. That's when the birds stopped showing up."

Mom said, "Your dad was fixated on the birds, and I had caught Grace coming out of Trinity's room in the middle of the night a few times. She always said she just wanted to use Trinity's bathroom, that it was closer than the one in the corridor. She always resented my giving Trinity the room with the bathroom. I wanted Trinity to have it because, well, it's the only bedroom where I can see the door with my head on the pillow."

"You suspected her that much?" I asked, stupefied. Trinity had had that room since first grade. Mom had told us she was bedwetting after the dog bite, but with the bathroom right there, she could make it.

"It was like anything else," Mom said. "Grace had answers. They made sense. Trinity's bathroom *was* closer. The toilet *had been* used. I had this picture in my head of Grace waking her up, tormenting her by whispering horrible things... I couldn't get rid of it; couldn't prove it, and couldn't catch her."

"So, you put in a video system."

"And nothing showed," Dad said. "At that point, we started to think we were crazy. Things got ugly. We started blaming each other. Your mom said I was gaslighting her. I accused her of...what'd I accuse you of, Lara?"

"Just some general paranoia," she said with an absent shrug like it no longer mattered. "I always bought the girls white pajamas, so I could see them in the dark. Things that would sound totally crazy if I told anyone. Especially because we had no proof."

"And you taped for four months and got nothing?" I asked in awe again.

"She called Trinity a brat in what looked like normal kid fights and tried to make perfectly normal conversation at other times. She never threatened Trinity. Nothing happened in the middle of the night—or in the day."

"Do you think Grace had found out about the videos somehow, and like, faked normal?" I asked.

Mom shook her head. "I don't. We were careful. The cameras were the size of grape seeds. I'll have to hear from the doctors, but I've suspected whatever she has would go into remission at times. That was the fall when Trinity made friends with the Twardy girls. Was she under less stress? It's the same year Grace started getting good at dance. Maybe she was distracted by getting some good attention."

Dad threw in, "Maybe we didn't compliment her enough. Maybe she got lost in the shuffle, what with Trinity being so smart and everything just coming so naturally to you, Toby..."

Mom said, "I always told her I started the dance school to focus her energy, because she never stopped running or bouncing into walls as a toddler. Maybe it made her feel, you know, *too* special—"

"Guys. Stop." Somehow, I knew this was going to be my mantra for a long time. Rachel was scratching her back with the ruler, suddenly, making some clatter. I'd almost forgotten she was there, and Mom and Dad had never tried to hide anything from her.

"We have to go get our bags at the hotel and turn in the rental car," Mom said, standing up. "I hope it doesn't make me a bad parent, that I just want to go home, love on my other two kids and not think about her for a bit--just for a month! Is that too much to ask for?"

"Mom! Stop!"

She looked ready to cry again, so I went on quickly. "Our flight doesn't leave until three. Just be back in half an hour."

I watched Mom and Dad leave and turned to Rachel. "What can I do for them? What? They're making themselves crazy."

"Nothing but wait. You're doing everything else. That was a great definition of *abomination,* by the way..."

-end -

About The Author

Carol Plum-Ucci is best known for her young adult novels that explore themes of psychological suspense, mystery, and the complexities of human nature. Her debut novel, *The Body of Christopher Creed*, won a Michael L. Printz Honor Book Award along with many other national honors. The novel's dark, atmospheric tone and exploration of identity and social alienation resonated with young readers, earning Plum-Ucci a spot as a notable voice in contemporary YA literature.

Following her debut, Plum-Ucci wrote six successful novels, five of which won national awards. She has twice been a finalist in the Edgar Allan Poe Awards and has received seven citations from the American Library Association.

Insane Possibilities is the first of Plum-Ucci's novels to be released in the mainstream market. The protagonist is an adult, but barely so. "Adults today enjoy reading slightly younger voices, as it carries them away from problems like divorce, corruption, the IRS and what-not, " Plum-Ucci said. "Everyone wants to be younger. Readers of any age who enjoy suspense can jump right in and become any age they want."

Plum-Ucci was raised in a funeral home on a barrier island in South Jersey. Both her home and the island have fed her dark side, of which she says, "I do *not* write horror. I just love to play with the dark." Her stories transcend age groups, appealing to readers of all backgrounds who are interested in layered characters and thought-provoking themes.

www.ingramcontent.com/pod-product-compliance
Lightning Source LLC
Chambersburg PA
CBHW070202310726
48976CB00001B/187